TWO WINTERS

Advance Praise for *Two Winters*

"*Two Winters* is an exceedingly clever adaptation that captures the heart of one of Shakespeare's most complex works—and it'll capture your heart, too. This multi-generational tale of self-discovery and the secrets we inherit needs a place on your bookshelf."—Stephanie Kate Strohm, author of *Love à la Mode* and *It's Not Me, It's You*

"*Two Winters* is a breath of fresh air; a sweet, nostalgic trip back to the 1990s, when music was *everything*, the angst was real and lifelong friendships were forged in the struggle of emerging identities. This modern retelling of Shakespeare's *The Winter's Tale* is a poignant and hopeful tale of love, tragedy and divided loyalties that will resonate with anyone who was ever a confused teenager. I just loved this book!"—Lillah Lawson, author of *Monarchs Under the Sassafras Tree, So Long, Bobby*, and the *Deadrockstar* trilogy

"Compelling characters lead complicated lives whose twists and turns will keep you turning pages of *Two Winters*."—Crystal Cestari, author of *Super Adjacent* and the *Windy City Magic* series

"*Two Winters* somehow magically, skillfully pulls off the feat of balancing two independent but interrelated narratives that are equally compelling, with complex characters who we get to see learn and grow on the page. Both stories are funny and sharp and dramatic and heartbreaking, and the way they ultimately weave together makes for an encompassing and satisfying read."—Michelle Falkoff, author of *How to Pack for the End of the World* and *Pushing Perfect*

Visit us at www.boldstrokesbooks.com

TWO WINTERS

by

Lauren Emily Whalen

2021

TWO WINTERS

ISBN 13: 978-1-63679-019-0

This Trade Paperback Original Is Published By
Bold Strokes Books, Inc.
P.O. Box 249
Valley Falls, NY 12185

First Edition: September 2021

CREDITS
Editor: Cindy Cresap
Production Design: Susan Ramundo
Cover Design By Jeanine Henning

Acknowledgments

In 2018, I played Paulina in *The Winter's Tale* and the idea for this book started to take shape. Thank you, Odd's Bodkins Theatricals.

The following people and places also made this journey a bright and happy one:

Sandy Lowe, Cindy Cresap, Ruth Sternglantz, and the Bold Strokes Books team, for their hard work and attention to this story.

Jess Moore, my first editor. You're worth your weight in gold and *Great British Baking Show* GIFs.

Sio Bast, Ali Aguilar, Vivi Valens, and Nikki Taguilas, for their insight into Mia and her family. I deeply appreciate your time and energy.

Kassie Davis, my day job boss, who screamed when I told her I was going to have a second book.

The Book Cellar, for support and delicious cake. Chicago is spoiled with so many incredible indie bookstores, and you are my favorite. Ditto Our Town Books, an asset to my hometown of Jacksonville, Illinois.

My beta readers: authors Stephanie Kate Strohm, Jayne Renault, and Lillah Lawson, and the brutally honest Rob Cameron. Thank you as always, all of you, for your intelligence, insight, and good vibes.

My A-team: Beth, Kyle, May, Hannah, Brian, and the rest. You know who you are.

My family: Mom, Dad, Will, Meghan (who loves space, just like Paulina), and Aaron. It's the six of us (plus various Whalens, Clancys, and Botos) against the world. Thank you for reading, buying, and applauding, even if Dad can't stay away from the cake.

Rob again: a million years ago I sent you a very rough short story and you emailed me back saying, "You have F***ING TALENT! You should be published!" I never forgot that, buddy.

Dedication

For Nora Manca Wickman.
Thank you for trusting me with Paulina.
And for Eowyn Manca Wickman,
the best Baby Perdita ever.

Part 1: Say It Ain't So
Paulina
Havendale, 1997

I will stand betwixt you and danger.
—Paulina, William Shakespeare's The Winter's Tale

PROLOGUE

February

Hi little one,
I have to burn this after I write it.
I wrote this letter in my pre-calc notebook where my parents are…unlikely to look, but you never really know with them. I know I shouldn't be writing this down at all, especially before your daddy knows, well, he's going to be a daddy.
But you're here. You're in me. Not big or strong enough to kick yet, just tiny flutters, asserting yourself. I have to do something to mark this milestone, even if I immediately set the record on fire with the verboten lighter I know your dad keeps in his locker. I won't tell him what I need it for.
I live in a town where girls are not supposed to get pregnant. If you get knocked up, they tell you before you even menstruate, it will ruin your life. It's not even a strictly Catholic thing. I know enough girls at the public school who say they, too, get that message.
No one ever specifies why or how, exactly, this life-ruining occurs. Young women have had babies since the beginning of time. My best friend's mother had her at nineteen and they're both still here. Lives definitely unruined.
I'm not stupid. I know this means giving up little stuff like the senior prom if I can't get a babysitter and big stuff like going away to college. Even bigger, I'm disappointing my parents, with all the

time and money and hope they've put into raising me, ensuring I'm a model for success while also giving me all the love I could handle. Even though we're not originally from this town, they buy into the life-ruining theory too. My getting pregnant as an unmarried teenager is their worst nightmare. In fact, that's the first thing they said to me when I got my period in sixth grade.

At the same time, I have the biggest feeling that you were supposed to happen—right here and right now. My parents and friends don't put a lot into faith or fate, but I believe in both. I'm sure others will call you a "mistake" and maybe that's true to a point. Your dad did, in fact, forget a condom, and I really should have stopped us because he would have listened, but we were finally alone for the first time in what felt like weeks. And honestly, the Church is wrong here: it doesn't matter if you're married; sex with the right person feels good. Really good. So good that just like all those dumb TV movies, you forget to think a little.

Still, though, you're here. You have a wonderful dad who will adore you when I'm ready to tell him.

Until then, you have me. And your auntie Paulina who, though she was shocked when I whispered my fears to her in the locked bathroom of Dairy Queen weeks ago, did what she does best— helped. There is no better person in the world than Paulina. I can't wait for you to meet her, and your dad, and Xander, and your grandparents, and all the people who make up my life that will soon be yours as well.

Not a ruin in sight.
Your mama,
Mia

CHAPTER ONE

Everything went to hell after the little girl was murdered in her house on Christmas.

Not that any of us knew her, though over the next few months, we'd come to see so many pictures of the six-year-old frozen in time. Blair-Marie Elliott, her first name a hyphenated combo of her parents' names, wore tiny ice skates and custom-made outfits festooned with beads and sequins and enough makeup to stock the Clinique counter at the Jefferson Mall. Her tiny figure, sassy little face, adorable pearly-toothed grin, sprayed hair in a cloud the color of a Hershey Bar, was shown gliding and leaping around the ice in old home videos. Her angelic appearance might have been sweet in the moment, but it came off positively garish on *Hard Copy* and in the newspapers after she went missing and was later found strangled in her house in Lake Forest, Illinois.

We'd already lived through OJ and his trial, the bloody glove and the crying sister-in-law. We listened to the "not guilty" verdict in the St. Cecelia's cafeteria, followed by a silence I'd never heard before. That was over a year ago, when we were sophomores. But there was something about that little girl, that ice-skating princess, that hit all of us where it hurt. As Tes pointed out, she wasn't much younger than his little brother, Max. Lake Forest, a wealthy suburb of Chicago, was only about four hours from here. And on *Christmas*. Season of trees and presents and mangers, and now, ransom notes and child corpses.

"I think it was the brother," Mia declared, cranking up the Dixie Chicks and taking another forkful of rotisserie chicken from its plastic grocery store shell. Normally, we weren't allowed to eat in her room, but Mia was constantly paranoid these days. She worried that someone would overhear her discussing the pregnancy, even though right now, we were completely alone in the house. We were meeting the guys at the movie theater in an hour, and her parents had been at work all day. We had the night off from her mom's restaurant, where they'd be facing the rush after 5:30 p.m. Mass, the one everyone went to so they could sleep in on Sunday morning.

"I don't know," I said, watching her dress. "The brother's only what, twelve? And puny. I'm not sure a seventh grader who hasn't gone through puberty yet has that much strength. Her mom's always given me the willies. Like, why wouldn't you call the police right away? And I know they haven't released the nine-one-one call yet, but something about the timing seems off. Plus...stage moms are freakish." I shuddered. I couldn't imagine my own mom showy-crying on TV like Blair-Marie's, while in the same breath refusing to talk to the police again.

"There you go, Miss Logic," she said, smirking.

"You love it."

"I do." Pulling on her jeans, she hopped around her bedroom. Her feet, with blue-painted toenails, landed softly on the newspapers with a crunch. The hopping had increased, getting more urgent Saturday after Saturday, as it became harder for Mia's pants to zip.

And apparently, tonight was the night they gave up.

"Oh, heck!" Mia exclaimed when she heard the soft but distinct rip.

I rolled my eyes. "You can say *hell*."

"No, I can't," she said, her brown eyes wide. Mia never swore, considering it a sin, thus missing the opportunity to flout one of St. Cecilia's rules that was hardly ever enforced. I never bothered to point out that premarital sex had way bigger repercussions than taking the Lord's name in vain. Bigger in every sense of the word. She'd already gone up a cup size.

Now Mia sat down on the bed, unintentionally ripped jeans at her knees and tears forming in her eyes. Not only was her body getting bigger, but her emotions were too. And because I was the only one who knew about her pregnancy, these larger-than-life feelings were usually directed at me.

"Okay," I said softly, stepping around newspapers and picking up the rotisserie chicken with two forks sticking out of it. "More protein?"

She shook her head, pushing away the plastic shell holding her favorite comfort food. On Mia's stereo, a gift for her fourteenth birthday—I could still hear her squealing as her dad proudly carried it into the dining room, his tie loosened and smile wide—the Chicks twanged about two best friends killing abusive husband Earl. Mia usually harmonized along, but not tonight.

"I still don't know what happened," she breathed, for what had to be the hundredth time since the pregnancy test (the one thing I'd ever shoplifted—if I'd paid for it, all of Havendale would've known within the hour) showed two little blue lines that meant the end of so much. Mia rested her head on my shoulder. Her warm tears soaked my dad's red-and-blue plaid shirt, the one I still wore every chance I got, even over my school uniform when my teachers looked the other way.

Would I have gone to him with this?

"Shhhh," I said, petting her crazy, curly, dark chestnut hair, which I envied no matter how many times she told me what a pain in the ass curly hair was. I kissed the top of Mia's head, and she stiffened. I kept smoothing her hair, pretending not to notice even though that hurt.

I bit my lip hard, wondering if I should bring it up. "You know," I said, and Mia lifted her head from my shoulder, sniffling and wiping her face. Even crying, she looked saintly, like one of the Holy Cards we'd collected after our first confession years and years ago.

Oh, what the hell. I took a deep breath. "I know you're past the first trimester, but it's not too late…"

Knowing what I was about to say, Mia shucked off her jeans and strode to the stereo, stepping square on Blair-Marie Elliott's newsprint smile. Shoulders tense, she cranked up the CD.

"Mia." I raised my voice. "If you really don't want anyone to know, we could forge a note from your parents and say you were staying at my house for the weekend. They're so busy, you know they'd never check. And I've looked into this place in Jefferson. It's a Planned Parenthood for Christ's…um, for Pete's sake. You'd be safe and—"

"I can't *believe* you!" she said. Burying her head in her hands, pantsless and defenseless, Mia sobbed over the plaintive whine of Natalie Maines's fiddle.

And I felt like shit.

Because no matter how many times I went over this plan in my head, lying in my bed at night and staring at my dad's photo on my bedside table wondering if he'd ever asked my mom to do the same thing, I *knew* Mia wouldn't agree with it. She considered "abortion" as much of a swear as "fuck"—wouldn't even say the word, let alone commit the act.

Sophomore year, she'd written a staunch anti-termination essay that won a diocese-wide prize and earned her a spot on the parish bus to Washington, DC, for the annual March for Life. Seniors went just to get away from their parents and sneak water bottles of vodka. Not Mia. A photo of her clutching a sign showing a shredded fetus (every bit as gross as it sounds), her mouth forming an O of holy protest, made the Havendale paper the next week.

While my faith in God was almost nonexistent at this point, Mia's was rock solid, impenetrable. Logic wouldn't overturn it. I couldn't convince her that a trip to Jefferson was the only real way that no one other than me would ever know about the pregnancy, or worse than that, that Mia'd had *sex.*

So why had I upset her all over again? And moreover, though I'd never admit my pro-choice status at St. Cecelia's for fear of expulsion (I wish I were joking), the decision was Mia's, not mine.

I just wasn't sure she was ready to deal with the consequences. Hell, she didn't even seem aware consequences existed, and in this case, they were six to eight pounds and depended on you for everything.

But right now? We had to meet the guys in half an hour, and there was a problem I *could* fix.

"Here," I said, whipping off my corduroys. Mia automatically averted her eyes. "These have a stretch. Just don't take a deep breath." Still looking away, she mustered a laugh as I put the pants in her hand. "Okay if I borrow a skirt or something?" I asked.

She nodded, so transparently grateful I felt guilty that I wasn't the one whose bottoms had ripped.

"Hey," Mia said, following me into her walk-in closet. "Love you, Pal." I turned around. She wrapped her arms around me, and I swear I could feel a flutter in her midsection. A mix of Mia and Tesla, asserting itself.

Our secret.

Chapter Two

The fuck is up with Mia?" Tes asked Monday morning as the Bear, his ancient Cadillac, possibly a station wagon in its former life, barreled through the streets of Havendale. It was Tes's first and only car, much to his car dealer dad's dismay. I knew Tes, and he only loved Mia and his little brother more than he loved pissing off his father.

Normally, I loved the drives to school with the smart boy I'd known since pre-K. Full of music or friendly patter from DJ Troy Strong, Tes and I would banter about who'd be valedictorian next year while his eight-year-old brother, Max, chattered in the back seat or showed me his latest art project.

But today, Max was home sick, the radio was off, and Tes was brooding. I strongly suspected Mia hadn't given him any last Saturday night.

Since he got his license last summer, I'd seen Tes's profile more often than his full face. Tes's looks were almost perfectly symmetrical, the way TV stars' were. It almost seemed as though his parents ordered up the ideal-looking kid, one who wouldn't be any trouble, who wouldn't *have* any trouble. Even his profile was one smooth, unbroken line topped off with impeccably gelled hair. Except for one thing.

He clenched his jaw. It was his signature tell when he was upset or when something in Tes-land was even slightly out of his control. He had a mouth guard he was supposed to sleep with to prevent him from grinding his teeth. He never used it.

Right now, his jaw was so tight the muscles on the side of his handsome face flexed. I wondered if it was only about Mia.

I decided to keep it light. "What crawled up your ass, Tezzie? You know she doesn't owe you sex."

Very few could get away with using Tes's baby name or giving him shit in any way, shape, or form. But I was different. I remembered when he'd had braces in sixth grade that ripped up the inside of his mouth so bad he'd cried, and even before that, when he'd always set aside the purple crayons for me in Mrs. Newport's kindergarten class. We'd taught each other how to swear in third grade, risking detention. I hoped Tes would remember and laugh.

Tes and I went further back than Tes and Mia. He called me his "friend to the end of the world." Of course, he had no idea said friend was guarding his girlfriend's secret.

Tes groaned, braking hard at a stoplight and reaching up to muss his own hair, another stress tell. "Touché, Pal. Touché." Once the pickup truck ahead of us moved, he pressed on the gas. The clock on the dash read 8:08. When we were little, DJ Troy Strong would call it "BOB o'clock" and we used it as an inside joke from there on out. I didn't feel right bringing that up now.

"It's not just that," he said, and I braced myself. I wasn't surprised Mia had held back Saturday night. We may have joked about it the next day, but the Pants Ripping Incident nearly destroyed her with its reality; the due date was one day closer. Her uncertainty, along with her body and the baby, were growing. I knew Tes loved her bigger boobs (I'd rather *not* know the details of my closest friends' sex lives, but what can you do?) but now she had to worry about her stomach.

"What if she's not into me anymore?" His voice broke. I frantically glanced at the back seat, as if Max might materialize and crack us up with a knock-knock joke. No dice.

I looked out the window to see if that'd provide me any relief. No dice there either. Just the usual sights: old men smoking and drinking coffee in the Kottage Kafé, the yawning empty storefront of the antique shop I never remembered being open, and the Gun Emporium building, tall and light pink, a scary presence pretending to be sweet. It always made me shudder.

I took a deep breath. "First of all, slow down."

"With the car?" Tes was now five miles over the speed limit. He knew I hated his lead foot, but I took the bad with the good because I had no interest in saving money for a car.

"With everything," I said, gripping the door handle until he got the message and eased up. "I don't think your girlfriend not being in the mood *one* night means she wants to break up with you."

"Paulina." Tes turned to me at the last red light before school, draping his arm over my seat.

He said my name right every time—with a long *i,* like "eye." It was the street my mom grew up on in Chicago before she and my dad bought a house here, three hours south, to be closer to my dad's parents while he was in the military. Years later, when I was ten, my dad was killed in Iraq. Friendly fire. Not even fighting the bad guys.

When I was little, my mom used to introduce me as "Paulina, like the street," but no one got that reference in Havendale. I'd lived here my whole life, yet I was still *Paul-ee-na* to most people. Never to Tes, who'd called me "Pal," like friend, since we were five. Since they started dating, Mia did too.

"I know you're not supposed to talk. *Chicks before dicks* and all that," he said.

I wrinkled my nose. "Sexist."

"Sorry. But I'm begging. You *sure* she hasn't said anything? Even something little, like…she doesn't like the way I smell or something."

In almost eleven years of friendship, I'd never seen Tes so serious. The golden boy, the great hope of Havendale, was freaking out. I had to make it better. No one else could or would.

"Green light," I yelped, and he sped ahead as I white-knuckled the armrest and got ready to lie. "First, no, she hasn't said anything big or little, and I think you're making something out of nothing." *Kind of like what happened when you had sex without a condom last November.* "Second, you're acting weird this morning. Anything else going on? Are you worried about Max?" Tes loved his "oops" baby brother more than anything.

"Max? Nah." He pulled into his assigned spot—the best in the junior lot, which was really just a gravel patch across the street from St. Cecelia's. "It's just a cold that's going around second grade. He'll be fine."

We slammed our doors shut, pulling our coats around us and bracing for the cold. Winter in central Illinois was no joke. We didn't have Chicago's bone-chilling lakefront wind, but black ice, with its invisible slickness blending into the pavement, could knock you on your ass or cause your car to swerve in two seconds flat. Snowdrifts abounded, and the February cold was often below freezing. Like this morning.

I sneaked a look at the Gun Emporium still looming in the distance. You couldn't miss that tower of candy-colored creepy. Havendale was so weird: part college town, part farms and cornfields. Oh, and no one could forget the prison just outside of town. People joked it was "a different kind of haven," and most households had gotten at least one collect call from "an inmate at the correctional facility" who'd just randomly pressed buttons.

The outskirts of Havendale looked like one of those establishing shots for movies where something seriously bloody was about to go down in the barn. The town proper appeared quaint on pretty days: kids playing in Nichols Park and people lined up outside the Westview Cone Shop. Come February, however, Havendale was a borderline ghost town. People skittered to and from their cars with bowed heads and chapped red faces whose expressions clearly read, "Fuck! It's cold!"

"It's my parents," Tes said over the sounds of other juniors arriving for the day, cars and trucks crunching on gravel. We looked left toward the antique store, then right to the dreaded Gun Emporium, and he automatically held a hand in front of my midsection, protecting me from traffic. Just like every morning, I rolled my eyes but secretly loved the gesture. It felt brotherly, not that I'd know as an only child. Tes looked over at me and raised his voice as a red Jeep whizzed by, scattering slush. "My parents told us last night they're going to Europe for the next two months. They leave Sunday."

"Two *months*?"

He nodded as we hauled ass across the street. "International car convention for Dad, vacation home real-estate convention for Mom, and they're hitting tourist shit in between. They won't even be here for Max's First Communion. Mom bought his little suit, but he'll probably grow out of it by April."

"For two *months*?"

Tes sighed, clenching his jaw harder. "That's what I said. They *know* this semester's crucial for college, and they're leaving me in charge of a kid. I do a lot for Max anyway because they work so much, but—"

"Taking care of him full-time is a whole other thing," I finished. My stomach sank. Sure, my mom drove me nuts sometimes, but what was the use of parents who weren't even in the *country*?

"Hey," I said, hitting his arm like I had since we were five, my glove making a soft *pow* on his parka. "We'll help. You know we will."

"Thanks, Pal," Tes said, slinging an arm around me as we stepped into St. Cecelia's to a *whoosh* of warmth, courtesy of the school's ancient boiler system. He'd started calling me Pal in first grade. Now everyone did.

We spotted them at the same time: Mia and Xander standing by her locker, harmonizing with a Boyz II Men song for a flock of adoring freshmen. They looked like something out of an MTV video about Catholic schoolkids making magic—even the fluorescent lighting seemed softer against Xander's dark skin and Mia's light brown. Tes's jaw clenched again, even tighter.

Not that you don't sound gorgeous together, but really, Mia? Maybe not the day for your boyfriend to see you batting your eyes at another guy.

I pushed away the nasty thought as we elbowed through the tiny but devoted crowd just in time for the final crescendo. The freshmen burbled and applauded before scattering to their lockers, gossiping away about how hot Xander was.

"Paulina!" Mia squealed as the guys did some bizarre handshake-half-slap-hug thing. Throwing her arms around my waist, she stood on tiptoe and whispered in my ear, "Thanks for your pants on Saturday." I giggled as she pulled away and rummaged in her backpack.

"Buñuelos," Mia said, proffering a foil-wrapped package that smelled like cinnamon nirvana (rest in peace, Kurt). "Fresh outta the oven. My mom said Roja is getting too skinny, and I happen to agree." Roja was Spanish for red, like my hair, thus Mia's parents' nickname for me. They rarely spoke Spanish with Mia, or at all, but nicknames and words of love were the exception.

I unwrapped the cinnamon and sugar fritters, my absolute favorite, that Mia's mother did *not* serve at her restaurant, preferring to save them for loved ones. "Oh God," I whispered, more reverently than I ever had at Mass, as I bit into my first. Only one experience was more ecstatic than chewing still-warm buñuelos, and I couldn't exactly do *that* in public.

"Cover me," I told Mia, since St. Cecelia's didn't allow food in the hallways. Hall*way*, technically. The high school was so tiny we only had one, the equivalent of Havendale's main drag, where all the action of two hundred students across four grades went down. After I shrugged out of my coat and draped it over my backpack, I checked to make sure my shirt was tucked in. Shirttails hanging out were punishable by detention, and at least three of the older teachers kept watchful hawk-eyes out every morning.

Thankfully, I'd remembered, and my white button-down Oxford's hem was snugly secured in the waistband of the navy pleated skirt all the junior and senior girls wore. Though teachers monitored shirttails flying free, nobody cared about skirt length for reasons I'd never known. Freshman and sophomore girls sported an ugly gray and blue plaid that had us all counting the days until we got navy. We could wear navy trousers like the guys November through February only (don't get me started) and long navy shorts at the beginning and end of the school year, which made us look like a bunch of religious camp counselors. The rest of the uniform consisted of white or light blue button-downs, navy or red sweaters, white or navy socks, brown or black dress shoes, and no sneakers outside of gym. Oh, and navy, white, or black tights, the latter of which I was currently sporting.

The public school kids always loudly wondered how we did it, but I was used to school dictating my wardrobe. St. Cecelia's was kindergarten-through-twelfth with uniforms starting in first grade: dark green-and-navy plaid jumpers. Most of us didn't know any different, and even Xander, who'd just moved here last year, said it saved him the trouble of remembering what was clean every morning. The *one* requirement I regularly flouted was gym shorts underneath our skirts because I found it incredibly sexist. Guys shouldn't be looking up our skirts anyway.

There were plenty of buñuelos to go around, so as Mia stood guard, I distributed one each to my friends. Mia waved hers off, saying she already ate but widening her eyes at me. I remembered just how bad her morning sickness was. I downed mine and licked cinnamon off my fingers, then tucked the rest into my backpack to share with my mom later.

It's then I really noticed Xander.

"Dude, you shaved your head!" I squealed, my voice going up an octave. "It's awesome."

Xander laughed in the sexy baritone that had all the underclassmen girls swooning and all the guys jealous. "I got tired of white people touching my hair." Despite the joke in his voice, I noticed a flicker of disappointment in his eyes. Xander was the only Black kid at St. Cecelia's high school, and it wasn't easy. People loved him, but I'd witnessed the hair touching, and if it was uncomfortable for me, I couldn't imagine how it made Xander feel.

After an awkward silence, Tes said, "Fuckers." Xander threw back his head, laughing and then bumping the fist Tes held out.

"Can I touch your head?" Mia asked. "I mean, I know you said..."

Xander softened, his expression warm. "Anything for Mary Magdalene." He bent over, and Mia slowly ran her hand over the smoothness, her cheeks pinkening.

Tes emanated a slow, low growl, but Mia and Xander didn't seem to notice. They were in their own world, just like when they were singing.

I squeezed Tes's shoulder with one hand and wiggled another buñuelo his way with the other. He shook his head, and I shoved it in my mouth so I wouldn't yell at Mia that she was very obviously hurting his feelings. Sometimes it *really* sucked to have your two best friends dating each other.

Behind me, there was a shout of laughter: more than one person and tinged with meanness. It sounded distinctly like a group of the athletes that populated our school. This wasn't good.

"Oh no," Mia said softly, taking her hand away from Xander's head.

The smell of shit hit my nose, cutting through the standard St. Cecelia's fog of rubber erasers and CK One. Not human, thank God, but from a cow—belonging to one of the ag kids—that would likely be hamburger at Havendale Meat & Locker soon. Not an unusual odor for any kid who grew up in this farm town, but completely unexpected indoors.

Solid and fetid, a host of large, petrified turds had tumbled out of Cameron Smith's locker, which didn't have a combination—no one's did, per St. Cecelia's policy. As always, Cameron's expression was unreadable.

I wasn't nearly as nice to Cameron, with her tangled dyed black hair and mournful, perpetually downcast dark eyes, as I could have been. Every class had a moving target. One person even the outcasts avoided, terrified they'd be prime bully fodder if they befriended or, God forbid, said hello. Cameron Smith was, and had always been, ours.

Tes and Mia weren't at the top of the popularity food chain (that was our state champion football team), but they were the It Couple. Tes had smarts, Mia had music, and they'd been together for longer than any of the higher-profile twosomes who broke up and made up with alarming frequency *and* volume. Xander came in junior year, new to a small class that had been together since grade school. He had a laid-back coolness everyone loved. Plus, he was even dreamier when he sang. No one messed with him either.

I, on the other hand, made excellent grades and was class vice president to Tes's president. I was keenly aware of my social status—one step above hanger-on thanks to my beautiful, gifted friends—which kept me from any word or gesture that might upset the apple cart that was high school. I loved math and science, which was considered weird for a girl, but I was cute enough to pass muster. I knew the rules and I followed them. Mostly.

Even if I had more power, I didn't know what Cameron Smith and I would talk about. She never talked at all. Never smiled. And even in a town this tiny with a school that was even tinier, no one knew much about her.

Except this: she was sick on picture day. Every year.

"The *fuck*," Xander said, his words echoing off the now-silent hallway. Laughter and whispers had died down, but the first bell hadn't yet rung. Residual sugar granules from the buñuelos turned to dust on my tongue. Even the teachers who poked their heads out from classrooms were at a loss for what to do. I heard footsteps— someone getting the principal, maybe?

St. Cecelia's was a Catholic school. We took theology from kindergarten through senior year; it was a requirement no matter your religion. In two days, we'd attend Mass for Ash Wednesday, the beginning of Lent, walking away with black smudges on our foreheads. We'd had Protestants, atheists, and the occasional Jewish kid whose parents didn't want them in public school. You didn't have to be Father Robert, our favorite teacher and the drama coach who'd just directed Mia and Xander in *Jesus Christ Superstar*, to know the real Jesus advocated not only loving thy neighbors but also helping them.

Yet right now, everyone was statue-still, watching Cameron and wondering if she'd finally snap.

The footsteps picked up, and I realized they were Xander's as he disappeared and reemerged from the guy's restroom. Wrapping a paper towel around his hand, he then knelt next to Cameron and started picking up the cow shit.

Chapter Three

March

"Tell me a story," I said to Max from across the dining room table. Just like always, I was awarded with the world's most adorable snaggle-toothed grin.

It had been two weeks since the morning of buñuelos and cow shit—the two would forever be linked in my mind. Upstate in Lake Forest, Blair-Marie Elliott's parents were cleared of any involvement in her murder, though I still suspected her mother. There was something weird about her insistence on slapping a bunch of makeup and adult-looking costumes on such a small kid. I couldn't picture my mom doing that, ever.

Here in Havendale, Mia was still pregnant and without a plan, now relying on uniform-friendly sweaters at school and hoodies at home to hide her rapidly growing belly. Tes's parents had left for their business-and-pleasure sojourn in Europe last week, and we were all trying to help. Mia's parents invited Tes and Max over for dinner most nights. Xander and I chipped in with homework assistance, multiple viewings of *Star Wars* on the VCR, and knock-knock jokes so Tes could grocery shop, prep for his second round of the ACTs, and just chill with Mia.

Max wasn't fazed by his parents' swift departure. He was used to them being gone. They were always working, schmoozing, or generally holding court as Havendale royalty. The Wrightwoods were hometown heroes: Dad, owner and operator of Havendale's premier new and used car dealer; Mother (always Mother, never Mom), a real estate maven. They were fixtures at the country club and the annual Beaux Arts Ball, a fundraiser for the Havendale Art Association that was also a bizarre sort of Midwestern coming out for the town's *brightest* (actually wealthiest) high school seniors.

Needless to say, the only time Tes's parents came into contact with *my* mom was when she rang up their groceries. Never mind that like my mom, Mrs. Wrightwood didn't finish college and put all her hope into making Tes a success. Max, on the other hand, was given stuff instead of attention. Kid had more toys than a Walmart warehouse, but it was Tes who signed permission slips, drove him to school, and gave him cuddles when he had a nightmare.

"What do you wanna hear?" Max asked, snapping me out of my reverie. He loved making up stories and wanted to be a famous author "like Dr. Seuss or Beverly Cleary" one day.

"Ummm." I tapped my pen against my chin, looking out at the frost on the floor-to-ceiling windows facing the deserted golf course. "Something with mythical creatures. And winter." Next to my elbow, Blair-Marie Elliott ghoulishly grinned up at me from the *Havendale Gazette,* teeth bright and eyes blurry. I pushed the newspaper aside. I didn't want to be sad right now.

"Oh, Pal." Max grinned. "Have I got one for *you.*" He always said that, cute as a kid on a Friday night sitcom. Looking at him, his little face shining under the soft lighting of the Wrightwoods' formal dining room, I had the strangest urge to freeze time, to keep him young and innocent and full of stories.

Max was deep into a tale involving a dragon named Ethan Embry (*That Thing You Do!* was his favorite movie) and a snowstorm, when I heard Tes calling my name with an urgent tone.

"Put a pin in that kickass narrative, bud," I said, pushing away from the long oak dining table, my notebook, and a worn, ink-stained copy of *The Scarlet Letter*. "I'll be back in a jiff."

Down the hallway, I found Tes in his dad's study.

Holding a gun.

"Holy shit!" I shrieked before clapping a hand over my mouth. Noise carried like crazy in this house, and I didn't want Max to come running and see the shiny silver weapon. It was pointed at the ground, but still.

Tes grinned at my outburst.

"Where did you find that?" I whispered. Even when my dad was home from duty, we hadn't kept weapons in the house.

I didn't think.

"I've always known about it," he said nonchalantly, setting the gun on the red walnut desk between us. I could almost see it pulsing, eager, ready to take away life with one touch. "Dad got it a few years ago. Protection, he said."

"Protection from what?" Havendale's crime rate was laughably low. And sure, Tes and his family lived slightly outside of town in a ritzy house five times the size of mine, but they also had a state-of-the-art security system. I knew the code, but I was the only non-Wrightwood who did.

Tes shrugged. "Dunno. But he took lessons a long time ago. Made me take them too." He grinned again, and I looked away, unnerved by the near blankness in his eyes. "Just in case."

What the ever-loving hell? Ever since our car convo about Mia, Tes had calmed down. He'd even seemed more jovial last Saturday at the movies and appropriately affectionate with Mia. I knew he hadn't figured out about the pregnancy because I'd be the first to hear about it. From both of them.

He was also remarkably unfazed about his parents leaving—hadn't talked about it with me since. I thought he was staying strong for Max, concentrating on school like he usually did when something was especially off. Maybe he'd shut down *too* much.

Still, getting out a gun when his little brother was three rooms away? What brought this on?

I shook my head, slowly inhaling then exhaling. I swear I heard my blood rushing into my ears. "Please, please, *please* put the gun away. It's totally ridiculous, and I have no idea why you'd get it out, like, right now."

"Fine. It's not loaded, by the way." Tes opened a cabinet behind his father's desk, put the gun next to several small boxes of what I assumed were bullets, twisted the combination lock, and turned back to me. "There. Happy?"

I shuddered. "I hate guns. Ever since my dad died, I hate them even more." When I said "dad," my voice shook, and Tes's face softened for the first time since I'd stepped into the room.

"I'm so sorry, Pal," he said. "I didn't think. I just wanted to make sure I still knew where it was now that Max and I are on our own, and I didn't want him in the room. And…I don't know, I guess I wanted someone else to know about it too, just in case something bad happens? It's stupid." He came around the desk and put both hands on my shoulders, meeting my eyes. "You okay?"

I nodded, blinking away tears. "Yeah. Just promise me you'll only use it if you really need to."

"Hey." He slipped a finger under my chin and tipped it up. We were almost the same height. "I promise."

Only he and I knew that Tes was my first kiss and I was his. It was nothing—a curiosity, a tentative press of our lips after we watched *My Girl*, followed by a mutual "Ewwww!" and lots of giggling. We were only eleven, like Vada and Thomas J., and luckily, no one died of bee stings afterward. "Let's never do that again," I'd said, tucking my legs under me on their porch. "Yeah," little Tes replied, and we shook on it.

We hadn't talked about the kiss since, nor had either of us ever told Mia. But moments like this, I remembered his lips on mine as if it were yesterday.

I nodded once more, and the moment was over. Tes looked away, muttering.

"Come again?"

"Sometimes I think you're the only real friend I have left."

I opened my mouth to ask about Mia, about Xander, about our classmates who all looked up to Tes (even the jocks), when the phone rang. We both jumped.

"Paaaaaal!" Max. Thank God he hadn't seen Tes with a gun. "It's Mia. She says you're late."

"Oh shit!" Leaving behind dragons, cryptic statements, and even *The Scarlet Letter*, I ran for my coat and backpack.

"Lemme drive you!" Tes called after me. "It's slick."

"I'll be fine!" I yelled over my shoulder, opening the heavy front door and feeling a blast of air on my face.

I didn't want to be alone with him.

❖

"Roja!" Mia trilled across the restaurant's bustling kitchen. Her St. Cecelia's sweatshirt looked new and much larger. She tossed me my apron and order pad. "We're already in the weeds."

"Hi, Carmen!" I called over my shoulder. I barely heard Carmen's response. She was bent over the stove—we really were in the weeds if she was helping out in the kitchen rather than working the front. I headed to my station, inhaling the aroma of fresh tortilla chips and smiling at Carmen's voice bossing around the cook and various bussers. It was my workplace now, but El Rancherito had been my happy place since grade school.

Carmen was the family's tiny but terrifying authority. Barely five feet tall, she used to be the one to spank Mia after we stole chips from the kitchen. She'd ruled with an iron fist since buying an empty storefront and building a successful restaurant from the ground up shortly after they moved here when Mia was seven, so Lin could go to law school on scholarship and later become Havendale County's first Latino prosecutor. Despite being in a mostly white town with a population who had definite thoughts about "the Mexicans," El Rancherito was wildly popular. Carmen attributed this to the recipes she'd tweaked for redneck palates. Mia described the fare as, "If authentic Mexican food and Taco Bell had a baby."

Mia's parents had been married before in Texas, and Mia had half-siblings fifteen and twenty years her senior. Her parents were older, but Mia had been very much planned: the baby, the only girl, and they treasured her. Put her on a pedestal even.

I met Mia on the first day of second grade. She was new—we didn't get a lot of new kids—and it was hard to miss that wild, curly, chestnut hair. But I first really *saw* her a few days later when Mom and Dad took me to El Rancherito, which was also new, to celebrate my first week of school and Dad's several months of leave. It had meant dinners out, trips to the Children's Museum in St. Louis, and my mom locking the door to their room so I couldn't crawl in to share her bed in the middle of the night. I was happy.

My seven-year-old classmate had dropped off a basket of chips and a bowl of salsa, balancing them perfectly on her tray. With a big smile at me, she flounced off, curls bouncing, confident and doing a job just like a grown-up.

I was in awe.

The next Monday, I sat with her at lunch, cementing our friendship. Mia's parents have always been warm and welcoming, taking extra care of me and my mom in the early days after we found out Dad wasn't coming home. And as soon as I turned fifteen and got my work permit, Carmen waved me away when I reached for a job application. She handed me an apron and winked. "You know what to do, Roja." They purposely didn't speak a lot of Spanish in public or private—Carmen was originally from Nebraska and barely spoke Spanish, period—so my nickname seemed even more special. Made me feel protected.

"Hi, Father Robert, I'll be with you in a minute!" I called, seeing the telltale smile and collar. He came every Friday night without fail and never paid. Mia's parents didn't go to church, but old Catholic habits die hard, and anyway, their daughter adored the priest. Plus, he always tipped on what he would have paid, which was more than I could say for my jock classmates.

Just then the scent of Vanilla Musk from the Body Shop wafted toward me, the ensuing rush so heady I had to keep from swooning.

I craned my neck and spied the back of her striped polo shirt heading toward a large group of volleyball girls. Empty chip baskets and plates smeared with refried bean refuse scattered all over the pushed-together tables. She had less of a walk and more of a lope—casual off the court and oh so confident—as if she'd get wherever she was heading when she was ready and not a moment before. The world could wait.

Her hair was messy tonight: a sort of half-assed ponytail where she didn't pull it all the way through the elastic, resembling a blond teardrop. Soft tendrils curled at the nape of her neck, meaning she needed a haircut. If she turned around, I'd see brilliant blue eyes. If she smiled, straight white teeth—no sign of the overbite she'd had for most of grade school. I remembered she was the first person in kindergarten to lose a tooth, and I'd suddenly become very aware of her presence. Maybe I knew about her, about me, even then.

Ani Donoghue. The girl who could ruin me.

I knew she brushed my shoulder on purpose.

CHAPTER FOUR

I can't do this anymore." She'd taken her lips off mine, and I felt every bit of the cold air between us. She brushed her bottom lip with her thumb as though trying to wipe away any trace of me, the girl she'd been kissing desperately just a moment before. My heart sank to my rubber-soled boots, the melting ice seeping in through the hole I really needed to patch.

Like clockwork, all of it.

Ani and I stood in the alley behind El Rancherito making out on my break. No one else was around, and we were hidden from plain sight in a convenient blind spot we'd found months ago. When she dropped this bomb—as she did every freaking week—I could still taste her Chapstick on my lips, a waxy strawberry. I never told her, but after our first kiss, I bought a stick of it that I kept under my pillow.

Ani was Anne Marie to her parents, our teachers, and her beloved volleyball coach. She nicknamed herself last year after discovering Ani DiFranco, whose smoky voice and authentic lyrics were ideal for two girls fooling around in secret. Unfortunately, calling herself Ani was her one and only act of outright rebellion.

She was the third of seven kids, living in an old farmhouse outside of town where there were still unpaved roads, the type of stereotypical Catholic family that was now pretty rare. In my dad's generation, twelve or thirteen kids in a family named Sheehan or O'Brien or Donoghue were as much a part of St. Cecelia's as the gray-speckled linoleum in the hallway. But modern Catholic parents knew the rhythm method didn't work, and I suspected most of them were ignoring church edicts and using birth control. I mean, I'd found Carmen's diaphragm in their bathroom last year.

Ani was a star in a way Mia and Tes were not. They were alterna-popular; she was mainstream: the cool girl in a Molly Ringwald movie. She was third in the class academic ranks after Tes and me, or me and Tes depending on the week, and varsity volleyball since she was a freshman. Her parents both grew up here but met at Notre Dame—the Holy Grail of Catholic universities. Her two older brothers were currently kicking ass on ND's football team, while one of her sisters was at the affiliate, St. Mary's, what they called a Smick Chick. Ani would be a shoo-in for either school with the trifecta of grades, sports, and legacy.

What Ani didn't have was a boyfriend.

The guys at St. Cecilia's found this personally offensive. The nicer ones made a big deal of asking her to homecoming and prom. She humored them, first come first serve, but it never went anywhere after the dance itself. The seedier types had a running bet over who could take her virginity.

Donna from eighth grade volleyball camp beat them to it, and nobody knew that but me, her third.

Ani was my first. And last and only, if I had my way.

Back in fifth grade, Ani, Mia, and I were a united front, forming the I Hate Boys Club that met every recess with an exclusive membership of three. When we were thirteen, though, Mia found music, Ani got into volleyball hardcore, and I focused on making my NASA dreams real through studying.

Then last year happened.

Mia had just started sleeping with Tes, and consequently, the two of us had drifted apart. I got into the habit of hanging out before and after my shifts, doing homework with ambient restaurant noise in the background. Lin patted my back as soon as he came in from the office and Carmen slipped me free chips and salsa, the telltale "we know our daughter's abandoned you for her boyfriend" expression written all over their faces.

I hated the pity, but I loved the free chips.

One Saturday afternoon after the lunch shift, Ani came in and slid across from me in the booth where I was working on pre-calc. Her forearms rested on the sticky table—salsa remnants I could never quite wipe clean. She was tan even in winter thanks to the local salon. Her wrists were strong, a silver charm bracelet dangling off the right. At the time, I'd wondered if a potential suitor had given it to her.

"Hey," she'd said.

"Hey," I'd said back.

I met her eyes, the bluest I've ever seen, like summer sky above the cornfields just outside of town.

And one thing led to another and another and another…

"You say this every time," I said, trying like hell to keep my voice calm and measured when really I wanted to scream in frustration. And not just emotional frustration, if you get my drift.

Ani fully broke away from me. The warm imprint of her body lingered on mine. I could still feel the soft cotton of her polo shirt and her bare back under my hands. But it wasn't enough. Never was.

"This isn't me," she said, gesturing between us. She paced the alley's blind spot furiously. Her huge Adidas sneakers inched closer to a patch of black ice. I wanted to reach out, pull her back to safety, to me, but I knew from experience she didn't want to be touched. "I'm not—"

"You're not what?" I lifted my chin. At this point in our relationship—or whatever you could call fooling around in an alley until Ani denied who she was, then ignored me for three days before we started the whole damn cycle again—I could recite her defenses word for word, and I was getting very tired of them. "The type who kisses girls? Because, news flash, that's what you were doing ten seconds ago."

"You know what I mean!" Ani threw up her hands, perfectly manicured with short nails, ideal for sports and, as we'd learned after the Christmas dance, other things. My dream girl, who'd said more than once she wished I were a boy so we could really and truly date. Those were the nights I went home and cried, and then *I* was the one who ignored *her*. For at least four days, until I couldn't stay away any longer.

"No, I don't know." I crossed my arms over my chest. "We've had *sex*, Ani."

She rolled her eyes and my heart hurt. "Oooookay."

"It's not wrong to like girls." My voice went from strong and true to small and weak in just a few words. Because as much as I wanted to believe my statement, I wasn't sure it could be so in Havendale.

"Really," Ani said. Now backed up against the other wall of the alley, she rested a sneakered foot against the brick wall, looking like an ad for the all-American girl. I wish I didn't find that type so sexy. "Why don't you tell that to Father Robert?" She smirked, knowing she had me.

Face flaming, I turned away.

"That's what I thought," Ani said over her shoulder, leaving me behind in the alley's blind spot. From here she'd go back into the restaurant and rejoin her volleyball friends. Tell them she left her Chapstick in her car or something. They'd believe her, laughing and spilling salsa without even leaving me a dollar. Never mind that their parents paid for everything and I was saving for college.

Didn't seem to matter to Ani that *she* was the one who always initiated things at my house when my mom was at work, in this quiet space that smelled like flour tortillas, and even once in the locker room shower when she swore everyone else had gone home.

What sucked the most though? Ani was right. I thought of Cameron Smith: no one really knew who she was into, but the worst of the bullies loved calling her "dyke" and "lil lezzie." They broke into her locker to leave Victoria's Secret catalog pages when they weren't leaving bovine turds. I'd heard of worse things in towns just like ours—kids getting beaten up, even killed, because they liked someone of the same sex. Those stories never got much coverage in the *Havendale Gazette*, but I read newspapers from bigger cities at the public library sometimes, searching frantically to find a mention of someone like me, even if it involved death, which it usually did.

Every time I learned about another incident, I shivered. I liked guys *and* girls. Others like me had to exist. But even on TV, everyone was either gay or straight. What would my meaner classmates think?

What would they *do*?

I hated what Ani said, but I was just as bad, fooling around with her in private, keeping my secrets because I was too chickenshit to deal with the fallout.

And now she was gone.

"Arrrrrgh!" I punched the brick wall behind me. No gloves to protect against the cold, I could still feel the scrape of brick against rapidly numbing skin.

"Hey!" a voice much deeper than Ani's boomed behind me. Xander, in a coat way too light for this weather, stood by the restaurant's back door. My knuckles stung, my break was almost over, and my coolest friend had caught me acting like a Rocky Balboa wannabe. Awesome.

The dim light of the alley reflected off Xander's shaved head as he stepped closer. "You okay?" he asked. "I saw Ani running the hell away and heard a scream."

"What are you doing here?" I asked, cradling my hand.

"Needed enchiladas." He sidled up next to me, our backs against the wall, shoulders touching. Ani was gone, but her cold breeze of Vanilla Musk remained. "You didn't answer my question."

"I love her." The three words came out softly. It was the first time I'd said it outside of my dreams. My breath fogged the March air, and I heard the *whoosh* of cars going in and out of the shopping center parking lot. Stores stayed open late on weekends, so that meant a busy night for El Rancherito.

I glanced at Xander, his strong profile backlit in the winter night. "You can't tell anyone."

"You small-town Catholics," he said. "I know gay people in Chicago. It's no big deal up there."

I sighed. "I'm not exactly gay. I don't think. I mean, I like guys too. Not any guys in our school, but guys in general. I know that's a real thing, being attracted to both, but I also feel like it's not quite right, like why can't I just pick a side? I just…" I trailed off, sounding like every lovesick character on TV shows written by people who thought they remembered high school, but really didn't. High school wasn't melodramatic every second of the day. More often than not, I was finding, high school was about longing. A quiet, desperate ache for someone I could never fully have hollowed me out. Sometimes I wondered if Tes felt that way about Mia.

Xander shrugged. "It's whatever. You know? Be who you are. Even in this farm town."

He made it sound so easy.

"Farm town," I said with a snort. "Why did you move here, anyway?" I asked, turning to face him. Something about the dark, the quiet, the rejection emboldened me. Xander opened his mouth and I cut him off. "I know, I know, your mom wanted you to live with your aunt and uncle because they're professors at the college and they'll help you get your grades up, but…"

"You've always thought it was bullshit?" he finished, chuckling ruefully. "You'd be right."

He rummaged in his pocket and pulled a photo out of his wallet. I recognized the baby's face as the same one taped up inside Xander's locker. I'd caught him looking at it once, between classes, with an expression of unbelievable sadness. When he saw me, he slammed the door shut, shouldered his backpack, and disappeared into French Three.

Now, though, he handed me the picture. "That's my son."

"Your son?" I always wondered about Xander's bring-your-grades-up explanation but never questioned him. That's the thing about living in Havendale: everyone listens to rumors, but it's practically against the law to ask people directly about personal matters. Anyway, he always seemed so confident when he laughed off his terrible marks.

Except he was in honors classes, had been since day one.

"He's a little over a year old now," Xander told me, studying the back of his hands as if they had the answers. "Actually, almost two." He smiled wistfully.

"His mom, Yolanda, she and I didn't last long. Well, we lasted long enough to get her pregnant. We get along fine; they live with her mom now. But *my* mom, she didn't want me getting too involved. Wanted me to go to college, so she had the idea to send me to my uncle and aunt. Out in the boonies. To the *Catholic* school, not the public. Didn't want me telling anyone here either, so, you know, I wouldn't be yet another young Black man with a kid out of wedlock." He took a deep breath. In the months I'd known Xander, this was the most personal we'd ever gotten. Even though we'd hung out almost every weekend, we'd never been alone. Until now.

All I could say was, "Um, wow."

He laughed, the kind that wasn't really a laugh. "Yeah. Wow. I know."

"Doesn't your mom know you can get a girl pregnant here too?" I clapped a hand over my mouth. "I'm sorry," I said, my face on fire. "Adults always think Catholic school is like rehab or something, when we're just as fucked up as everyone else."

What I was really thinking: Xander was the first person I knew my age with a kid. And soon, I'd know another. I wished Mia would come up with a plan. Tell her parents. Or anyone who wasn't me. Tell someone who would know exactly what to do.

I shivered. Suddenly, the night air seemed a lot colder.

Xander grinned. "That's what I said to my ma." I handed him the photo and he carefully put it back in his wallet. "Then I got here, and yeah, I wish this town wasn't so white, but I don't hate it. And St. Cecelia's music department kicks my old school's ass. Also..." He got a faraway look in his eyes, and I knew, I just *knew*.

"Mia?"

"Damn, Pal," he said. "She always says you can get anyone to tell you anything, but I didn't believe it till right now. You've got powers."

I rolled my eyes. "I don't know about *powers*." Keeping everyone's secrets was not all that. "And honestly?" I said, leaning back to look him over, tall and strong and handsome. I liked guys, but I didn't like Xander that way. I wished I did. Everything would be so much less complicated. "You can't feel that way about Mia."

He lifted his chin, a challenge glinting in his eyes. "You can't tell me how to feel."

"Fair enough, but she and Tes are serious. Like, really serious."
Like "they're going to have a baby even though Tes doesn't know yet" serious.

Right then, I wanted to tell Xander. It was so hard being the only one who knew. As the snow melted outside only to be replaced day after day, Mia's body changed and her emotions got bigger, and I worried for her. I bit my lips till they almost bled just so the secret wouldn't burst forth.

"I *know* they're serious," Xander said, snapping me back to the present. "Trust me, Tes is ass over teakettle for that girl. He only talks about her every second." He sighed, shoulders slumping, then looked right at me. "You can't tell anyone about my son. It's not like I'm ashamed or anything. I just...I don't want it following me around here, you know?"

I nodded. "I know." I knew he worried what Mia would think. "And you can't tell anyone about..."

Xander crossed his heart. "I'll take it to the grave." He shook his head, looking to where Ani had left me stranded. "You deserve better, you know that?"

"Whatever."

"Not whatever, Pal. Really. You're a good person." He smiled, but his eyes were sad. We both wanted what we couldn't have.

"Roja!" Carmen's melodious voice rang out over the back alley. "Break over!"

"I gotta go," I told Xander. But before heading back into the warm kitchen, I stepped toward him and hugged him tight. He wrapped his arms around me, warm under his light coat, heart thumping.

For just a moment, I breathed him in.

Chapter Five

I haven't felt this shocked since Mia showed me the blue line on her fourth pregnancy test.

Speaking of Mia, I didn't have to look at my best friend to know her eyes were bugging out of her head. A puke-green plastic tray slopped with the cafeteria's Salisbury steak was on the table in front of her, completely forgotten. Next to her, Tes clenched his jaw.

Xander appeared relaxed and confident as always, but I saw the fear in his eyes.

"Everybody know Cameron?" he asked, gesturing to the Cousin It double standing next to him. Cameron Smith's hair hung in two dark and stringy curtains that covered her face, as if she wanted to hide from us.

"Sit next to me," Xander said gently, putting down his own tray. After a slow, deliberate pause, Cameron did the same. She still hadn't made eye contact.

"Hey," she mumbled, a single gravelly syllable. I could almost see it hanging in the air only to plop down smack in the middle of our lunch table. I tried to remember whether I'd heard her talk since the first day of freshman year, when she transferred from the public junior high and said her name in front of homeroom. Nothing came to mind.

"Hi, Cameron," I managed to squeak, and Tes and Mia muttered greetings. Their expressions had morphed from outright disbelief to frozen politeness. The manners our parents and various clergy had instilled in us wrestled with the fact that our peaceful lunch routine had been turned on its head.

I tried to catch Xander's eye like, *What the ever-loving hell is going on here?* Since that night in the alley last week when we traded our life-altering secrets like Mia and I used to trade Lisa Frank stickers, I'd felt closer to him. Now I saw Xander for who he really was: a fellow outsider, part of the golden circle but not quite *the* golden circle, with secrets of his own.

He'd been kind to Cameron after the cow shit incident, which I admired, still guilty I hadn't had the guts to do anything but stare. But bringing Cameron to sit with us was a whole other animal.

Cameron usually ate in the bathroom. Last fall, I had to change my tampon during lunch, and her scuffed Doc Martens were poking out of the biggest stall. She was sitting on the floor, not the toilet. With a flash of her hands, she opened a Ziploc bag of bright orange baby carrots, and I heard the *crunch* as they made their way into her mouth. Coupled with the fact that I was taking something out of myself and putting another one in, the whole thing was oddly intimate. I'd left in a hurry, back to the solace of my cozy table and my cool friends, and away from the fear that I, too, was one faux pas away from eating carrots in the place where people crapped.

Today, Cameron ate her carrots out in the open, chomping loudly and staring down at the Ziploc bag full of neon sticks. Mia masticated the cafeteria's Salisbury steak that was her weakness. Tes picked Doritos out of the bag and looked at each one as if he wanted to kill it before crunching down. Xander and I stuffed mashed potatoes into our mouths. At one point, I coughed politely, apologizing to no one.

The dead little girl, Blair-Marie Elliott, flashed into my mind. What did her last night look like? Her last meal? I'd read she ate pears just before, that the medical examiners found them in her stomach. Did someone in her family give them to her, in a bowl with a spoon? Were they sitting around a table, watching her chew her canned fruit, marking time until she was no more?

The worst attacks come from the inside.

Just a few minutes before the sixth-period bell, Xander widened his eyes at me, a silent plea to break this uncomfortable silence punctuated only by the slap of the butter pat Mia pressed on her roll and the *shhhhh* of Tes opening a Dr Pepper.

"Uhhhhh," I said, ever the great conversationalist. "How was everyone's last class?"

Cameron mumbled something, grabbed her carrots, and rushed away. We all exhaled. I couldn't shake the months-long feeling of being on edge, skittering along on a rickety train about to go shooting off the tracks, into the unknown.

But I didn't break the silence again. Tes did.

"What. The. Hell," he spat, looking straight at Xander. Under his white Oxford shirt, Tes's shoulders were hunched up, as if he was ready for battle. He'd told me about the night before: Max had bad dreams that kept him up into the wee hours, and they barely got out the door this morning. Earlier, he'd bombed a pop quiz in Honors English because he hadn't read the short story last night; Max had needed help with a worksheet. Some people don't freak out about one bad grade, but a sleep-deprived, stressed out Tes was not some people.

"What?" Xander asked with an unmistakable edge. Mia caught my eye, wondering what to do, and I shrugged, hoping if we stayed silent nothing would escalate. "I just wanted to be nice. Don't make a federal case out of it."

"This is the one time," Tes said, "the *one* time, the twenty-five minutes of the day I get to hang out with my friends without worrying about ACT prep, grocery shopping, and reassuring my eight-year-old brother that yes, Mommy and Daddy are coming back someday. And you had to *fuck it all up* with that *freak.*"

"Hey!" Mia said. She tapped Tes's arm and he looked at her sharply. There were bags under his eyes, and I wondered how long they'd been there. "Don't talk to him that way."

Tes would do anything for Mia, and normally just her hand on his arm, soft and sweet, would have calmed him straightaway.

This time, Tes jerked away. "Of course you'd say that."

"Tes," Xander warned.

"What's that supposed to mean?" Mia folded her arms across her chest. Her sweater was larger than ever, and I swore I'd seen it on her dad in the past.

Tes glared at her. "I think you know."

"Hey, man," Xander said, shooting me a confused glance. I shook my head. More and more lately, I didn't know what to do.

"The way you look at him," Tes said, still glaring at the girl he repeatedly told me he loved more than anything. None of us needed to ask who "him" was. "The way you guys are always *singing*. For fuck's sake, what is there to sing about, like, all the time?"

"You know how I feel about the *F* word," Mia whispered, staring at her lap.

Tes leaned in, and for a second, I thought he would apologize, kiss her, make it all better.

Just as I started to relax, he looked Mia right in the eye and hissed through his teeth, "Fuck. Fuck. Fuck."

"Jesus, Tes!" I said. Now *my* jaw clenched.

"What the hell is wrong with you?" Xander said, rising from the table, looking down at Tes, tone steady and profile noble as a monarch's. "Why would you talk to your girl like that?" He started to say something else, but instead took a deep breath and focused on his orange plastic tray with a pile of paper napkins and Salisbury steak smears.

I glanced frantically at the clock—three minutes left of lunch—and prayed for an early bell, which had never happened in the history of St. Cecelia's lunch. Fire drill, maybe?

"Say it," Tes challenged, rising from his seat. Without even thinking about it, I rushed around the small table to Mia's side and grabbed her hand. She squeezed hard.

"You have *everything*," Xander said. His hands curled into fists against his navy blue Dockers. "The money. The respect. The grades." He hesitated, gave Mia the most fleeting of glances. "The girl." He reached his hand across the table, put it down just as quickly. "I get that you're going through something, man. I do. But you can't take that shit out on people who haven't done anything to deserve it."

Mia's fingernails bit into my palms.

By now, the whole cafeteria was silent. No one had ever seen the golden boy freak out. Moreover, no one challenged Tes—not even teachers.

Yet Xander *was* challenging him. And what's more, he was absolutely right.

Tes's jaw looked like it was about to pop out of his skull.

Two minutes.

Before I could say, do, think anything more, Tes lunged at Xander with a scream that wouldn't be out of place in the wild. He picked up his cafeteria tray, then wielded it like a deadly weapon, a violence in his eyes I'd never seen before and hoped I never would again.

Chaos.

Xander tried to head him off, but once Tes landed a punch square to his eye, his instincts kicked in. Xander was bigger, but Tes had several axes to grind, making him infinitely more dangerous. Soon there was full-on rolling around and more animalistic yelling from Tes as the puke-green cafeteria tray he tried to break over Xander's head ended up flung against the wall, shattering into three pieces and splattering brown gravy—that looked disturbingly like blood—everywhere.

I grabbed Mia's arm and pulled her into an awkward hug-hold, the words "the baby" frozen on my tongue. Tears ran down her face as Tes and Xander went at it, and she looked for all the world like a saint, or more accurately, a martyr, watching the world go down with absolutely no control.

A few punches in, Kevin "Moose" O'Brien, lunged in and grabbed Tes while another football player got ahold of Xander. Father Robert rushed into the middle of it all, glasses askew and a sandwich dangling from his hand. He yelled for quiet, please, order, his office, Tesla and Alexander, immediately.

And then Mia fainted, slumping against me. I scrambled to keep her steady. My grasp was firmly around her middle when the baby moved, this strong pulse that came from inside, an impossible to ignore statement. *I'm here.*

I screamed.

❖

After Father Robert's office, Xander and Tes were sent to Dr. Foley with their heads down, shoulders not touching, as the bell rang and the rest of us watched.

All except Mia, who was hauled to the nurse. I would have been more nervous, except all Sister Bernice did was take your temperature, give you a cup of juice, and let you lie down until next period. She was almost ninety years old and blind as a bat.

"Bless me, Father, for I have sinned."

We went to confession every quarter, and as timing would have it, today was the day. It was also Lent, the big Catholic pre-Easter season of even *more* guilt than usual and self-sacrifice that extended to meatless Fridays. Mia observed to the letter, and I not at all. I was already having premarital sex *with a girl*. I didn't think eating chicken on Friday was going to up my sinner status much.

Normally, I was not into the confession ritual. Telling a man in a collar about the time I said "fuck," only to be assigned ten Hail Marys and my soul was clear? How did anyone buy that?

But Father Robert was different, and today I was grateful.

After Moose exited the confessional, I padded in, my shoes silent on the thin carpet. I closed the door and sat on the other side of the screen, tuning out the organ music courtesy of ancient Mrs. Darby pounding away and trying my damnedest to calm down. The cold leather bench bit the backs of my thighs where my navy skirt didn't cover.

"Would you like to tell me what that was all about, Paulina?" Well, we were getting right into it. Squinting, I could see Father Robert through the screen. His hands were folded on top of his black shirt, glasses slipping down his nose and his round head resting on his nonexistent neck, like a friendly turtle from a children's book.

"Not really," I said.

All the strict rules and rituals and uniforms from the time I could tie my own shoes weren't something I really thought about until Xander, coming from a Chicago public school, pointed out how strange it all was.

On the one hand, I and my classmates developed an unmistakable urge to rebel, to quietly bend or openly flout regulations. We tried little things like pulling out our tucked shirts in front of the strictest teachers right after the last bell, then bigger, like smoking cigarettes outside in full view of the older nuns and buying beer from the gas station cashiers who always looked the other way. Especially where the athletes were concerned.

On the other hand—though I couldn't speak for my classmates—I took comfort in the black-and-white penguin outfits of the clergy. The words of the Our Father that I whispered at school assemblies were as much a part of me as my hair. And though I bitched about uniforms, the fact that in such an uncertain world— where dads get shot overseas in friendly fire and little girls die in their own houses during the holidays—knowing something small had already been decided for me helped me get through the day.

"That was a lot for you to witness," Father Robert continued as I concentrated on the weak sunlight streaming under the door. "Dr. Foley will handle the discipline, but I know you're friends with everyone at that table. I wanted to check in and make sure *you* were okay."

I tucked my hands under my butt and crossed my ankles, uncomfortable with the fact that someone was worried about *me*. Should I make this a real confession and tell Father Robert everything? If I squinted harder, I'd see his kind turtle face empathize the way it had during my first confession in second grade.

I wanted those simple, clear instructions again. *Say these words and all will be well. Your friends got into a fight and your best friend's pregnant? Call this doctor and he'll make it all okay.*

For a moment, the words were on my tongue, the texture as unmistakable as a Communion wafer.

But he'd have to tell someone about Mia's pregnancy, and I couldn't make this all about me and my feelings, my fears. I had to protect her and Tes and Xander.

The baby.

So when Father Robert repeated the question, I thought of the Communion wafer and let the truth dissolve. "I don't know what got into Tes, Father. I'll keep an eye on him, I promise."

"That shouldn't be your responsibility," he said.

But it is! I wanted to scream. *I don't want it to be, but it is!* I gulped away the lump in my throat.

"I—" I sputtered.

I what? *I was scared of how angry Tesla seemed these days. I wanted Ani to ask me to the spring dance. I worried I'd love the baby more than Mia. I couldn't stop thinking about Tesla's dad's gun. Technically, it was wrong to like boys and girls, but the more I thought about it all, the more it felt right.*

Father Robert's gaze burned through the screen so hard I was surprised the thing didn't spontaneously combust.

He *knew.*

Maybe not the details, but in that freaky way only priests and nuns had, he could sense I was holding back, that I wanted desperately to talk, to release some of this steadily accumulating weight.

I had to deflect. I had to.

"I'm, uh…" I mustered my best sheepish smile. "I'm stressed about my Honors English essay."

Father Robert sighed heavily, shoulders sinking. The moment was over and we both knew it. "I worry about you, Paulina. I know you hold a lot in. People tell me their secrets too, but I have to work hard not to let that…overtake me."

So, clearly, he wasn't going to assign me three Hail Marys and call it a day. Sometimes I really missed being a kid.

"I gotta go, Father."

I could hear the shuffling of jackets as everyone got ready to walk across the blacktop elementary playground back to school. Rushing out of the confessional, I nearly knocked over Stevie Little, one of Max's classmates who also played peewee baseball.

"You okay?" I asked, squatting down to his level. I glanced around St. Cecelia's Church for a teacher, another second grade class, another second grader even. The kid was alone.

"Fine," Stevie answered me in his tiny, squeaky voice, rubbing his perfectly coiffed hair. When he opened his mouth, there were three gaps where his teeth hadn't yet grown in. "You done?"

"Yeah," I said. "Go on in."

I half-ran through the cold outside and back into school, mind racing with thoughts of Tes and Mia.

Much as I hated to cause even more trouble, I had to reason with Tes. I could talk him down and doubted Mia could do the same, especially with a person growing inside her. I knew from the copy of *What to Expect When You're Expecting* hidden under my mattress (I'd tried to give it to Mia, but she wrinkled her nose and turned it down) that fainting sometimes happened to pregnant women.

Because no matter how much she tried to deny it, to the world and to herself, Mia was pregnant. And sooner or later, we would all have to deal.

I'd barely gotten into the hallway when I smelled Vanilla Musk, then felt something press into my hand.

I looked over my shoulder to see Ani's swinging blond ponytail as she disappeared into chemistry, then opened the delicately folded triangle.

Her familiar bubbly scrawl read, *Your place Saturday night? BURN THIS* in smeared black ink on blue lines.

I grinned. I never would.

And then I saw them.

Tes knelt in front of Mia with his cheek pressed against her stomach. Her hands were in his hair. Even in their uniforms, they looked like fine art. The Virgin Mary and Joseph plunked down in the hallway of St. Cecelia's, goddess and supplicant. Delicate. Priceless.

I drew in a shaky breath. People seemed to slow down as they passed by, taking in the silent but powerful spectacle. As I came closer, I heard Mia humming.

We were in so much trouble.

❖

Baby,
We were kings.
Once I found out about you, I dug out an old English notebook and started writing everything down, making notes. Not just about

diapers, formula, what to do when you wake up screaming—anything I could find at the public library before I shoved the books back in the stacks—but on me, your mom, the you we made one night at Nichols Park.

My parents never tell me anything, so I want you to know everything.

You came to be in November on closing night of the fall musical, Jesus Christ Superstar. *Your mama played Mary Magdalene, because of course she did. We're only juniors now, but she's had the best voice at St. Cecelia's since she was in eighth grade, and something just clicked.*

I was there that day at all-school Mass. We had mandatory music class through grade school, but she never stood out, whispering syllables and notes in the back of the classroom with our friend Paulina, your soon-to-be auntie. During the Gloria, she opened her mouth and out came a sound that I can only describe as otherworldly from three seats down. That day I looked up at the stained glass windows, sure I would see the Virgin Mary, or Jesus, or some kind of heavenly being that would land us on Unsolved Mysteries, *but there was nothing, just dust motes in sunshine and your mom's voice. The stellar high school music department at St. Cecelia's took her under their wing right then and there.*

From then on, she was golden, the light shining through her hair as she got all the good solos and made the senior girls jealous. I was the smart kid, the one who threw the best parties once we hit eighth grade, ensuring my "in" with the jocks (very important) despite my chicken legs and lack of hand-eye coordination. For real, baby, I spent two years trying to work up the courage to ask her to a movie. And when I did and she said yes, and we sat in the encore screening of The Crow, *surrounded by our classmates hurling candy and flirting loudly, even as poor Brandon Lee got for-real shot on screen, she frowned at their disrespect and crossed herself like the hardcore Catholic she was.*

I was a goner.

Anyway, we made you the first semester of our junior year. After the closing night cast party, we were tooling around on Havendale's main drag in my ancient Cadillac. The thing's the size of a boat and older than dirt. I call it vintage; your mom and our friends call it the Bear.

Green Day blasted from the tape deck, and we sang along to "When I Come Around" and reminisced about how the album changed our lives as flannel-clad, just learning to be angsty fourteen-year-olds. I was in the driver's seat, and she scooched over to the middle of the bench, laying her head on my shoulder and twirling her fingers through her curls.

I dreamed about her hair. I hope you get it too.

In the back seat was your auntie Paulina, and Xander, who was new to St. Cecelia's and fell right into our group. Almost too easily. He was as good a singer as your mom, played Judas in JCS and nailed the high notes and the angst that came with betraying your best friend. His voice matched your mom's, finding an easy harmony.

I saw the way he looked at her and I didn't like it. He was doing it while we sang, sneaking glances at your mama in the rearview mirror when he thought I wasn't watching. I recognized that look: like one of those kids in The Goonies when they find the pirate cave full of gold and jewels. My eyes met your auntie Paulina's, and she shook her head, mouthing along to Billie Joe Armstrong.

Today I took the first step to make sure Xander stopped looking at your mom that way. Got me suspended, but it was worth it.

Havendale's small, less than twenty thousand, and St. Cecelia's with fifty kids per class is even smaller. I know every face. And that night, harmonizing to Green Day after your mom's star turn, the four of us were kings of everything. Wheels. Tunes. Each other.

I won't go into detail about what happened after I dropped off Paulina, then Xander.

Your mom and I pulled into our usual spot, next to a white Chevy whose windows were already plenty steamed up.

I turned to her. She looked at me, warm brown eyes full of anticipation. And I'm not going to lie to you, baby, something that night felt different. I'm not talking about what I forgot because I *was so absorbed in the moment, in the smell of her hair, the taste of her mouth, the little sighing sounds she made. It was more intense. Binding. What my English teacher would call "foreshadowing" but in a good way. The best possible.*

Don't ever let anyone call you an accident. You were meant to be.

Love,
Somebody You Don't Know (Yet)

Chapter Six

Tesla knew about the baby. Mia told him; she'd blurted it out the second he left Dr. Foley's office with a purple bruise on his cheek and three days of detention.

They still hadn't told their parents. Instead, Tes proposed.

Two days later, we were still whispering about it in the back room of El Rancherito.

We filled saltshakers out of Carmen's earshot, and I tamped down my sense of foreboding that had bloomed the minute the fight started.

"I can't believe you'd take him back after he did that to Xander," I muttered, carefully making sure I didn't spill one grain of salt.

Mia glanced at me, brown eyes wide from behind a pepper shaker. "He loves me, Pal," she said. "He apologized so many times and he even cried. He's just tired and taking care of Max has been a lot lately." She broke into a smile. "He even started a notebook so he could write letters to the baby, isn't that the sweetest?"

This was really starting to sound like one of those made-for-TV movies. I knew Tes wasn't abusive. Of course he wasn't. But shouldn't he have to suffer some consequences? Especially from the mother of his child?

I took a deep breath. She wouldn't want to hear this, but I had to say it. "You and I deal with a lot too, Mia, and we don't start fights. I don't swear at you after you ask me to stop."

"Well, you're not in love, are you?" That hurt, as she knew it would. After twisting the top on the final saltshaker, she huffed off. Her ruby engagement ring caught the harsh fluorescent light.

Leaving me standing there, alone. I blinked back frustrated tears like the closeted idiot I was.

❖

The Saturday lunch crowd was dying down at the restaurant. Mia and Tes sat in a corner booth. They were holding hands and making plans, and I sat across from them trying my best not to feel awkward and failing. Mia glowed in the way pregnant women do, the way I thought was a myth until I saw her that morning. The promise ring Tes gave her adorned her wedding finger. Festooned with a tiny ruby, it was his great-grandmother's, stored away until he'd presented it to Mia, down on one knee in the study where he kept his father's gun. I wondered how close they'd been to the safe. I also wondered what, exactly, Tes promised.

"I need to wipe tables," I told them. I didn't actually, but I couldn't sit there any longer. Tes kissed Mia on the nose. She giggled, and they didn't hear me.

I felt a tug on my pants pocket, looked down, and saw Max.

"How's it going, buddy? Do you want to help?" I asked. He nodded, carefully handing me a clean rag in exchange for my dirtier one. My feet ached and my face hurt from my standard-issue "What can I get you?" smile. I heard Mia giggle again.

"Eh." Max shrugged, sounding a lot older than second grade. "Could be better."

"How's that?" I concentrated on scrubbing a particularly stubborn piece of dried salsa, sneaking a glance at Tes and Mia, whose foreheads were touching, in a world all their own. I thought of Ani and tried not to scowl.

"Tes got in trouble at school," Max said matter-of-factly. I shook my head back to the present: my damp rag, his sad eyes.

"I know, bud," I said. So did Xander, who got suspended even though he didn't start the fight. Completely unfair if you asked me, which no one did. I stopped scrubbing the last table, reaching out one arm to Max, who snuggled into a sideways hug.

"He didn't use his words," Max whispered, his little face falling. Like the rest of St. Cecelia's, he thought Tes hung the moon.

I was grateful he hadn't seen his beloved brother fly off the handle. The look in Tes's eyes, his clenched jaw, had haunted me ever since.

"That's right," I said. I desperately needed to get off my feet, and the place was now officially empty. Salsa stain wiped away, I perched in the now-clean booth, closest to the door and farthest away from the happy couple. Max joined me on the opposite side. His feet didn't touch the ground.

"Dad yelled at him on the phone last night. They were cursing," Max told me as a big laugh came from Tes and Mia's booth. Even though I wasn't happy with either of them, I couldn't help but feel distinctly...uninvited. Mia and I'd had a secret, just the two of us. Now that Tes was in on it, which he *should* have been as the father, everything had changed. My intimacy with Mia—one I hadn't felt since she and Tes first started having sex—had slipped away. Again.

"Hey, Max?" I asked. "Did Tezzie tell you anything about Mia?"

Max wrinkled his forehead, thinking. "Just that he loves her so, so, so much and he wants to marry her and he's giving her Great-Grandma's ring." He smiled. "And they're going to move to a new house, and he'll take me with him."

"Really," I said, my smile frozen in place as my blood pressure shot up.

"All good here?" Lin asked, approaching us with a warm basket of chips and a bowl of tomatillo salsa. He hadn't been at his office today, was just here helping Carmen and wearing a T-shirt and jeans instead of his usual jacket and tie. He glanced over his shoulder at his beloved only daughter and smiled. I noticed Mia now had her hands under the table, hiding the ring.

"Sorry, Lin." I hopped up, hoping my face wasn't giving anything away. "I know I'm still on the clock."

Lin smiled, ruffling my hair like he had when I was in second grade, only he had to reach up now because I was taller. "Sit back down and have a snack. You too, Max." He bounced off to the kitchen, humming just like Mia did. Tes's and Mia's excited chatter lowered to the barest of whispers.

"You look sad, Pal," Max said, reaching for a chip. "Want to hear my new story?"

I grinned at him, grabbed a chip of my own, and dunked. "Absolutely."

As Max told me about a dragon named Daniel and his adventures with the Blue Power Ranger, I crunched on warm homemade chips with just the right amount of salt and tried to ignore Tes's and Mia's twitching and giggling as her parents carried on in the kitchen, utterly unaware.

When I glanced over my shoulder, Tes grinned and put his hand on Mia's stomach. His eyes were shining, jaw relaxed.

I looked away.

❖

Baby,

Your uncle Max is my life.

The two of you will always be eight years apart in age. Max and I are nine. If things work out the way your mama and I want them to, he'll live with us, at least part-time. The four of us will be our own family.

Our parents didn't plan for either of us (sound familiar? Ha ha, bad joke). Basically, I was an accident and Max was an oopsie. My mom had me when she was a junior in college. She was a physics major, really brilliant, as she never hesitates to tell me when she's in a bad mood or has had a few too many. She and my dad didn't believe in abortion like your ma, so here I am. She named me after Nikola Tesla, her favorite physicist whose footsteps she wanted to follow in. Now she's a real estate agent, and Max and I have college funds.

Not a bad deal. Especially considering Pal's parents were in a similar situation. Then her dad died, and her mom started working at the grocery store. Kate is the best. When you talk to her, she really listens. My parents just throw money at problems.

Anyway, Max. My parents dropped me off at Pal's when my mom went into labor. Her dad was God knows where, probably a desert in the Middle East. Kate let us stay up late and share a bag of Doritos. We watched Dallas *because Kate had a crush on Bobby*

Ewing, then The Three Stooges *because that's what was on Nick at Nite. Pal and I were still little enough we could share a bed without it being weird, and her mom sat with us and gently bounced on the mattress until we fell asleep.*

The phone rang early in the morning; it was still dark. I was in a sleepy fog, but Kate held the receiver to my ear, and Dad said I had a baby brother. The next afternoon, I got to hold Max. He was so tiny, but he opened his eyes and I swear he smiled at me. There's no way that could be true, but that's what it felt like to nine-year-old me. I promised to look out for him.

My parents work a lot. My dad seems resentful of me in a way he never has been of Max, and I don't know why. I'm kinda relieved though, in a weird way. I'm older; I can handle it. He actually goes to Max's peewee baseball games, which he never did for me, and I try not to feel hurt. Maybe when I was Max's age, he was working at the dealership even more.

I wish they hadn't just jetted off to Europe though. It's not like they spend a ton of time with us, but still... This has been a lot to manage.

You will love your uncle Max so much. He smiles all the time and makes up stories that are seriously good. He knows all the words to Green Day's "Basket Case" even though I lied and told him "stoned" has to do with rocks. Probably strange for a teenage guy to be so all about his kid brother, but whatever. When he loses teeth, I play Tooth Fairy. When he has a bad dream, he comes into my room and I check both our closets to make sure there aren't any monsters. I take him to school every day, and we cheer whenever the local DJ says "BOB o'clock" at 8:08. All the little, corny details that make up a real family.

To our parents, we're part of the Christmas card picture, or the occasional newspaper ad showing the perfect nuclear family to the public. Two boys who don't complain (too much) about wearing matching sweaters. To each other, Max and I are everything. And once you're born, we will welcome you in.

Love,
Someone You Don't Know (Yet)

Chapter Seven

Mmmmm," Ani hummed as I pushed aside her hair to drop kisses along her neck.

My feet still ached from my double shift, but I was happier than I'd been in weeks. She smelled like vanilla and sweat and me. My room, papered with posters of astronauts and my map of the sky, felt like a fourth dimension. A universe all our own.

And so far, she hadn't spewed the whole "I can't do this" crap. As we kissed and touched to our hearts' content, I tried to project a message: *You can do this. We can.*

Maybe this time, telepathy would work.

We hadn't had sex tonight, but were down to our underwear, skin to skin, burrowed under blankets. Ani's room was more comfortable, but with all of her siblings and stay-at-home mom, my room was easier. Quieter. So, on the rare nights I wasn't studying or working, and she didn't have practice for whatever sport was happening that season, we came here.

Ani pulled me on top of her, running her hands down my ass, so soft I almost couldn't stand it. Before we started messing around, I had no idea someone else could do what I did by myself, bring me to that point that was so intense it would almost hurt if it didn't feel so otherworldly. After Ani, I knew what the characters on *Friends* meant when they said they saw God.

"I wish we could stay here forever," she whispered, biting my earlobe.

I shivered, both at the temperature and the words she'd never said before. Ani wrapped her arms around me and smiled, probably thinking I was just cold. "Better?" she cooed, rubbing the nape of my neck with her strong fingers.

"Much," I murmured.

I felt my muscles unknot one by one, the most exquisite pain I'd ever experienced. I rested my chin on her chest, that sweet space between her breasts.

Ani giggled, looking around the room. "I've always meant to ask, why all the space stuff?" She hitched her chin at my poster of John Glenn. "Were you always so into it, or was that a recent thing?"

I planted a kiss on her left boob, right where smooth skin met lace bra, and she giggled again. I loved making her giggle. "Hmmm," I said, blowing a strand of hair off my face. Ani tucked it behind my ear, and I kissed her palm. "That's right, we didn't really hang out here in grade school 'cause my mom was always working." I felt a pang in my heart. I didn't talk about my dad much these days, but with Ani, I wanted to try. Taking a deep breath, I looked into her blue, blue eyes and thought of the summer sky. Maybe by then we could go outside, out in public, together. "You sure you want to hear all this?"

Ani rolled out from underneath me and onto her side. Leaning on her elbow and running a hand through her messed-up locks, looking for all the world like Pamela Anderson Lee, she uttered the most beautiful syllable in the world.

"Yeah."

I rolled on my back, the glow-in-the-dark stars on my ceiling coming into focus. In a fit of inspiration, I reached over and snapped off the lamp. This might be easier in the dark. The plastic constellations were green and eerie, but in a good way.

"Long story," I said. "It all started with my dad."

I knew how my love of space *should* have developed: my dad and I lying on our backs counting the stars, him telling me about Ursa Major or whatever, like in one of those tender Sunday night movies my mom and I laughed at but secretly loved.

In reality, it had started with a boiling hot summer. I was five, he was home on leave, and we were lying on the couch watching a rented tape on the VCR. *The Right Stuff* was about a bunch of guys in puffy suits yelling about solving problems and lighting candles before blasting off to the moon.

When it was done and Mom went to bed, my dad said, "Feel like another round?" in that central Illinois drawl that never went away even though he was gone all the time. I nodded eagerly. At first, I didn't care about the movie. I just wanted to stay up late with Daddy, who was an idea more than a parent. He was always flying away to places I'd never heard of and didn't want to know about, no matter how many times Mom pointed them out on our living room globe.

Like me, underweight since birth, the world I knew was very tiny: my preschool, the grocery store where my mom worked, the occasional playdate, and the library. I didn't want to think of anything bigger because it overwhelmed me. My dad was just a speck in whatever wild blue yonder, far beyond my imagination.

Space, however, was another story. It was vast. It was beautiful. It was new—everything that happened there was happening for the first time. An action as common as walking took on a whole new meaning on the moon. People on the ground helped, but astronauts were mostly on their own. Constant problem-solving and endless rewards—both appealed to me. I was never sure what or who my dad was fighting for, but what the astronauts sought? I couldn't quite name it, but even at five, I deeply understood.

"Good, huh?" Daddy said, turning to me and grinning. "You didn't fall asleep once, babe!" We high-fived, then he scooped me up and carried me to my room.

From then on, I was obsessed with space. I devoured every book and TV special my parents could find.

"Anyway, the whole 'you're going to college' thing was instilled in me young," I said. Ani nodded—Notre Dame was a foregone conclusion for her. She pulled me closer, kissing my temple in a way that felt far more intimate than sex.

My parents weren't pushy like Ani's, but they expected a lot. My dad had asked about my grades in every letter and phone call. I didn't mind. I loved school, started reading when I was three.

Space gave me a focus, an end point. I focused even harder when my dad died. I had to get there, even if it just involved talking to astronauts from the ground for a living.

"It's still my absolute favorite movie," I finished and raised my head to meet my girlfriend's gaze, eyes adjusting to the dark. My girlfriend. I vowed to call her that from now on, even just to myself. Because this, *us*, was real, even if Ani hadn't yet made up her mind.

I bit my lip, hoping she wouldn't laugh at the stars, the space, the pipe dream of a career at NASA, and leaving a town where everyone always returned sooner or later.

Instead, she reached over and stroked my arm. We lay there, facing one another. In the dark with toy stars above us, it was the most intimate I'd ever been with anyone. If I were struck down for being with this girl, I'd be fine with that.

Ani scooted closer and kissed me, long and slow, and my happiness increased tenfold.

"Um…" I said after we broke apart. I didn't want to ruin the moment, but I was really tired of sneaking around, keeping one secret too many. "Have you thought about telling anyone about us?"

I expected her to get out of bed, start dressing, make excuses, tell me once again about *conservative* Notre Dame—though I was hard-pressed to believe everyone at that school was one hundred percent straight like she said. Didn't people at least experiment in college?

She bit her lip, and I wanted to kiss it. Instead I held my breath, waiting.

Ani said, "You're right, Paulina."

I loved how she called me by my name. Not Pal. Not Roja.

"About what?" I asked, treading lightly. Always so careful. When could I stop looking over my shoulder?

Her warm arms, strong from volleyball and softball, tightened around me, and she pulled me even closer, not an inch between us. "I want everyone to know about you. About us. I don't want to hide anymore."

We kissed deeply, until she pulled away and continued. "I know you like guys too, Paulina, but I've thought about it…well, a lot, since we started…"

"Doin' it?" I cracked, pronouncing it like the title of LL Cool J's song that was constantly on MTV last year. Ani'd stolen the single from her younger sister—ostensibly because Mary was too young, but really because the lyrics got Ani going. She'd then introduced it to me, and I bought my own copy.

"Shut up," she said. I giggled. Ani was the only person who made me giggle. "I know you like guys too, but..." She took a deep breath, closed her eyes. Her long eyelashes against her smooth, pale cheeks were so heartbreakingly beautiful I had to swallow hard to keep the tears at bay. Then she opened her eyes and all I saw were pools of blue I could drown in.

"I like girls," Ani whispered. She reached for my hand, entwined our fingers together. "Just girls. I like *you*." She leaned closer, lips brushing my earlobe. "And I want everyone to know."

"Really?" I asked, still wondering if this was all a big joke.

"Really." She reached over me and snapped the lamp back on. Instead of the stars, I was looking up at her, Ani, smile like the sun. "I love you, Paulina."

It was a good thing we were lying down.

I rolled flat on my back, bra straps dangling off my shoulders. Even with the lights on, I could see Orion's Belt—my dad's favorite constellation—where, in a fit of grief mixed with mania, I'd looked it up in our dusty 1960s encyclopedias and meticulously re-created it on my ceiling. I could see it every night, but now it was more than a shrine to my dad. The fake constellation was the first thing I saw after my girlfriend—*girlfriend*—said she loved me. Amazing how a bunch of plastic would always bring back the way my skin buzzed, my face flushed, a sense of contentment I'd never felt.

And then I started to cry. Not loud sobs, but saline leaking, dripping down my face. I couldn't take my eyes off Orion's Belt. I didn't move for fear this was a dream.

Ani saw my face and flicked the light off again. She tucked her face in my neck and held me, saying nothing. Her skin was so warm, the muscles in her arms comforting as I slid my hands over them.

I closed my eyes and felt Ani's forehead against my own. "Is it weird to cry when you're happy?" I asked.

"Look at me," she said gently. I obeyed. Her gaze burned into mine, face completely serious. "It's totally weird."

I burst out laughing as she pulled me on top of her and started undoing my bra. Her long fingers were surprisingly delicate for someone who hit balls over a net.

Ani murmured, "*I love you, I love you, I love you.*" The fact that she wasn't even pressuring me to say it back, maybe sensing I wasn't ready, just made me love her more, even if I couldn't tell her yet.

How could any of this be wrong?

Fuck Catholicism and the ancient monsignor's prayers for "gays and lesbians."

"Oh shit," I purred, straddling her hips as her tongue brushed my neck and she tossed my bra to the floor. One of Ani's hands cradled my breast and the other was traveling down my stomach.

Creak.

My door opened, and my mom cleared her throat.

❖

"We should probably talk," said Mom, setting another brown bag on the kitchen counter. Behind her, our refrigerator hummed in agreement. I thought of Ani's little hum earlier.

I froze, my hand closing around a box of cornflakes. After Mom caught me and my secret girlfriend on the verge of having sex, my bedroom light blaring, she'd had the courtesy to go out to the car and finish bringing in the groceries. It had given us enough time to shoot out of bed and get dressed, and for Ani to mumble something about calling me before dashing out the back door like a bat out of hell. Probably faster.

I concentrated on the cereal box's happy rooster as I carefully put it away. "I, uh, thought you were working late tonight."

"Stock room got cleaned early." Unlike Ani's bouncy blond ponytail, Mom's hair was dishwatery with split ends, badly in need of a trim. "Look at me, sweetheart." Her voice was soft, understanding.

We knew who was the parent and who was the kid. But my relationship with my mom had soft curves, friendly edges. We didn't go to church most Sundays. We had popcorn for dinner some nights, when we just didn't feel like cooking. And nothing cheered us up after a shitty day like Molly Ringwald movies from the last decade. She trusted me, treated me like an equal, and I knew how unusual this was.

Still, talking to her about my relationship—and Ani said she loved me, so this *was* a relationship now, not just two girls kissing in an alley—wasn't going to be...fun.

I dove into the brown paper sack and pulled out two dented cans of turkey chili. "We haven't exactly told anyone."

"That wouldn't be the case if she were a guy, would it?" Mom set a bag of Smartfood, our favorite white cheddar popcorn, on the table. As usual, she cut right to the heart of things. Midwestern to her very core.

"If she were a guy, we'd be king and queen of the prom."

For a moment, her expression was unreadable.

Mom hauled a gallon of milk in the fridge, then opened the Smartfood. "Leave the rest for a sec," she said. I nodded, taking a tiny handful of popcorn.

"Hon, I figured it out a long time ago." She smiled.

My eyes widened mid-chew. Mom fished out a piece nonchalantly.

"When your dad and I took you to *Beetlejuice*, you said you wanted to marry Michael Keaton *and* Winona Ryder."

"I did?" They *were* really hot in that movie. I'd still marry either.

"Yeah." Her eyes got that faraway look, the one that showed up whenever she talked about Dad. We each took a bigger handful of popcorn this time—just like always, this family-size bag of Smartfood wouldn't last a day. It was hard to be nervous while licking white cheddar off my fingers.

"So..." I let my voice trail off. "You're okay with all this?"

I never thought a "no duh" look from my mother would fill me with such gratitude.

I crunched for a minute, fixing my gaze on the glowing green digital clock of our microwave.

"What are you thinking, Paulina?" Mom started to fold and put away the empty grocery bags, a familiar action that soothed me.

I took a deep breath. This was going to kill me, but I had to know, and she was the only one who could answer.

"What about Dad?" I bit my lip as if I could trap the words back in my mouth, but they hung in the air between us. My face on fire, I reached for the Smartfood bag, now half full.

After shutting the drawer, my mom stood up and brushed leftover cardboard box dust—a fixture of every stock room shift—off her jeans. "Give me the corn," she said. I did, and she reached in for just one piece, crunching it in her mouth and swallowing as she contemplated.

"I think…" She paused, then looked right into my eyes. "I think your dad was very Catholic, as were *his* mom and dad. It's how they all were brought up. His parents were about God, mine were about science and reason, and you and I are more like them." She held the bag out to me, and I took a tiny handful. Even though my heart was sinking, I'd still have the comfort of processed snack food.

"I *know* that he loved you more than anything." She smiled sadly, and I could see every line in her face. She'd had me young, sure, but losing a husband and working overtime aged anyone. When Dad died, we got a government payout that took care of our house, but as a college dropout in a small town, she didn't have many job options. Plus, she insisted my monthly survivor checks went straight to my college fund. In the soft kitchen light, she looked about twenty years older than Tes's mom. "Even if he didn't understand, he'd learn. And he wouldn't stop loving you."

I sank in the kitchen chair, hearing every beat of my heart. I knew I'd be wearing Dad's flannel tomorrow.

He loved you more than anything.

We weren't a hugging and crying type of family. Instead, I touched her messy hand full of popcorn with my own. "Cheers," I said, and my heart flooded with an emotion I didn't recognize at first, though I eventually realized it was the first time I felt accepted, understood, on such a base level. Crunching down on my popcorn, I blinked very hard so my mom couldn't see my tears. I have no doubt she saw them anyway and pretended not to notice, affording me my dignity. She was good like that.

"Just make sure she treats you right," my mom said, turning to the next grocery bag.

I grinned, remembering Ani in my room, in my bed. I hoped that once she broke the news to her parents, we could start going on real dates.

"At least I don't have to worry about you getting pregnant."

My head snapped up. Her back was to me as she opened a cabinet to put away the Golden Grahams. I eked out a laugh, swallowing hard and wishing I could truly come clean.

I could tell her about Mia right now. Put an end to everything wrong with the whole situation. Just as I opened my mouth, Mom looked over her shoulder. "No regrets on my end, though. I'm sure glad I have you." She smiled, still standing on her tiptoes, cereal box in hand.

My smile back was genuine, my pangs of guilt equally so. I turned back to the bags, clearing my throat. No. I couldn't risk losing Mia and Tes, and if I blabbed, I would.

"Oh, and, Paulina?" Mom stopped, just as I pulled out the ice cream. "You didn't check the mail yesterday, did you?"

I shook my head. "Totally forgot, sorry."

"Well." She reached in her pocket and pulled out a bent envelope. "This may complicate things with your girlfriend."

❖

Baby,

I wish I could say the day I found out about you was all pure and happy. You deserve that. But I won't lie to you, not ever. You deserve honesty, transparency. Even if sometimes it hurts.

It wasn't a great day. Right before your mom told me, I fucked up and punched Xander, my friend. I shouldn't have, and I know I need to apologize… But I still don't like the way he looks at her.

See, my dad had an affair when I was in third grade. I don't know much about it, and I don't want to. She was one of his employees at the dealership who moved away.

My mother was devastated. She blew off work and stayed in bed for days. That's when I taught myself to cook from the recipes on boxes and cans, then cookbooks. Not long after, Mom got pregnant with Max.

I shouldn't hold it against Xander. I was glad he and Mia were friends. The four of us, along with Pal, became this tight little posse I'd always wanted. We went to the movies and sat together at lunch and helped each other study because we were all smart and wanted the same things.

And I'm not stupid. I see the way people at school look at Xander. They're in awe of him but a little afraid too, and I know why. Mia's Mexican, so she probably knows what that's like, kind of. To be different in a really obvious way.

I get that they have music in common too. I just wish Xander wouldn't sing all those hallway duets with her. Every time they're performing and looking so goddamn beautiful together, I hear a voice in my head say, "You're never enough." *On the day of the fight, when Mia stood up for him, the voice was louder than ever.*

Once some football douche hauled me off Xander, we were sent to the principal's office. And when we got out, your mom was waiting.

"I'm pregnant," she whispered.

Suddenly, the nagging voice in my head—the one that insisted I wasn't enough—faded.

I am enough. I'm your dad.

He still looks at her that way.

Love,

Somebody You Don't Know (Yet)

Chapter Eight

A nyway. The letter.
My grandpa had a little bit of family money, which he used to help pay my St. Cecelia's tuition after Dad died. And then last year, Grandma scored a professorship at Chicago University, a really prestigious college with a high school attached. Nicknamed U-High, it was a wet dream for someone like me. They even had special clubs and programs for girls interested in math and science. Way bigger than St. Cecelia's, as in multiple buildings and over a thousand students. Best of all, Chicago University professors' families got free tuition, if they were accepted.

Families included grandchildren.

Even the smartest St. Cecelia's graduates tended to stay at the local colleges or go straight to work. Teachers tried their best, but Havendale was a farm town in the middle of nowhere and perspectives were limited.

I was in senior math and science as a junior, and they were easy. Also...I loved my mom and friends, but I could do more. I really did want to work for NASA. When I told that to adults in Havendale, they laughed like it was cute. When I got older, they laughed like it was sad.

So last November, I applied to U-High. Only my mom, my grandparents, and the school office who had to send my transcripts knew.

I got the acceptance letter. And Ani loved me. I didn't know what to do.

Now we all had secrets.

It was Monday. Ani brushed past me in the hallway.

"Hey!" I said, or started to say, my voice tinged with optimism. She'd not been home yesterday when I called, and I knew better than to leave a message on their machine.

Instead of returning my greeting or (in my wildest dreams) coming up to me for a kiss that rivaled what Mia and Tes were doing in front of the lockers, Ani widened her summer-blue eyes, a look I was well-versed in by now.

Don't talk to me.

She was surrounded by her volleyball girls, and I was all alone. Still without a girlfriend I could call my own outside the shadows of my bedroom.

I squinched my eyes shut and bit the inside of my lips until I tasted blood. I wanted to punch a locker. Or a football player, even. Get punished for fighting like the boys had. Then I'd have proof my feelings were real.

When I opened my eyes, Moose—the dude who'd pulled Xander off of Tes during the cafeteria fight and who I'd known since kindergarten when we helped take care of the class hamster, Pickles—loomed in front of me

"You okay, Pal?" he asked. Moose wasn't the smartest guy, but he was genuinely sweet. In third grade, I used to quiz him on multiplication tables at recess. He had big problems with the nines.

Normally I would have given him my best student council smile, squared my shoulders, and marched off to French.

Today, I was just too goddamn tired.

"Um…" What even could I say without getting in trouble with someone? In that moment, I hated everything. I was perpetually in fear of breaking some rule. My voice caught—shit, I would *not* cry in front of the guy who, despite his size, still looked exactly like he did in third grade, puzzling over the nines.

Moose looked supremely uncomfortable. He didn't know how to deal with crying girls. Then his small, mud-brown eyes lit up.

"I know what you need," he said, extending finger guns. In spite of myself, I managed a small smile. "Where ya goin', my lady?"

"French," I mumbled. "But what—"

I didn't have a chance to respond. Moose tossed me over his shoulder and headed to Madame Marie's classroom.

"Moose!" I squealed, thankful I'd worn shorts under my skirt that day. And despite the fact that he really should have asked first, I loved how everyone's heads turned when they saw Moose charging through the hall, the smartest girl in the junior class slung over his shoulder.

Ani was standing in front of the Spanish room, ready to learn tenses from Señora Haynes.

I looked her straight in the eye, laughing extra loud.

❖

"Hey, you," I whispered, sliding into the pew next to a kneeling Mia the next morning amid our yawning classmates. Nothing like the monthly all-school Mass to start an already cold and wet day.

She held up a finger, then after a long silence, crossed herself as the organ music rang out. I was used to Mia's long conversations with God. She sat back and either the curve under her red sweater was more pronounced than yesterday, or I was just getting paranoid. With her long curls and clear, soft skin reflecting weak March sunlight, she looked like the Madonna in the third stained glass window on the left of St. Cecelia's church.

Mia squeezed my hand with a beatific smile as the junior high choir started the opening hymn. Her talk with God must have been a good one.

"Where's Tes?" she asked.

"He's parking, then he'll drop off Max in the second graders' section," I said. Mia nodded and hefted up her backpack to the pew to save Tes's seat. "We ran late this morning," I explained. "Max threw a tantrum."

"Again?" She raised her eyebrows.

"Shhhhhh!" Mrs. Nergenah, the school's oldest teacher—seriously, she taught my dad—gave us both the evil eye.

I lowered my voice and leaned closer to Mia. "Maybe see if your mom and dad want to have them for dinner this week? I think he could use the support."

She winced, curls brushing my face as she whispered in my ear. "I would, but my parents aren't exactly thrilled with him, you know?" She held up her left hand. The ruby ring twinkled in the light.

My stomach jumped. "They know?"

Mia shook her head. "I told them it was just a promise ring, but I don't think they believe me. My mom wants to take me to the doctor because I'm *still* throwing up in the mornings, even though I should be past that now, right?"

I nodded, biting my lip to try to rein myself in, but I couldn't resist.

"Mia," I whispered. "You need to go to *some* doctor, though. You haven't been at all, and I'm worried. What if something goes wrong?"

"It won't," she said, putting her hand on my arm. "I know it won't."

The choir went into the second verse of "On Eagle's Wings" and I tried not to think about hearing it at my dad's funeral. What a depressing fucking song.

Mia inclined her head toward the giant wall sconce behind the altar, a resurrected Jesus with holes in his hands and feet. Her peaceful expression matched his. "I'll be fine."

My dad went to church and prayed every chance he could, and still got blown apart, Mia.

Just as I was debating whether to tell her that—or a gentler version—Tes slid in next to us, shaking the rain off his coat. The weather couldn't make up its mind this morning.

"Morning, mi princesa," he said with a loving gaze so private, I was embarrassed to be in the vicinity. I'd been wondering whether they were having sex again and with that look, I had my answer.

"So I talked to Father Robert," Tes whispered. "He said he'll meet us after school in his office."

"Wait," I said softly, "meet Father Robert about what?"

Tes and Mia turned to me, and this time, she wasn't the only one glowing.

Fuck.

"You guys," I hissed, trying to keep my voice level and undetectable as we sat for the first reading. I took a deep breath, ended up with a mouthful of spicy incense scent, and coughed. "You can't be serious about getting marr—"

"Yes," Mia said, eyes full of hope.

With that one syllable, my heart dropped into my imitation Doc Martens.

"We're *seventeen*." I restated this obvious fact through teeth clenched tighter than Tesla's jaw this morning when Max poured juice on his homework. I'd never seen Tes as deliriously joyous as he looked now. His fingers laced through Mia's. That traitorous ruby ring mocked me, winking in the sunlight pouring through the stained glass windows.

Mia looked at me with the type of motherly gaze she usually reserved for Max. Only, since I wasn't eight years old, it came off as really patronizing and I didn't appreciate it.

"Your parents did it," she said.

"My parents were nineteen and twenty! My dad was living on his own. My mom was in college!" I hissed. "Not a *junior* in fu—" I bit back the curse word. Even I had limits in an actual church. "*Friggin'* high school."

"The word of the Lord," the student reader, some junior high girl with dark braided pigtails, said into the microphone at the lectern.

The entire church murmured, "Thanks be to God." Kindergarten through twelfth grade, we all paid tribute to the big guy in the sky.

Mass was usually forty-five minutes long. To his credit, Father Robert kept his homilies short and to the point, aware (unlike some of the much older priests) that that was a long time for the grade school kids to sit. He incorporated music and TV references into his sermons too, so they were actually relatable, not just some dried-up text from thousands of years ago. His was the kind of sermon I could stomach. He also never did the "pray for gays and lesbians" crap like Monsignor. Father Robert cared about all of us and wasn't afraid to show it. He smiled at Max's class when he talked about Jesus and the little children. So sweet.

Or at least it would have been if Stevie Little hadn't chosen that moment to freak out.

His screeches sliced through the quiet Wednesday morning air. Every head in St. Cecelia's Catholic Church—mostly students and teachers, but also a few dedicated old people—swiveled toward him. I shot a quick glance at Father Robert, who for once seemed at a loss. His arms dangled by his side, hands obscured by the long drapey sleeves of his green vestments. As this kid just *stared* at him, still screaming like he was possessed.

Finally, Sister Sara grabbed Stevie's hand and led him out through the double doors, shooting an apologetic look at Father Robert.

Up at the ambo, Father Robert cleared his throat. "Well," he said with a nervous laugh. "Who knows? Maybe Jesus had to deal with that too."

The teachers tittered uncomfortably. The second graders' eyes were wide as dinner plates. My stomach dropped, remembering Stevie outside the confessional.

Something seemed...off?

Next to me, Mia clung to Tes's hand. Her eyes were closed, and her lips were moving. I knew what she was doing: praying for that poor little boy and whatever was troubling him.

I've always known Mia was really religious. It was unusual because her parents *weren't*. Supposedly, Carmen's mom had been devout to an extreme, and Mia spent a lot of time with her grandma when she was very young, which maybe explained her conviction.

Faith was a thing I respected but didn't quite understand. It's not like St. Cecelia's did a whole lot for us after my dad died— maybe they'd sensed my mom and I weren't into Catholicism, that my dad was the one holding us to it. After Dad, I broke away from God for good.

My grandparents were proud atheists. I wasn't sure I agreed with them, but I didn't feel like praying anymore. I went through the motions at school, got As in theology. Every month, I ate a dry cracker that tasted like nothing and sipped from a glass of wine that was supposed to be Jesus's blood. I zoned out during the scripture readings and mouthed the words of the hymns.

What I never told anyone and hated to admit, even to myself, was that I took comfort in the rituals of it all. The smell of incense, the pretty stained glass: Mass was as much a part of my life as grocery shopping with my mom, bullshitting with Tes, or my dad's flannel shirt, soft and worn. The trappings were fine. It was the blind belief I couldn't stomach.

Mia never understood my lack of faith, even knowing my background, but to her credit, she didn't push. She continued with her devotion on her own. I looked over at her kneeling after the Our Father without fidgeting once, her right hand clutching Tesla's left. As if they were both afraid to let go.

Stevie's outburst was soon forgotten. After Communion, the little kids wiggled. Junior high boys covertly flicked spitballs at each other, and a couple were led out of the church by an angry-looking Sister Jean. I looked for Max. He sat with the second graders, his head bowed. I wondered if he was praying, and then I realized he was actually asleep, probably tuckered out from the fit he'd thrown earlier.

I worried about Max.

I worried about Tes and Mia.

I worried about us all.

❖

"Why won't you come back and eat with us?" I asked Xander after school.

Holding on to a whining Max, I turned and gave him a Look. He immediately quieted down, and I felt a little guilty. Max didn't want to be here any more than I did, but Tes was our ride and he and Mia were meeting with Father Robert.

"Uh, let me think," Xander said, slamming his locker shut. "The last time I was with y'all at lunch, Tes kicked my ass and got me suspended." Ever since the fight, Xander'd sat with Cameron at the table farthest from us.

I sighed. "Fair. But there's *no* chance you two could work it out?" I didn't even know why I was begging Xander. Maybe because too much was changing—absent parents, new babies, a possible marriage between my friends—for my comfort. I missed Xander's smile, his jokes, the way he'd break into song and make Mia laugh. He balanced things: whenever it was just me and Tes and Mia, I was the ultimate third wheel.

"Walk with me." Xander shouldered his backpack, and we made our way outside, breathing in the muggy post-storm March air.

"I don't wanna go outside!" Max bellowed, as loud as ten kids. I muttered, "Jesus."

He heard and stared down at his little sneakers, ashamed. Then I felt worse. He was just a kid who'd had a rough morning that got even rougher when his classmate started screaming in church and had to be carried out. I wondered if Stevie Little was okay, but I felt strange asking Max, who was clearly going through some shit of his own—stuff he probably couldn't even articulate.

Xander turned to Max, as if seeing his former friend's little brother for the first time. He squatted down to Max's eye level. "If we're not outside, I can't give you a piggyback."

It was the absolute right thing to say. Max's eyes lit up and he yelled, "YEAH!" He looked like the eight-year-old he was instead of some little old man, stooped over with the weight of the world. Not for the first time, I thought his parents should go fuck themselves.

Once Max was propped on Xander's back, we began a lap around the school. Max pulled a leaf off a tree, mesmerized by his new height.

"I'm going back to Chicago when the school year ends," Xander said. "My mom said I could, as long as I don't knock up any more girls." His laugh wasn't really a laugh. When was the last time we all laughed together?

"Oh, Xander," I said. "I'm sorry." *Dammit, Tes. Why'd your jealousy have to get violent? Why can't guys just talk to each other?*

He shrugged, careful not to disrupt Max. "Just didn't work out here. At first, I was happy to be in a music department that actually knew its shit, and you guys took me in right away…" He soldiered on, kid on his back and a faraway look in his eyes. "But that's all gone now. Ever since I pissed off the king of the junior class, you and Cameron are the only people who'll speak to me."

"Cameron speaks?" Now Xander gave me the same glare I gave Max earlier, and I immediately regretted my snark. "Sorry again."

Xander's expression turned sympathetic. "You know, Pal, I can't wait for you, and Cameron, and Mia even, to get out of here and learn there's a whole world outside this cow town."

"We have a college," I offered lamely, but I knew what he meant. I loved that Xander singled me out. Looking around at the green lawn, hearing the gentle sound of cars rushing by St. Cecelia's, I felt a tug that was becoming more and more present in my heart lately. I wanted so very badly to leave, to be part of a thriving city, and one day, among the stars. And at the same time, I never wanted to be away from Havendale, the cornfields, my bike, and my mom. The little house and little life that was all ours, with popcorn for dinner whenever we felt like it. The air wouldn't smell the same in Chicago, or in space. Like grass and sunshine poking through the wet, spring making itself heard. Winter finally ending.

Xander hoisted up Max, who giggled. "Tes'll never leave Havendale. Why would he? He's a king. This one"—Xander cocked his head at Max, watching the sun through the clouds—"is a prince. But Cameron, no one gets her here. And you…" He shook his head. "You're a watcher. You see everybody and everything, but no one really sees you."

I looked down, blushing.

"I'm right, yeah?"

I nodded, thinking of the U-High acceptance letter burning a hole in my backpack. It was tucked in the innermost zippered pocket for safekeeping. Would people see me in Chicago?

"Mia, she's like me. The little Mexican girl with the angel voice and the restaurant. But I'm sure she's been followed around Walgreens more than once." I glanced at him, confused, and he clarified. "Wondering if we'll steal anything."

My mouth dropped open.

"Yeah, that's the tip of the iceberg," Xander said, picking up his pace and bouncing Max on his back. Max giggled. Xander would be a good dad. "Our classmates don't look like me. Neither do the college profs who aren't my aunt and uncle. Since Biggie Smalls died last week, I can name five people at St. Cecelia's who've asked if I'm related to him. Same when I was new, and when Tupac got shot."

I wondered if I was missing something. "Because you're Black?"

Xander nodded.

"That's so fucked up!"

He shrugged. "Yup, but what can you do about it, especially here? Happens in Chicago too, but a hell of a lot less." We reached the front lawn again and Xander turned back to Max. "Full stop, kiddo."

"Okay," Max said, and his voice sounded a hundred times brighter than it had that morning.

"What do you tell Xander?" I prompted him.

"Thank you!" he cried and threw himself at Xander's legs for a bear hug.

"You're gonna bruise me, little man!" Xander joked. He turned to me, ruffling Max's hair. "This is another thing I want to get back to." He meant his son.

"I get that," I said. "Well, I mean, I don't have a...you know, but—"

"I know what you mean, Pal." He smiled sadly and held up his hand. "Wait. *Paulina.* Like the street."

A flood of warmth rushed through me. The end of the school year was two months away, but this, Xander calling me by my real name, felt like good-bye.

I reached for his hand and shook it. Not hard, but a gentle press of flesh that felt like a promise. "I'll see you tomorrow, Xander." I almost said, "I'll look you up next year," but bit back the words just before they escaped my mouth.

"See ya." With another sad smile, Xander disentangled himself from an armful of Max and crossed the street to the junior lot, holding up a hand in farewell and glancing over his shoulder at us one last time.

Next to Xander's tiny Pontiac, Tes's Bear loomed.

❖

Baby,

Here's what I've never understood.

People have kids young all the time: my parents, Pal's parents, countless other couples around the globe, and single people too.

So why was everyone making it so hard for your mama and me?

We were trying to do the right thing!

The two of us set up a meeting after school with Father Robert. We liked him. We trusted him. He could marry us in the Catholic Church, which your mom wanted more than anything. Made the marriage legitimate in her eyes.

Plus, again, this is what we were supposed to do. I loved her and you. There's no one else for me. I had always wanted and planned to marry Mia; now it would just happen sooner.

So imagine my shock when the old priest, who looks like a damn turtle, said, "No."

That was it. Unequivocal, if you want to get fancy about it. "No."

When we asked why, he started rattling off reasons. St. Cecelia's allows pregnant students but not married students. It's in the handbook, I guess, and it makes no fucking sense.

He talked, lectured really, about how we were too young— blah blah blah. And I tried, baby, I really did. The way I figured, if we're old enough to make a baby, we're old enough to get married. I brought up my parents, Pal's, and all the other people who've done it and been fine. I told him about the plans we'd already made. There was more than enough money in my college fund to buy us a house, I said. My mom, the best real estate agent in town, could get us a good deal. If we needed to, we could live in the spare room at my parents' house for a while. When I was a baby, we lived with my grandma and grandpa, so it could be done.

Then he asked how we planned take care of a baby, who would depend on us for everything. He emphasized everything, *and his beady eyes about popped out of his head. It would have been funny if I weren't already so steamed.*

At this point, I couldn't even look at your mom. Yes, Father Tightass, I know how to take care of a baby. I reminded him, through clenched teeth, that I was nine years old when Max was born. So, yeah, I could do bottles and change diapers.

But the priest didn't seem satisfied, and I got the feeling he wouldn't listen to us, ever. We couldn't win. I looked over at your mom, and she'd sunk in her chair. Her huge sweatshirt pooled over her stomach. She'd been borrowing clothes from her dad, telling him baggy was the style. Of course he believed her, his precious only daughter. Her parents' worst nightmare was her getting pregnant as a teenager. But they were so busy with work, they had yet to catch on. She wished she could tell them, but we agreed we should have everything in place first.

Too bad Father Robert didn't want to do his part.

Screw him. In fact, I said that to his face. Which would probably be punishable by detention if it had happened during school hours, but by that point I didn't give a shit. I grabbed your mama's hand and dragged her out of the office. I did feel a little guilty—she loved Father Robert, idolizing all priests and the Church—but I needed her to understand, they were failing her. Failing you. Failing all of us.

Looking back, I guess I can be grateful he didn't ask about our parents knowing or whether your mom had been to see a doctor. Pal and I tried telling her we'd take her to another town, lie about our ages. She brushed us off and said that women have given birth without medical care since the beginning of time and she would know if something was really wrong. She wouldn't budge on this. It kept me up at night, if I'm being honest with you.

Once we got out of that hell-office, I looked at your mama. The disappointment was written all over her face. Even in that moment, I wondered if you'll have her features or mine, or the best possible combination of both. I'm hoping for that last one.

I apologized automatically.

She shook her head and that gorgeous curly hair, the hair I first noticed when we were little, bounced around her shoulders. My love for you and your mama, baby, is deep and never ending and there's no way in hell Father Robert could understand that.

I pulled her close in the empty hallway and touched my forehead to hers. She looked up at me with those soft brown eyes. Baby, I made a promise right then and there that I'll do anything *for her and our family. My dad always told me to man up. The time is now.*

"Let's just get married at the courthouse," I said. "We don't need a church."

"We're not eighteen, Tes. We'd need permission," she said.

I could smell the cinnamon gum she sneaked between classes on her breath. I kissed her nose, and her eyelashes fluttered against my cheek. I flashed back to holding Max when he was tiny. I can't wait to hold you.

"We forge notes. It can't be that hard."

I pulled back just enough to look at her, and I swear to God, even with her round pregnant face and worried eyes, she looked holy.

My Mia. Your mama. We are both so lucky.

"Okay," she said. "Yes. Let's—" The last part of her sentence got lost because I picked her up and whirled her around. And for the first time, I felt you kick, baby. You're excited too.

This is the right thing. We'll have everything: you, a house, Max. We'll finish high school; I'll make sure of it.

When I went to tell Pal and Max, I swung him around too.

For some reason, Pal wouldn't look at me.

Love,

Someone You Don't Know (Yet)

Chapter Nine

April

I checked the bathroom mirror and saw I wasn't alone. It was straight out of the movie *Scream*, except instead of a guy with an Edvard Munch mask, a semicircle of volleyball girls lurked behind me. Ani's teammates. Looking right at me. Looking mean.

This wasn't good.

Inhaling quietly, and noticing one was blocking the door, I turned around, feeling the porcelain of the sink press into my lower back.

"How's it going, dyke," said Laura Frink. She had both a mean serve and the biggest ass in our grade, which she proudly showed off with an incredibly short skirt. Her eyes were slits, so narrow I could only see navy blue eyeliner.

A scream froze in my throat. The last bell had rung, which meant everyone was making a break for the parking lot or after-school activities. Who would hear me? No one.

"Ani says you've been hitting on her," said Michelle Casey, who had terrifyingly broad shoulders. Even her untucked shirttails looked menacing as she advanced on me and poked her stubby finger into my sternum. There'd be a bruise tomorrow.

Dammit, Ani. As if ignoring me wasn't devastating enough, she'd outed me. Probably to get me off her back—not that I'd even tried to contact her. I doubt she had any idea how devastating this could be.

Or maybe she did.

Standing there trapped, my mind whirling with how to get out of this circle of ripped, angry girls with nasty smiles, I realized I didn't know Ani at all. That despite her words of love, what we'd had was anything but.

"You see, Paul-lee-na," Laura said, stepping toward me. I winced, trying my hardest not to let her see me sweat. "We don't like when someone fucks"—a dab of spittle hit me in the face— "with one of our girls."

"Yuuuuup," drawled Gretchen Keithley, cracking her knuckles the way she always did.

"We don't like muff divers," squeaked Melissa Morrison, trying to inject threat through her Kewpie doll voice.

"Hey." Nora Cox came forward and gave me a light, stinging slap on the left cheek. "What the fuck are you smiling at, lesbo?"

Oh no. I'd smirked. Shitshitshit.

"Weren't you listening in theology, smart girl?" Laura asked, motioning the other four girls forward so they were crowded around me, in my face. Except for Amanda Simon, now guarding the door. "God created Adam and Eve, not Adam and Steve."

I sucked in my lips, shaking, with no way to hide it. I'd mostly avoided bullies through the years—my friendships with the golden boy and the most beautiful, talented girl in our class gave me a cushion I was grateful for every day. But Mia wasn't here. She and Tes were probably holed up somewhere planning that godawful secret wedding.

My mind raced with everything that could happen in the next few minutes: my forehead banging against the sink, being held under the water, their tough girl fists beating me to a bloody, unconscious pulp. These girls could kill me for loving another girl. I could be the next headline.

"Whaddaya girls think?" Gretchen rasped, lumbering closer so we were nose to nose. The cafeteria meatloaf from hours ago lingered on her breath, not the good kind with ketchup like my mom and I made.

Mom.

Tears welled in my eyes. What would she do without me?

"Awwwww," Laura said, eyes dark and glinting. "Are you gonna cryyyyyy?"

They were like bullies out of an after-school special, so clichéd and unoriginal. If I weren't afraid for my life, it would be funny.

As the volleyball girls squeezed closer, I spotted a body-sized hole and, hoping I could overpower Amanda at the door, pushed forward, trying to make a break for it.

No dice. Five sets of hands grabbed at me, all over my body: my breasts, my ass, yanking the tail of my shirt out of my skirt. Someone pulled up my skirt, laughed at the fact I wasn't wearing shorts, and smacked my butt hard and fast.

Every unwanted touch burned, like poison seeping through, disabling me further. We moved, a six-person unit with me thrashing and desperate, losing my ability to breathe out of fright. The second story window was open. I hadn't thought of that; they could throw me out. I tasted salty tears and metallic fear and something else... blood. I'd bitten my own tongue.

Suddenly, I was over the toilet, someone's hands holding my hair back, pulling at the roots.

And I laughed.

Maybe it was gallows humor. More likely, it was relief that Ani's friends were so goddamn stupid they couldn't think of anything worse than a swirlie.

"The *fuck*?" Laura yelled behind me. I sneaked a look over my shoulder and saw five volleyball players, who three seconds ago were violently defending their teammate's honor, staring down at me dumbfounded. They couldn't believe I'd dared to laugh.

This was it.

Feeling completely out of my body, I slammed my head as hard as I could up into Gretchen's nose.

"SHIT!" she screamed, doubling over in pain.

The other girls let go of me, and I shoved past them, successfully this time, my vision blurred. Amanda ran to the team captain's aid, completely abandoning her guard dog post, so I knocked open the door with my shoulder and hustled down two flights of stairs, through the empty main hallway, and to my bike, which I unlocked with the speed of light while silently thanking a higher power that Max had a dentist appointment and Tes couldn't drive me today. I headed straight to El Rancherito, a public place, where Carmen would feed me chips and salsa and Mia would give me a bear hug and sing me some Dixie Chicks and no one would hurt me anymore.

❖

Baby,

My dad called from Europe at three a.m., half an hour ago. He likely won't remember tomorrow that he just turned my whole world on its ass.

Our landline jangled through the hallway, jarring me out of a dream about a house with just me, you, Mia, and Max. Sort of set apart from town like we are now, but little and cozy. Not cavernous and constantly cold like this place. I'm realizing more that I've never liked it here. I was so tiny when we moved out of my grandparents' house, but I still miss how it always smelled like Grandma's oatmeal chocolate chip cookies. They died before Max was born. He never knew them.

Anyway. The phone. The one in my dad's office. I was closest to it since I'd passed out in front of Jay Leno after getting Max to bed. I ran for the jangle and picked up, my heart racing. What if it was Mia? What if you were coming early?

It was my dad.

Now this was weird. My mom called every week or two to check in, but I hadn't heard from Dad since my fight with Xander. He worked, my mom worked and did whatever parenting she didn't farm out to me. He wasn't the dad who asked if you did your homework and actually cared, like Mia's dad, or Pal's when he was alive. My dad was the suit-wearing kind who was basically a pair of legs behind a newspaper, like what you saw on Nick at Nite. Or he would have been if he'd sat around with us at all.

What's weirder: he was wasted. At a party from the sounds of things. I could hear it behind him, the loud clinks and soft murmurs.

He was slurring, then over-enunciating. My polished, intelligent dad said he had something to tell me and now. I had to be up in four hours.

Something kept me on the line though. This is your grandpa, after all. He's always been slightly cold to me, but I still looked up to him all the same. It was like nothing could touch him, and I wanted that for myself. Maybe he'll be more gentle with you, the way he is with Uncle Max.

Then he dropped a bomb. Four words I'll never forget.

"I'm not your father."

I sank down in his chair and I swore I felt the grooves of my dad's butt underneath my own. Or not-my-dad's, I guess.

What the fuck.

Then he was babbling—talking more than I'd ever heard, aside from the car dealership commercials he did. He didn't even let me have a minute to digest the biggest news of my life. He'd been wanting to tell me for years. Apparently, my mom was dating someone else around the time she got pregnant. He might be my dad, actually, but they hadn't wanted to get me tested because then I'd ask questions. He figured I was man enough now.

He doesn't even know about you yet.

I was numb. The house was still, my ear pressed against the phone, starting to itch. But I couldn't move.

I have to tell you this next part. I think it's important you know, because it means I do have a protective instinct. And I will use that for you your entire life. Because I am your dad. I know it.

My eyes went toward the cabinet where he locked his gun. The one I showed to Pal and immediately regretted it—not just because it freaked her out, but now she knows it's there.

I leaned toward the cabinet.

My fingers closed around the box of bullets. I took them out with the case and opened them. I've heard of "silver bullet" but these were gold.

My dad—should I call him that anymore? I was too tired to care, really—was silent on the other end.

"I mean, it prolly doesn't matter anyway?" He was slurring again, but there was a question in his voice. *"I raised you. I made sure you ate, went to school."*

Really, my mother did that. But I didn't correct him.

Loading a gun is amazingly easy.

We'll never keep one in our house, baby. I don't ever want you to stand at my desk, thinking how easy it is to click the damn thing open and start putting in deadly pellets. It's like my old Pez dispenser with the Donald Duck head on top.

You and I, we won't be anything like this.

"So yeah, I thought you were old enough to know, kid." He sounded like his usual pompous self, selling a brand-new Chevy to the parents of someone in my second-grade class. *I used to think my dad could do anything. I guess he still can.*

I clicked the barrel shut and held the gun in my hand. Ran my fingers over its smooth surface just to know what was at stake. I'll never let you experience this, if I can help it.

I don't know why I did it, baby. I wasn't going to shoot myself or anything, and I knew I'd unload it later. I wanted something to do with my hands so I wouldn't have to think about the bomb my drunk dad just dropped.

More than that, I wanted to feel in control.

The line went dead. No apology. No, "I love you." Not that I'd expect it.

I hung up the phone and the thump *of the earpiece going back in the cradle echoed through the quiet, shadow-still house. Like I was waking up from a dream.*

A dream where I held a loaded gun in my hand and stroked it like a pet.

"Tezzie?" Max called, sounding panicked. *His little voice cut me to my core.*

"Coming, buddy," I called back. *My voice came out high, shaky, thin, as if I was the eight-year-old. I cleared my throat and repeated myself. My normal voice came back.*

I was halfway out of the study when I realized I was still holding the gun.

I shoved it back into its hiding place, gently shutting the cabinet door, and ran up the stairs like someone was chasing me.

In my mind, I repeated what I know to be true:

I'm your dad, baby. No one else. You'll never doubt that.

I need to marry your mom.

I need to get us out of here. All of us. Whether it's a house on the other side of town or a hut in Timbuktu, you and me and your uncle and your mom. We won't live here a second longer than we need to.

I love you, baby. More than you'll ever know. I will do anything and everything to keep you safe.

I'm losing it. Tomorrow I'm going to burn this letter.

I love you. I love you. I love you.

Someone You Don't Know (Yet)

CHAPTER TEN

They did *what?*" Tes's voice shot up to pre-puberty heights. I added it to the list of things that would be funny if we were talking about anything else.

Mia lifted her head from his shoulder, where it'd been permanently planted since they agreed to go to the courthouse in Springfield that coming weekend. It was open Saturday mornings. "Pipe down," she hissed. "You'll scare Max."

At the mention of his name, Max looked up from his Game Boy in the next booth and waved with a gap-toothed grin. We smiled back, all *nothing to see here, kiddo.* A coloring book was open next to him, along with all the crayons Mia could dig up from the kitchen.

Tes turned back to me, fake grin fading as quickly as it had appeared. "I cannot fucking believe this." His jaw clenched and his blue eyes were a mix of horror and sympathy I found deeply comforting. "What the hell is wrong with people?"

We were in a corner booth at the Ranch, an hour before the dinner rush, when Mia and I would be on duty. Just as I hoped, Carmen brought around chips and salsa, then quietly went back to prep. I didn't know Tes would be here, but I shouldn't have been surprised.

Mia, however, did surprise me. Normally, she was a great listener, an *active* listener. I could always count on her for laughs, gasps, "And then what happeneds," sometimes to the point I had to laughingly shush her to finish the actual story.

Not today.

Tes grew more shocked as I revealed the details, taking my hand to steady my shaking. He asked detailed questions, made all the right noises, pushed the basket of chips toward me when I paused to take a quivering breath and the memories of a bathroom I'll never use again started flooding back, threatening to drown me in sadness and anger.

Mia, on the other hand, stayed quiet, expression inscrutable.

Then she leaned toward me, took my other hand.

"Paulina," she said softly, eyes gentle. She rarely called me by my full name, and I automatically sat up straighter. "Don't take this the wrong way, but…maybe you brought this on yourself?"

I snatched my hand from her grasp and laughed out loud, just like I had in the bathroom when I feared for my life. No way was she serious.

"Are you kidding me," Tes said. A statement, not a question. His eyebrows were practically in his hairline.

Mia took a deep inhale, then exhaled. After checking to make sure her mom wasn't in the vicinity, she rubbed her belly in a smooth, circular motion, hidden under a voluminous navy sweater. She looked as tired as I felt.

"Mia," I said slowly. "I was *cornered*. Ani's teammates knew I was alone. They blocked the door. I'm lucky I got out."

I swallowed hard as the impact of those words hit me. Whenever something really bad happened, my adrenaline temporarily took over, but once it wore off, I was screwed—the well-wishers long gone, leaving me alone with the godawful feelings. It had happened after we got the news about my dad, and when Mia had shown me her final pregnancy test, blue lines against white—no more denial. And it happened now. My stomach hurt, and I pushed the chip basket away. The salsa looked like clumps of blood.

Those girls were strong. Porcelain, water, glass windows were all enough to hurt. Badly.

Mia sighed. Her eyes closed, and she rubbed her belly again.

But something was growing inside me too: resentment.

Mia had someone who loved her enough to marry her. She had two parents who gave her everything she wanted and more. She had real Doc Martens that she saved her tips to buy instead of using every dollar to save for her future, like I was.

I, on the other hand, bought all my clothes myself: uniforms and otherwise. I had one living parent who worked overtime for retail wages and was lucky to have health insurance for both of us, and I wanted to take care of myself as much as I could, because she'd made so many sacrifices to take care of me. I had an ex-girlfriend who may have put a *hit* on me, not to mention all of my friends' secrets that they just assumed I'd keep because I was good old reliable Paulina.

Eyes blinking open like a sleeping princess coming to consciousness, Mia asked softly, "Have you even *tried* liking a guy?"

I didn't think it could get worse. I was wrong.

I could've driven the Bear through Tes's wide open mouth. Slowly but deliberately, he removed his arm from around her and reached for the last chip, biting down with an extra loud crunch. His worried eyes were focused on me.

I sucked in my lips, willing my voice to remain calm so as not to scare Max or alert Carmen just feet away. "You know I haven't, Mia. You know everything about me." *Almost everything.* "I'm attracted to the person, not the anatomy. And Ani is—" I cut myself off, squeezing my eyes shut to ward off tears. "*Was*," I corrected myself, "that person."

Mia bit her lip, looking down before meeting my eyes again. "Pal, you think you like girls—"

"She doesn't *think*," Tes interrupted her, his voice rising. He knew about Ani, our secret and all the drama that went with it. "She knows." Our eyes met, and I mustered a tiny, grateful smile before Mia went on.

"I've tried," Mia said, oh-so-tentative in a way that made my blood boil. "I've really tried to support you and your…girlfriend, Pal." Had she actually just shuddered before she said *girlfriend*? I couldn't be sure. I prayed to a God I didn't believe in that I was wrong about where Mia might be going with this. "I tried to wrap my head around his whole—" She lowered her voice. "*Bisexual* thing. Is it even possible to like guys and girls? I don't know. But I can't get past that the Bible says one man, one woman. You know?"

Just as rapidly as it boiled, my blood turned to ice. Because I knew, I just *knew*, Mia was only trying to help. She really thought everything would change if I just got a boyfriend—because I liked them too, right? I could keep the *sinful* part of me inside until graduation, go hog wild in college, and then marry a man. I knew her train of thought as clearly as if she'd spoken it out loud.

Memories *whooshed* through my synapses: the early days of Ani, when I couldn't get enough of her lips and tongue, our first kiss in her bedroom when no one else was home, the way I'd known it was coming from weeks of secret looks, passed notes, and hidden smiles, yet was completely surprised all at once. When I'd tried to tell Mia about it, those gushy confessions you're supposed to share with your best friend, Mia smiled and listened tolerantly, then quickly changed the subject. Never mind that months before, she'd called me the second she got home after losing her virginity to Tesla, speaking in hushed whispers on her kitchen phone, sharing way more details than I'd wanted. When Ani and I had sex, I'd already known I couldn't confide in Mia.

And now, she'd played her God card. As if I hadn't gotten the same eleven years of theology.

"The Bible also says," I replied, the edge in my voice sharpening, "you can't eat shellfish. Or get haircuts. And yet you had leftover shrimp for lunch yesterday. You got a trim last week. People don't take the Bible *literally*, Mia. You of all people should know that." I couldn't help adding, "Isn't that Tes's sweater you're wearing?" Mia glanced down, briefly chastened. I felt a small flash of triumph before she regained her composure.

"That's food. My curls." She giggled, as if this was all a big joke. "*This* is people. Love. There's no comparison."

Flames. On the side of my face. A line from an old movie my dad used to like. She was stomping all over my heart.

"And besides," Mia continued, totally oblivious to Tesla's glare. "Even if we're not going by the Bible, the Catholic Church says you can *have* gay feelings, but you can't act on them. And you did. A lot." She shrugged. "I'm not saying it's okay, but you had sex with a girl, and it was going to get out eventually."

You got what you deserved, Pal.

Carmen kept the restaurant warm, but now I was cold all over. I reached for my dad's shirt, debated stuffing it into my mouth so I could scream, but decided that would look stupid and pulled it around my shoulders instead. Mom said even my dad would have understood, eventually. Mia wasn't even trying.

"Are you *blaming* her?" Tesla whispered. I heard danger in his tone, and even more disbelief. "Our best friend's sitting here, telling us how she almost got her head shoved into a toilet for kissing another girl, which isn't anybody's business. Not to mention Ani lied to her friends about it." We both stared daggers at Mia, and my heart thawed just the tiniest bit.

She looked down at her ballooning stomach, cheeks round and pink.

Tesla turned away from her. "What can I do, Pal? Do you want me to call my mother? She's on the school board. I think they're in France this week, but I can find the number of the hotel. Or you can tell Dr. Foley. I'll go with you. Does your mom know?" He gulped from his water glass, throat working furiously, a man on a mission. "Those bitches can't get away with this. They *won't*."

"Wait." I held up my hand. "Tezzie, I really appreciate that you're trying to *help* me"—I couldn't help but level a long gaze at Mia, who only stared back, smug in her hypocrisy—"but that'll only make things worse." He opened his mouth and I cut him off again. "And yes, I've thought about this. If any adult does something about it, the volleyball team'll just double down. I'll not only be a dyke, but a dyke who couldn't keep her mouth shut."

I stared at the stained cloth napkin in my lap and concentrated on staying level. I had to work soon, and I couldn't take orders if I was blubbering. Carmen might ask what was wrong. At this point, I might just tell her everything.

Tes let out the longest sigh in the world, crunching ice between his teeth. "I wish they wouldn't get away with this shit." He paused, and I saw the wheels turning. "Can you at least talk to Ani?"

"I've tried." But ever since she started ignoring me at school, her little sisters always said she couldn't come to the phone, even with her voice in the background obvious as a tornado siren. Today, I didn't even make the effort, just came straight here. I sure as hell wasn't going to call her from the school pay phone. Clearly, Ani was done with me, and there wasn't anything I could do to change her mind.

I'd talked to my mom, though—called her from the restaurant, asked Carmen if I could use the phone in her office. One phone call from my mom later, she and my grandparents were filling out the paperwork for U-High. Grandma agreed to get Mom's old room ready in their apartment on the Northwest Side.

I didn't tell any of them about what happened in the bathroom. What good would it do? I'm sure my mom heard the urgency in my voice, and that's what spurred her into action. But because she loved me, she didn't ask.

"Ladies!" Carmen trilled, sounding scarily like Mia, approaching our bench and clapping her hands. "Work time." She patted Tes's back. "Go sit with your brother. Dinner is on us tonight."

He grinned, turning on the parent charm. "Thank you so much, Carmen." She nodded, quick and efficient, before checking in on Max, making sure he had enough crayons.

"Gracias, Carmen!" he chirped. She replied with a light chuckle.

Mia looked at me, tentatively smiling in a way that meant she *knew* I wasn't happy with her but hoped I'd forgive. As if. "Back to the salt mines," she said. Tes scooted out of the booth and she rose, with more effort than she used to, and kissed his cheek.

"You coming, Pal?" Mia asked. As if this were a normal day, a regular conversation over chips and salsa like we'd done so many times.

"In a minute," I told her. Her resigned nod told me she understood my need to sit, if not my sexuality. Rubbing her lower back, she made her way toward the kitchen, school bag in tow.

"Hey," Tes said, and I turned back to him. "Don't take it to heart, okay? What she said." He leaned closer. "Hormones, probably." He was smiling, but I could see in his eyes that it bothered him too.

"Yeah right," I said drily, shouldering my own backpack, prepared to soldier on. "Hormones."

Tes and I watched Mia's retreating form, her mom swatting her with a dish towel, likely admonishing her to get to work with love in every syllable. "I hope it's hormones, Pal. Because..." Tes shook his head. "Never mind."

"What's up?" I asked, trying to keep my voice light but hoping he was reconsidering this whole elopement. They were planning to come back from Springfield on Saturday afternoon, legally linked for life, done with it. That was three days away. Tes was throwing a huge house party on Friday night to make the big announcement and celebrate, as if the whole school hadn't already seen Mia's engagement ring.

Tes sighed. "I love Mia. I know this is the right thing, marrying her and raising our baby together. Even if it seems wrong right now." I raised my eyebrows and he snorted. "Don't look at me like that. It's obvious you don't approve. When you don't like something I say, you suck in your lips. You've done it since kindergarten."

"What?" I protested, realizing immediately that I *had* sucked in my lips.

"See, like that," Tes said. "I know you, Pal, and I always have." He paused, looking down at his new Doc Martens made of buttery oxblood leather. They were St. Cecelia's uniform-friendly, and I coveted them hardcore. "I thought I knew Mia. And then she drops some bullshit like what she just said to you, and..."

Wait.

Maybe there *was* hope. Maybe Tes would change his mind. They'd tell their parents, and Mia would actually see a doctor, finishing out the pregnancy under adult supervision.

Right then, I crossed all my phalanges that this secret wedding wouldn't happen.

"Roja!" Carmen called.

"Coming!" I yelled. Before I took another step, I gave Tes a fierce hug, then pulled back and looked into his eyes. He hadn't been perfect this winter, but he was my best friend too. Maybe now my only friend. "You need anything, you call me. *Anything.* Okay?"

He nodded, eyes as serious as mine. "You do the same? I mean it."

"Deal."

I was halfway to the kitchen when I heard a little crunch under my left foot.

Curiosity getting the better of me, I squatted down to find a crumpled piece of notebook paper. Under any other circumstances I would've tossed it into the big trash can in the kitchen without a second thought.

But today was different. I was unsettled, for obvious reasons. Thrown way off my efficient waitress-student-friend game.

Today, I unfolded the note and smoothed out the rough edges. I saw Mia's name in Xander's handwriting. It must have fallen out of her bag.

"Roja!" Carmen sounded none too pleased with my dillydallying.

"Be right there!" I called.

I should've handed the note to Mia without reading it. Respected her privacy.

Instead, I shoved it in my pocket.

❖

My Mia Mary Magdelene,
I remember the first time I saw you.

Advanced Vocal Music, eighth period, September 1. I was brand new. The only Black kid in the junior class and one of three in all of St. Cecelia's, even counting the grade school. Believe me, I was counting at that first all-school Mass.

People were friendly enough, but mostly they seemed scared of me. The first Black person some of them had seen in real life, probably. The collar of my shirt itched—I wasn't used to Oxford button-downs yet. Also, I was completely out of my element because I'm not Catholic.

I was ready to turn around and call it a day. Talk to my aunt and uncle about going back home. I'd promise my mom that I'd stay

*away from my ex-girlfriend, except to be a real person in my son's
life. A photo taped up in my locker didn't count.*

Then I saw you.

*I guess I heard you first. I'm not great at flowery shit. You
sounded like an angel, reaching notes so high. And that was just the
warmup. I looked around to make sure I hadn't suddenly died and
gone to heaven (yeah, right). I had to steady myself against those
weird painted cinderblock walls.*

*Then the door to the music room cracked open, and Sister gave
me the first genuine smile I'd seen all day. "Alexander? We've been
expecting you. Everyone?" She opened the door wider, and there
was a sea of faces. "This is Alexander, our new tenor."*

Everyone gave those hesitant waves and muttered hellos.

*You really looked at me though. That dark hair springing
around your face, your round cheeks, your warm brown eyes, you
looked like a painting at the Art Institute back in Chicago. I just
knew you had to be the girl behind the angel voice.*

I knew I had to have you.

*I'm sorry for what happened during the fall musical. It was
totally my fault. When I asked you if it was okay, even though you
breathed yes and it was the purest syllable I've ever heard in my life,
I already knew you wouldn't choose me.*

*The second my lips touched yours was a mistake, even though
we kept on going. The heat of you against me and you smelling like
the nutmeg in Christmas cookies. I know we agreed we'd never talk
about it again, but I haven't stopped dreaming about you since.*

*No matter who you're with, no matter what happens with the
baby, Mia, know that I don't regret what we did. And after I leave St.
Cecelia's and Havendale and put it all far behind me, I'll remember
that you understood me, touched me, kissed me at a time when
nobody else could get through. (Colleen Grady from Homecoming
doesn't count. Ha ha.)*

I love you,
Your Judas

Chapter Eleven

H ey, Pal!"
I twisted around in the Bear's front seat. "Yeah, buddy?"
Max was all smiles. Tes had left him a basket from the Easter Bunny last weekend, and he was still riding the high of chocolate, egg hunting, and not having to go to Easter Mass for once. He'd also lost a tooth the night before and woke up to a dollar from the Tooth Fairy. The new gap in the top row made him look really young and really old at the same time. I wondered who Max would be at my age. "Wanna hear a story?"

"We're almost at school, Max," Tes said, glancing over at me as he braked hard at a stop sign. I braced myself.

I'd been quiet most of the ride. The secret wedding was one day closer, the big celebratory shindig tomorrow. Max had been bribed with a new Game Boy to stay in his room the whole night. Granted, his room was bigger than my kitchen, but I made a note to check on him from time to time.

"Maybe on the way home, huh?" Tes said.

Max heaved a huge sigh. "Okaaaay," he said, and I had to laugh. After a beat, Tes joined in, but his jaw was still clenched.

I should've listened, should've set all the bullshit aside and let myself disappear into one of Max's dragon tales. But I couldn't think beyond the weekend. Even if Mia was my least favorite person right now, I couldn't let them go through with this stupid charade. I had to stop it.

Xander's letter took up space in my pocket as if it were alive. I kept checking to make sure it hadn't crept out.

"So…how *you* doin'?" Tes asked in his best Joey-from-*Friends* voice once we dropped off Max at the grade school. He looked over at my poker face while pulling into the junior lot. "Really, Pal? That always makes you smile."

With a strained smile and bags under his eyes, he looked like I felt. Something was off about Tes and had been ever since his parents left. No matter how much he tossed Max over his shoulder when he dropped him off, Tes couldn't fool me. I knew my best friend and I knew he was hurting. I also knew that when Tes was like this, no amount of cajoling would get him to open up. He had to do it on his own terms. But, like a naive idiot who thought things would always be the same, I didn't even ask him to try.

I twisted my skirt, the pleats of navy cotton softened from wash and wear. Green grass poked through dull brown on St. Cecelia's front lawn. April 5, Saturday, was tomorrow. If all went right, Tes and Mia's wedding anniversary would be very close to April Fool's Day. I wondered if they realized that.

"It's Mia, isn't it?" Tes hung a right into his parking spot. The Bear's tires on gravel gave a telltale crunch.

I swallowed hard. "Not easy to hear that your best friend disapproves of you as a human being." I wasn't looking forward to facing her. Wednesday night was hard enough, but luckily, the dinner shift had been busy, and we were mostly rushing around. Mia had been out sick yesterday. Just a cold, Tes assured me over the phone last night.

Today, though, she'd inevitably want to talk. I'd have to see her ring, and her face, and whatever big sloppy sweater she was sporting. I'd have to pretend I was excited for her and Tes while also trying to take them down. I'd have to ignore my newfound knowledge that she and Xander had gotten together, and that Xander definitely still had a thing for her—more secrets on the pile.

Tes put the Bear in park and turned to me. "I'm so sorry about that. I'll talk to her after the wedding once things calm down, I promise."

I sighed. "I appreciate that, but I don't think it'll do any good. She has her mind made up about people like me."

"I have to try though. It isn't right she thinks that way." Tes was both sincere and sympathetic; I could see it in his eyes. But he was a straight guy, so he didn't really get it and never would.

But he tried. He was in my corner. Where less and less people hung out these days.

"You got a minute?" I asked. He'd barely nodded before I pulled the sheet of paper out of my backpack and handed it to him. "I need you to read this and tell me what you think."

Tes was a speed-reader. He wasn't trained or anything, just really fast. Before most people would get through the first sentence, his eyes were back on me.

"You're going, aren't you." In true Tes form, it was more of a statement than a question.

I looked out the window and saw Xander's small red Pontiac. Parked next to it was Ani's yellow Toyota, bold like she pretended to be. She'd avoid me in the hallways like always, which was just as well because I wouldn't fucking look at her ever again. The back of Havendale Video faced the parking lot. We'd snuck into the legendary porn section freshman year (per town tradition) and ran out, giggling at the gigantic breasts and...other parts while the owner, a grizzled old man named Gene who always smelled like stale cigarette smoke, kindly looked the other direction.

Did I really want to leave?

"I have to, Tes," I said, realizing how my voice trembled as the words came out. "You know I can't stay, not after..." I trailed off, remembering my head near the toilet. "And their math and science departments are incredible. They have *departments.*"

"I get it here," he said, tapping his head. "But here," he added, thumping his chest. "That's hard."

I thought of all the conversations we'd had in the Bear. Of us sharing crayons, lunches, the occasional short answer in Honors English. Of him and Mia, stumbling toward an uncertain future. Even if I stopped the wedding, they'd be linked for the rest of their lives with a baby to raise.

Reality was hitting all of us with a baseball bat.

I held out my hand to Tes, who squeezed it. For a second, we looked at each other, saying nothing.

Tes lifted my hand to his mouth and pressed a kiss to it. "They just better treat you right, Pal," he said, a catch in his voice as he looked away.

"I mean, that's a low bar," I said, glancing toward the school that had once been a safe spot to chat with my friends at lunch, to ace a geometry test, to sneak glances at Ani's ass in the hallway. Now St. Cecelia's was a place where I couldn't even think about the girls' room without shuddering.

U-High would be so different.

"Besides, I can always sic Professor Grandma on any bullies," I continued. "She's like, seventy, but she can probably throw a textbook at their heads."

It wasn't funny, but we burst out laughing anyway.

As we crossed the street, Tes held his hand in front of me, making sure I wouldn't walk into traffic. As always, I rolled my eyes.

"Hey," he said as we crossed. "Gotta get that in while I can."

Forget Mass. *This* was a ritual I'd miss.

And then I remembered what I'd wrestled with all last night, and again this morning as the Bear crept into my driveway. I didn't know what was bothering my best friend, and I was fully aware what I was about to do could make things even worse. This could be the moment where everything went off the rails.

All because of me.

Because I thought Tes needed to know, and because I was still mad at Mia. Because Xander was leaving anyway, back to his city and his son and away from the narrow minds this town produced. Because even though no one would ever know it, Tes was my first kiss and I had the security code to his house and the memories of shared purple crayons and the stories from his precious little bro. If I could halt one stressful thing in his life, this joke of a marriage, then maybe it would have a domino effect, and those worry lines on his face wouldn't grow any deeper, his jaw wouldn't clench so hard he broke a tooth.

"Tes?" I said, just before we got to the doors. My cheeks stung from the lingering winter cold, my lips freezing, but I couldn't risk Mia seeing us.

He turned to me, a question in his eyes.

I handed him Xander's note. "Read it later."

And with that, I sealed all of our fates.

❖

Baby,

I need to tell someone.

We got in a fight. He kept his distance. I thought he knew your mama was off limits. I thought he'd stopped looking at her the way he used to.

So why did I see what I saw today?

The bell rang. I headed to your mama's locker as usual. I've been checking in with her between classes religiously, just making sure everything's okay. If she won't see a doctor, I'll be her nurse.

But someone beat me to her locker.

Xander.

They were chatting, and she was smiling up at him like she used to when they sang in the hallways. That was annoying enough. I could deal with it though.

Here's what I couldn't deal with.

Before he walked away, he gently touched her stomach under her billowing sweatshirt.

Why would he do that?

If I ask your mama, she's just going to get upset. That's not healthy for you or her. If I tell Pal, she'll just defend him. So that leaves you.

Though it just occurred to me as I write this:

What if I'm wrong about you, baby? What if I'm wrong about all of this?

I'm going to burn this letter.

Love,

Someone You Don't Know

Chapter Twelve

The smell hit me first.

"What the fuck..." Tes said as we made our way down the hall. The commotion was high—people talking and laughing, gathered around another decimated locker.

I'd been naive enough to think they would stop at threatening me in the bathroom.

Once I got to my locker, I was greeted by Mia on her knees, paper towels around her hands like white hooves. She was cleaning up the mess, just like Xander had done for Cameron forever ago.

Cameron stood nearby, eyes huge, taking in the scene. I didn't blame her for not stepping in. As the object of ridicule, I'd quickly learned, flying under the radar was a survival tactic.

"Hey, *hey*," Tes said, gently lifting Mia to her feet.

I saw her tears.

"I can't believe this," she whispered. "What is wrong with people?"

The hallway quieted. Everyone was looking at me to see how I'd react. There was my shredded pre-calc textbook. The pictures of me and Mia and Tes, our faces scribbled over. The photo of my dad and me at my First Communion with my face cut out.

Really, the cow shit was the best of it.

I walked up to my locker and slammed the door shut, knowing my suspicions were likely true. There it was: DYKE, scrawled in black Sharpie.

Two volleyball girls had lockers nearby, and I swore I heard them snicker.

Tes and Mia looked at me...for answers? For orders to get the principal, the janitor, anyone? I wasn't sure.

I stood there, shaking, thinking back to my First Communion. I knelt and picked up the picture. My little white dress. I'd felt so special wearing it. My now-missing face had been full of hope and happiness. Daddy was there. He'd taken special leave. My mom snapped the photo, trying to get me to stand still as if I hadn't already been doing that all day. Even as she cajoled and scolded, she laughed in a way I hadn't heard before or since.

My only copy.

People nudged each other, giggling. They expected me to freak out, to cry, to unleash my dyke-y fury or whatever.

They'd be waiting a long time. My body was numb. My brain was two-hundred-plus miles away, in Chicago, at a school where no one had even *seen* cow shit, much less put it in a locker.

I turned around, seeing them. All faces I'd been in kindergarten with, whose voice changes I'd heard firsthand. Some of the girls crossed their arms over their chests, probably to protect themselves from my wandering bisexual eyes.

I wouldn't give them the satisfaction—not now, not ever. They'd never leave Havendale, and I'd be gone soon. I would work for NASA, have girlfriends *and* boyfriends, and one day I'd laugh.

I quietly shut my locker and announced, "Nothing to see here, assholes."

St. Cecelia's had a strict no-swearing policy, punishable by detention, but there were no teachers around, not that I gave a shit anyway. The bell rang. I ignored my friends' pitying eyes, the rising stink of dung, and the audible disappointment that I hadn't cried.

I realized right then how much time I spent looking: up at the endless sky, down at the ground of Havendale that rooted me, out the window as the gun shop and antique mall blurred by on the way to school. Now I needed to look straight ahead. My reality, even if it currently included violence, doubt, and animal excrement, was in front of me.

"I'll see you later," I murmured to Mia and Tes.

And in the midst of uniformed people gathering books and streaming into classrooms, already on to the next round of gossip, I gave my locker door a good, hard kick.

Then I headed to the janitor's office, passing Ani in the hall. Our eyes met, but this time I was the one who looked away.

❖

Baby,

I'm so sorry for that last letter.

I realized I was dumping all my paranoid shit on you. And that's not what a good dad does. So I am going to destroy it.

We're so close. We get married tomorrow. Everything will all be right soon. Tonight, we celebrate.

I can't wait to meet you.

Love,

Someone You Don't Know

Chapter Thirteen

Humming "Wide Open Spaces" under my breath, I answered the phone on the second ring.

"Are you coming tonight?" Mia sounded breathless and excited. And for the first time since this all began, I heard a tinge of fear.

Fear of what exactly? She was getting everything she wanted, while all I got was shit in my locker.

I tried to shake off the bitterness. Other people's bigotry wasn't her fault. She'd helped me clean it up and sat by me in the principal's office while I lied through my teeth, saying I had no idea who would do this. Though she hadn't apologized for her comments at the restaurant, doubting whether my identity was real, and that *was* her fault.

"Long as people leave their cow patties at home," I said, a lame attempt at humor.

Mia was quiet. "You don't have to do that around me," she said.

I sighed, sinking down on my bed at the memory of that horrible smell and the evil word on my locker. I'd changed the sheets that Ani and I had lain on. I wanted to burn them, but I didn't know where, so I'd stuffed them in the back of my closet. A few more months and I'd leave it all behind. As of now, only Tes knew about U-High.

Maybe I wouldn't tell anyone else. Maybe I'd just go.

"So," Mia said. "Tomorrow's the big day."

Don't do this, Mia. I didn't say it out loud. Instead I asked, "You nervous?"

I wondered if she was missing Lin and Carmen, who'd left last night for a family reunion in Texas. They'd been planning this trip forever, Lin taking rare time off from the state's attorney's office and Carmen calling in reinforcements to run the restaurant. Mia had begged off a while back, claiming she had really important tests she couldn't miss, and because she was their precious only daughter who would absolutely not get pregnant and disappoint them forever, they believed her. There was a time when I would have offered to sleep over.

"You mean, nervous about marrying the love of my life while I'm carrying his secret baby? This is the stuff of *telenovelas*, Pal." She laughed.

I knew she wanted me to laugh too. I couldn't.

"You know, you don't have to marry Tes," I said, casting a look at my closed bedroom door. I wished I could leave for Chicago tomorrow. How had I ever felt tied to St. Cecelia's with its big rules and bigger hypocrisy, or to Havendale with its dusty storefronts and gun shops?

Silence. The phone was warm against my cheek. I pulled my dad's shirt closer around me. I was wearing it tonight, for protection.

"Look," Mia said softly, "I know you've had a rough day, and I get that—"

"*Do* you?" It came out sharper than I'd intended.

I turned around and saw myself in the mirror. Pale. Tired. In the corner of the mirror, my dad in fatigues, unaware he'd get blown away in a week, smiled at me from a worn photograph. Outside the window, the sun was just setting. It was unseasonably warm for April, but in Illinois, you learned to expect anything at this time of year. There could be a blizzard next week.

I felt like tonight could turn too—so many different ways— just like the weather. Maybe a cyclone upending Tes's house would destroy us all.

On the other end, Mia was silent. "I'm sorry," I said quietly.

Mia took a breath. "Don't worry about it. But you know, Pal, it's going to be okay. We'll have the wedding, we'll have the baby, we'll have the summer, and everyone will forgive everyone else."

And then I'll get the hell out of here, Mia. But I didn't say that. When exactly was I supposed to tell my friend I was leaving her? *Maybe when she apologizes for being such a bitch at the restaurant.*

"Anyway," Mia said. "I'll see you tonight?"

Just before I hung up, I heard a *clunk*, both through the phone line and in the kitchen.

Oh fuck.

"Paulina Mary, get out here right now." My mom's tone meant she was not messing around.

I timidly stepped out of my room.

"Sit down," she said, pointing at the couch.

Mom wasn't a yeller. When she raised her voice, it was out of frustration at burning dinner or when I forgot to take the garbage out and it stunk up the kitchen. Little things.

For the big stuff, she got scarily quiet. I still remembered that Sunday night we got the phone call about my dad, the *ring, ring* in the midst of her putting away groceries and me setting out my uniform for the next morning. When she sat me down to tell me, ten years old and unaware my life was about to change forever, I had to ask her to speak up.

I understood her now, loud and clear.

"How far along is Mia?" my mother asked, sitting on the love seat across from me.

"How did you know she was—"

"How. Far." She looked straight at me, blue eyes almost silver with repressed rage. The same as mine.

I took a deep breath. "Six months. Almost seven."

"Okay." She rose and started pacing the room. Mom spent all day on her feet at the store, but she was always more comfortable in motion. "Paulina. Tell me she's seeing a doctor. A clinic, whatever. Tell me she's been *once*."

I looked at my hands, throat drier than the Sahara. "She won't go."

"GodDAMMIT!" Mom yelled, a strangled cry I'd never heard before. "I told myself I was paranoid, but I just *knew*. I don't know how Carmen missed it. Maybe she's in denial, but still, mothers know. I'd see Mia over here and at the store, wearing those baggy shirts and buying chips. Her skin was so clear, and her face was round…" She barked a sarcastic laugh. "Everything that happened to me when I was trying to hide *you* from your grandparents."

She sank back down onto the love seat. "Why? Why did I not talk to her? Why did I not reach out to Carmen? *Why?*"

A silence hovered over the room. We were so rarely awkward with one another. My stomach churned as I pulled my dad's shirt tight. If I inhaled hard enough, maybe I could still smell him: pinecones and cold air, with the faintest hint of cigarette smoke when he and Mom went out.

"Paulina." My mother's voice jerked me back to our messy living room and the even messier situation I'd been living with all winter. "I don't even know where to start here. Why, *why*, did you not come to me with this? To *any* adult?"

"Mia made me promise not to?" I asked, my voice going up at the end in the way I hated. What was once a sacred vow now sounded pathetic.

"Look at me," Mom said in that low voice again, giving me no option but to obey.

A tear slid down my face at her sheer *disappointment,* and I scrubbed my face roughly with my shirtsleeve.

"I know I've put too much on you. You were so young when… when your dad died, but you stepped up and did so great in school, got a job the second you could legally work. Maybe, probably, I didn't supervise you as much as I should have, but I didn't think I *had* to."

She swallowed hard, the same way I did when trying to collect myself, before focusing on me again. "Now I see it: you are *such* a kid, because this is more serious than you can imagine, and you don't realize. There could be so many things wrong with the pregnancy. Mia might be eating and drinking things she shouldn't, not taking her vitamins or getting enough rest. Not to mention she's been on her feet at the restaurant, there could be genetic issues we don't know about…" She gazed out the window at the melting snow. "This isn't just about Mia anymore."

"I know," I said. I wanted to make this better, to make my mom feel better, to make Mia better. "I *know* all this."

"I don't think you do." She pinched the bridge of her nose. "Tell me this, and no more lying. Does any adult know? Anyone at all?"

I shook my head, then remembered. "Wait. Father Robert knows. He said he'd give them time to tell their parents before he did."

My mom's voice caught. "He's gone, Paulina."

"Where did he go?" Without thinking about it, I crossed my fingers, hoping like hell he wasn't dead.

My mom swallowed again, this time squinching her eyes shut. "No one really knows, but when someone takes off like that without warning, it's never good."

Like Tes's parents. Why did almost every adult leave just when we needed them most?

"Did Father Robert ever…" My mom paused, clearly weighing what she was about to say next. Whatever that was, I got the feeling it wasn't my fault. "Say things to you he shouldn't?"

Huh? "What would he say?"

She pinched the bridge of her nose again. "That answers my question. I just worried that if you were keeping something so vital from me, it might not be your only secret." Mom looked hard at me. "There's a reason kids have parents, Paulina. You can't handle everything on your own and you shouldn't have to. If *anything* ever happened to you…" She trailed off, burying her face in her hands. After a moment, I saw her shoulders shudder.

Without even thinking about it, I crossed the room in two steps and took her in my arms.

We sat like that for a long time, her crying, wetting the shoulder of my dad's shirt. My stomach was in knots and my head spun. When would it all just stop?

I rarely drank at parties, but I knew I would tonight.

"I'm sorry," I said into her shoulder. I knew she understood I wasn't just talking about my own lies.

After a long pause, she released me, looking me straight in the eye. "Thank you. And know this: yes, you should have told someone, but you aren't Mia or Tes. You aren't pregnant and handling it very badly. Don't take the fall for them." She reached up, held my face in her cool hands, and I instinctively closed my eyes. "You have a future, and *you are getting out of here.* Understand?" I opened my eyes and nodded shakily. "You're not off the hook, though."

I sighed. "I know."

"I've been trying to reach Carmen, but when I call the restaurant, they say she's out," my mom said.

"Family thing in Texas. It's been planned forever, but Mia didn't want to miss school." Mia was the only one outside of the restaurant staff who had her aunt and uncle's phone number. That's why she and Tes had planned for the elopement this weekend. They had forged notes and real birth certificates at the ready. I was supposed to babysit Max.

Unless I could talk them out of it.

I still had tonight. Tes played hooky this afternoon to party-prep his house, and I hadn't heard from him. I hoped Xander's note to Mia would delay a quickie marriage. I knew I should tell my mom, but maybe if I made things right in time, I wouldn't have to.

"And of course, Tesla's parents..." My mom continued, then trailed off. "I'd *never* leave you to jaunt off to Europe. Just so you know."

I managed a small smile. "I know."

"About Chicago," Mom said, putting her hand on my knee and squeezing. "This is probably the wrong time to tell you, but what the hell."

I wasn't sure what to expect, especially when the last two months had thrown me so many twists and turns, but luckily, my mom didn't keep me in suspense for long. "I decided I'm coming too. When you leave, so will I. I wanted you to know before I put the house up for sale."

Holy shit.

She pointed at me. "That's *not* to say I want you keeping any more big secrets from me. Understand? At the same time, I'm not going to overprotect you."

I nodded.

"But the more I thought about it," Mom continued, "the more I realized we both could use a new start. Broader horizons. And I don't want to miss your senior year." She looked down for a moment, suddenly shy. "I was thinking I'd give college another go."

Mom took a deep breath and gave me a small smile. "I'll get an apartment with a room for you, but if you want more space from your old mom, you *can* still stay with Grandma and Grandpa…"

She didn't get to say anything else, because I was hugging her again, as tight as I could.

A torrent of emotions flowed through me. Mostly happiness, because now I wouldn't have to navigate a whole new city alone and Mom would get a second chance at her degree. I wouldn't have to live with grandparents I liked fine but didn't know very well. I wouldn't have to miss my mom, because she'd be right there, like she always had been. Regret too, because we were *really* leaving Havendale behind. I wouldn't be coming back for weekends and summers. The house would no longer be ours.

Tes and Mia. Would I ever see them again? When I realized I might not—that honestly, I didn't have to if I didn't want to—the last emotion I experienced was relief.

Mom broke our hug and pulled away, studying me carefully. "There's something you aren't telling me."

Wrong. There are three things: a secret wedding, a bathroom attack, and a pile of turds.

She'd heard me joke about the cow patties. I thought of the volleyball girls, their expressions. The way the photos in my locker were shredded and scribbled on when I arrived at school this morning. The smell. My head in the toilet, how close I'd come to not being here at all.

"Am I right?"

Pulling Dad's shirt around me again, I nodded.

"Anything I can do?"

I'd done enough damage. We were so, so close to getting out of here, to making a brand-new start in the big city. I could shake off the bullying. I could stop the wedding. If there was a way to make the house sell faster, I'd do that too.

I pressed my lips together, shook my head.

"No one else is pregnant, are they?" Now Mom wore a tiny smile, and I felt myself smile too.

"Nope," I said.

"Okay." She pulled me toward her, kissed the top of my head like she had a million times throughout my life. When she released me and sat back, she looked older than she ever had. I hadn't realized till now: by going to Chicago, I'd be leaving her here, a widow with a faraway daughter and a grocery store. All alone. Maybe once we got there, she'd look younger.

Mom patted my knee. "I have to work tonight. I know you're going out, but *please* be careful. Talk to Mia. Lin and Carmen need to know about the baby, and they need to know now." I nodded and got up, heading back to my room to grab my jacket.

"Paulina?"

I looked back at my mother, Kate, on the couch. For some reason, I got the strangest feeling that this, right now, was the last time I'd ever see her. I felt a sudden, weird urge to run to her, sit in her lap even though I was taller now, and tell her over and over how much I loved her.

Instead, I stayed rooted to the spot.

"Be careful tonight."

She'd already said so, but I didn't point it out.

"'Kay," I said.

❖

Baby,

Everything's going to shit. I haven't slept a full night since my parents left. My grades are slipping. Xander is in love with your mom and she might love him back. I hate Father Robert, but I didn't want him to leave without warning—and what if he told someone about us? On the other hand, did he leave because *of me and Mia?*

And my best friend, your auntie Pal, the person who was supposed to get away from all this scot-free because she's smarter than all of us put together, is getting shit dumped in her locker just for being who she is.

I'm worthless. I can't even protect Pal.

I tried.

I'm sorry. I'm so sorry. I know I said I wouldn't do this, but again, you're the only one I can tell. Even if it's in a letter I'll rip up. And if I forget to rip it up, well, you learn more about Pal, who's going to be a huge deal in your life. She's so strong and brave for falling in love with who she damn well wanted to, no matter how much the Catholic Church and Havendale told her it was wrong.

Today, right before I pulled over to write this, I found Ani.

Scratch that. I tracked her down. Like some crazy stalker. I'm not exactly proud of that, but Pal is way more important to me than some stupid bitch who treated her like shit and then sicced the volleyball team on her.

I was waiting outside Ani's Spanish class today.

"I need to talk to you," I said.

She shrugged like "I don't give a shit."

I crossed my arms and hissed, "It's about Paulina."

Ani's eyes widened and she glanced left and right. People we've known since kindergarten were opening their lockers, chitchatting, sitting on the floor trying to finish a worksheet before sixth period— usual shit. Only now that I'd mentioned her secret girlfriend, Ani was paranoid. On edge.

Right where I wanted her.

"My porch, after school," she muttered before dashing away like she'd just heard the fire alarm. I was skipping out to get ready for the party, but of course, I know when the final bell rings, and about when Ani would be home.

In a place like this, you have farm kids and town kids. Ani is the former; I'm the latter. My dad sells cars, and Ani's sows and plows. She's been de-tasseling corn every summer since she was ten, and my dad never let me try, implying that kind of work was below us. Her address starts with RR (rural route). When she had a birthday party in fifth grade, her mom told us to wear "icky clothes" so we could ride the four-wheeler through the fields that make up their backyard. So basically, Ani and I go to the same school—have kissed the same girl, even—but otherwise our worlds are very, very different.

When I showed up, banging on the storm door, Mrs. Donoghue couldn't have been happier to see me, the class president coming to call on her daughter. So enthusiastic, in fact, I wondered if she suspected anything about Ani.

We sat on the porch, looking out at the cornfield across the highway while Ani's younger sisters shrieked inside the house, playing some demented game or other.

Ani said softly, "I know why you're here."

Ignoring the plate of Oreos her mom insisted we take outside, I crossed my arms and twisted around on the step to face her. "Oh yeah?"

She looked down, her face red, and mumbled.

"Come again?"

"I didn't mean for it to go that far." Her voice broke as if she might cry.

I wasn't sympathetic.

"Okay. You thought your jacked-up pals would corner my best friend in the bathroom to have a chat*? You didn't think they'd put cow crap in her locker when their basketball bro friends did it to Cameron Smith?"*

"Stop!" She looked up and I could see tears in her eyes.

Didn't work. I don't trust anyone these days.

Ani shifted as far away from me as she could without falling off the step altogether. A blue VW drove by, going way over the speed limit.

She whispered, "I love her."

I snorted. "Bullshit. You like the attention."

"No, I love"—she checked behind her, making sure her mom wasn't listening—"her. Your parents think the sun shines out of your ass. They also don't go to church every week, I've noticed. We have our own goddamn pew. Not official, but everyone knows it's for the Donoghues." She lowered her voice. "My dad caught my oldest sister kissing a girl when she *was a freshman. She got...sent*

somewhere. She came back, started dating a guy right away, and none of us ever talked about it. Then they got married right after college and had five kids." Her chin quivered. *"I could never tell Paulina."*

If this were about anyone but Pal, baby, I might have felt sorry for her.

"Pal wasn't trying to out you," I said in my best class president voice, just quieter. I'm not a monster. *"You told her you loved her, that you wanted to go public. And she didn't tell anyone outside her own circle. If you'd been honest about your family, she would have understood."* I thought of Pal, trying not to cry at the restaurant, how she'd been worried at school ever since. *"She's worth way more than you and your volleyball bitches."*

"I know that!" she said. Her voice went all loud, and she scrubbed at her eyes furiously. *"I know,"* she repeated, as if I wasn't there.

"You need to apologize."

"Yeah," she said, whispering now.

"And tell them to leave Pal alone. For real this time."

"I know."

"They could have killed her, Ani."

She said nothing. A motorcycle whizzed past, and I covered my ears against the deafening motor. The sun peeked out from behind the clouds.

"You're right," Ani said. Now her voice was clear, strong. Determined. *"You're right."*

Duh.

I stood up, gave her a long look, sitting there small and alone. She deserved how she felt and worse. *"I'm having a party tonight, in case you hadn't heard. Come. Tell her you're sorry. Tell your buddies to leave her alone and mean it this time."* I hardened my voice. *"Just you. Your teammates show up, I'll call the cops and say they're trespassing or stealing or something. Don't test me."*

Ani nodded, still looking down at her hands.

"Good? Good," I said, grabbing a cookie for the road.

I was halfway to my car when I heard her yell, "Hey!"

I turned around and she jogged up to me. No tears anymore.

"I'll think about it," she said. "I really will."

"It's one thing to say you love her," I called over my shoulder as I unlocked my door. "This time, maybe act on it."

I was sitting in the car when she banged on my window, making me jump. Everything makes me jump these days.

I rolled down my window. "What?"

She bit her lip and I rolled my eyes. Ani took a deep breath. "How do you always have it figured out?"

I couldn't help it. I laughed. She was serious.

I left her in a cloud of dust, staring out at the corn.

Baby, since I found out about you, I've gotten way more protective of my friends and family. And Pal is my family, more so than my mom or dad ever were.

I'll always fight for you just as hard.

Speaking of Pal...shit. Here I am, writing all this out, pulled over on the side of the road, and the note Pal gave me yesterday is sitting right here in the passenger seat. From the look in her eyes, I know it's important, but with everything going on, I forgot.

Time to read. I'll be back.

Love,

Someone You'll Meet Soon

Chapter Fourteen

I knew how bad it was the second I opened the door.

Tes was drunk. Shitfaced, off his ass blotto.

When Tesla Wrightwood threw parties, he was the consummate host, happy but dutiful. Tes knew how to stand out. He had designated sources with fakes to buy the liquor—and there was always actual liquor, and mixers, not just beer. Keys went in a bowl by the door. Valuables were put away and guest bedrooms opened to anyone who couldn't drive by the end of the night. Normally, Max went somewhere else for a sleepover.

Tes had had a talk with his parents at the end of eighth grade, and they had *terms and conditions* for this kind of thing. He reasoned with them: parties were going to happen, so why not here, in a safe and controlled environment? (Yes, he did this at fourteen. Always the prodigy, Tes, even when it came to teenage drinking.) The consequences were strict, but he never once broke the rules.

But tonight was different.

"Paaaaaal!" he cried, stumbling toward me like every caricature of a drunk person, only far more disturbing. This was my straitlaced best friend who allowed himself two beers, three if he'd had a long week. A half-empty bottle of Wild Turkey dangled from his hand as he hugged me fiercely, spilling on my dad's shirt.

"Heyyyyy, Tezzie," I said, returning the hug and trying to keep my voice light. Not only was I an ace secret keeper, but I could also talk down drunk people, a skill I wasn't exactly happy to have. Often Tes enlisted me to do this at his parties, paying me in donuts the next morning and his eternal gratitude. "Where's Mia?"

He gestured around him, to endless St. Cecelia's people and a lot of faces I didn't recognize—word must have spread to the public school. "Not here." Then he spun, arms thrown out like that old TV show where the city girl threw her hat in the air, face bright with expectation. "But she's eeeeeeverywhere."

"Okay," I said. "Let's go to the kitchen and get you some water." So far, I couldn't see or hear any of my tormentors, and Gretchen's voice was famously loud. I breathed a tiny sigh of relief before asking, "Where's Max?" *Please tell me he hasn't seen you like this.*

Tes gave me a lopsided grin. "Here, there, everywhere, my Pal. My best, best pal." He slung an arm around shoulders, then started to lean on me. Heavily. It wasn't an act; he really couldn't walk straight or upright. I tasted the dread I'd felt earlier when my mom sat me down. My mom who now knew about the baby.

I dodged two sophomores making out against the refrigerator and filled a glass for him. "Drink it all," I said sternly. "You're gonna feel this tomorrow."

"Tomorrow!" His voice went up about a million octaves and he leaned in with a drunk whisper-yell. "I'm getting *married* tomorrow, Pal."

"Yeah. About that..." *Should I try to reason with him? Can I reason with him?* Time was running out though. I had to—*had to*—stop this.

But then I realized what'd been growing alongside my dread, creeping up like ivy vines in latticework my grandma used to have. What I'd felt the other day in the restaurant when Mia all but laughed at my assault.

Resentment.

My so-called friends had forced me into this role. I was elected class vice president, *not* the Secret Keeper, but they'd turned me into someone who couldn't fuck up. I was compelled to keep it all together—for them. But when I faced anything major, I had no one.

My mom was right; I shouldn't have kept Mia's pregnancy secret. She was also right that Mia's pregnancy *wasn't my fault.* I wasn't the one who threw birth control and caution to the wind, who went ahead with heavy breathing and pure feeling, knowing the whole time what could result.

Yet here I was, feeling guilty about not being a good enough friend, about sneaking around with Ani for the few moments of joy I'd felt all winter, about secretly applying for a better school, a better *life*, because deep in my heart, I was afraid my friends would be mad at me, and then I'd have no friends.

And for what?

Right then, I hated Father Robert for skipping town. He was the only one to check in with me, to *care about me*, while I was carrying everyone else's weight. And now I couldn't even count on him.

I'm done.

"I need to talk to Mia," I said, more to myself than to Tes. I left him with his glass of water and the horny sophomores, praying like hell I didn't run into the volleyball girls or if I did, they'd be too drunk to attack me again. Pulling my dad's shirt around me, I made my way out of the kitchen, more clear-headed than I'd been in months.

"Pal?" I felt a tug on my shirttail, heard a tiny voice.

Max, utterly confused and, what was worse, disappointed. He'd never seen his brother like this. He shouldn't.

I squatted down to his level. "Hi." He gave me a fierce hug, puny arms squeezing my neck and nearly choking me, but I let him take whatever comfort he could.

New mission: once Tes sobers up, kill him.

"Buddy?" I smoothed back Max's hair (which had not been brushed today) and looked into his eyes, just like his beloved older brother's. "Let's find a place for you to hang out until I sort through things, all right?"

In that moment, I decided I'd do one more thing for everyone. I would get the party people the fuck out of this house, and then I would sit down Tes and Mia, like my mom had with me. I would protect this sweet little boy who'd done nothing to deserve seeing his house turned upside down by people who didn't give a shit. I wouldn't fail him, the way Blair-Marie Elliott's parents had failed her.

"Let's see," I murmured, leading him through the throngs of drunk people bouncing to Snoop Dogg. I was almost afraid to check Max's bedroom, because I *knew* what happened in bedrooms at parties. The poor kid was traumatized enough.

I peeked my head into their dad's study. Miraculously, it was empty, though the globe full of liquor bottles had been purged.

Good enough.

"Here." I led Max into the room, shutting the door behind me. I got down to his level again so we were face-to-face. "Listen to me, buddy. Harder than you've ever listened in your life." He nodded, eyes way more serious than a second grader's should be. This winter had been rough on him.

"I want you to lock the door and do not let *anyone* in who isn't me. When I get everyone out of here, I'll tell you it's me and do this special knock." I rapped on the wooden desk three times in quick succession, then a big, loud *BANG*. Max smiled, probably loving that we now had a secret code. "I know your dad doesn't let you play on his computer, but you can tonight. It'll be our little secret." When would I get away from secrets?

Max's eyes widened, and I knew he was thinking about messing around on his dad's big, expensive Macintosh. If he broke anything, I'd figure out a way to pay for it.

I held out my pinky. "Pinky swear you'll lock the door and play quietly until I come for you?"

He nodded solemnly as we locked pinkies.

I kissed him on the forehead.

"Ew, girl cooties," he said, wiping the kiss away and sounding more like himself.

I ruffled his hair. "Good boy. Sit tight." I shut the door. Once I heard Max click the lock, I left, dodging sweaty, writhing bodies, to find Mia.

"Pal?"

I shrieked, wrenching around to see Moose's hulking form behind me.

"Sorry, sorry!" He held up his hands, each the size of a small dinner plate. "My mom always wanted to put a bell on me."

"It's okay." Still a little shaken, I craned my neck to see around his massive bulk into the living room. No Mia. "Did you...did you need something, Moose?" The downstairs bathroom was all the way down the hall, but Tes had been throwing these parties since freshman year, so I'm sure Moose knew that.

"I was lookin' for you, actually," Moose said. He reached for me, then thought better of it and put his hand in his jeans pocket. I appreciated that, having been touched enough by St. Cecelia's athletes to last a lifetime. "Got a minute?"

"Sure." I wasn't exactly looking forward to holding Tes's head while he puked or telling Mia the jig was up. Anything to put off the inevitable.

He leaned against the wall, facing me, and I did the same. Aside from one cheerleader staggering past us, giggling at nothing, we were alone. Maybe I should have been afraid, but I wasn't. He'd been kind to me.

"I heard about the volleyball team," Moose said, just loud enough that I could hear. He stared down at his beat-up Nikes. "Not till after, or I woulda stopped it."

Moose leaned in so I could hear him over the hubbub. Weirdly, I couldn't smell any alcohol on his breath. "You okay?"

Someone was asking about *me*? Maybe I needed to sit down and honor this momentous occasion.

Then I realized Moose was waiting for my answer. I shrugged. "You know. Same shit, different day."

"You're funny." He smiled a little bit before once again focusing on his sneakers. "Um...would you want to go to a movie sometime?"

And there it was—my escape hatch.

A movie would lead to the spring dance. Maybe we'd make it official and I'd wear his Jostens class ring, the weight of legitimacy on a chain around my neck.

Football was king in Havendale, and as a team member's girlfriend, nothing and no one could touch me. Sure, a brain and jock couple was unusual, but not unheard of. This could save me for the rest of the school year, even through the summer if I played my cards right.

And he had all the right parts. *Boy* parts.

Ani could be written off as an experiment, like overdoing it on sour apple flavored Puckers and puking green or trying out for cheerleading sophomore year when you'd been a drama geek all along. I *did* like guys. I wouldn't be lying to myself if I had a boyfriend now and saved my next girlie crush for Chicago.

His eyes lit up—my face must have given me away.

But I knew it wouldn't be fair to Moose.

"I can't," I said, and his face fell, eyes back to his sneakers. But he was sweet, and though I knew I didn't owe him anything, I wanted to acknowledge that he'd at least tried to reach out amid the chaos. I put my hand on his shoulder, the faded plaid flannel not unlike my dad's shirt, just about five sizes larger.

He nodded, looked down at his sneakers. "I get it." Then he looked up, mustered a small smile. "Do you want to have lunch together on Monday? As friends?"

"Uh…yeah," I said, then felt the corners of my mouth turn up. "Yeah, I would, Moose."

"See ya then." He grinned and lumbered off.

I was glad I could make one person happy tonight.

I finally spotted Mia on the soft, worn leather couch in the living room. She held a tiny green bottle of Perrier. A beautiful light blue top draped over her burgeoning stomach. It was as though she existed within a force field that the party chaos couldn't permeate. She was a queen, a fertility goddess in teenage girl form, the portrait of serenity, from her glowing skin to the smile on her face. For a moment, I had to catch my breath before I approached her, a willing lady-in-waiting.

How stupid we all were to think she could hide a very obvious pregnancy. Lin and Carmen were always busy, but our classmates weren't. Of course they saw.

"Mia," I said, passing a little freshman girl (did we ever look that young?) running to fetch her another Perrier. She was surrounded by underclassmen girls, like handmaidens, the opposite of a pariah. Word of her upcoming marriage had spread, and it was sooooo romantic if you were fourteen, the age Juliet was, oh my God!

Not my words. I heard it all from the gaggle of admirers around us.

"Hey, can we talk?" I asked.

"Yeah, absolutely." Was she relieved? I couldn't tell. Either way, she seemed happy to see me, reaching for my hand and positioning me beside her on the couch. She set her Perrier on a coaster on the coffee table and pulled my legs onto her lap, the way she used to when we watched movies. That was before she knew I was bi and became uncomfortable with my touching her. She always thought she was being sly, subtle, but I'd noticed.

Mia beckoned me to lean in. "I wanted to say," she whispered, curls brushing my ear, bringing me back to all the secrets we'd shared since we were seven. Her voice caught, and she pulled back. I scooted closer so I could hear her over Busta Rhymes reverberating through the living room. I thought of suggesting we go somewhere quiet, but other than the study where Max was probably playing solitaire, there wasn't such a place. And he'd heard enough grownup talk.

"I wanted to say," she began again, huge brown eyes serious and deep. "I wanted to thank you for being the most supportive friend I could ask for." I started to reply, but she held up a hand, nails manicured a pearly pink. The ruby ring was back on her wedding finger. "I'm serious, Pal. You've stood by me and Tesla and Xander, and you always listen, and you never complain." She smiled, and it was different from the serene goddess-smile from a minute before. This smile was vulnerable yet strong, like an icon of the Virgin Mary.

And just as quickly as it appeared, Mia's smile was gone, and her face grew serious. "I wanted to say too…" She took my hand again. "I was wrong the other night at the restaurant, and I'm so sorry." Her face crumpled. "Not even wrong, I was awful. I read a story in the news the next morning, about a boy who's gay and his classmates beat him up and I thought, that could've been you. And then what happened today…"

Tears were in her eyes, and I pictured her kneeling by my locker today with the paper towels wrapped around her hands. Her frantic glance when she saw me, trying to get rid of the bad stuff before I had to bear witness.

"And all I could do the other day was quote the fu—the freaking Bible, instead of being compassionate to my best friend." Her hand tightened around mine. "I have to be honest; I'm still wrapping my mind around two girls together, but from now on, I'm gonna be better, Pal. I got your back."

I wanted to cry. Not only because my best friend was finally—*finally*—supporting me. Not only because I had to tell her I'd be leaving in August and probably never coming back. But also because yesterday, I gave Tes that love letter from Xander to Mia, the one that alluded to them being together.

Five minutes ago, I was full of righteous indignation—the Jesus, the misunderstood hero. Now, I was the Judas. The betrayer.

I didn't deserve any of them.

"Mia," I said, "we need to talk. In private. Right now."

"Tes has a surprise for me," she said, eyes glowing. She reached for her Perrier as if I hadn't spoken at all. "He's going to give it to me in front of everyone." She took a sip, bubbling over just as much as the sparkling water. "I think it's a wedding ring!"

"Okay." I hadn't heard about this surprise, but then again, Tes couldn't string together a sentence when I'd come in. I had a moment of panic—was this about the letter? But Tes seemed happy-drunk. It couldn't be that. It couldn't.

Even so, I needed to get this off my chest. "Mia," I whispered, touching my face to her curls again. "My mom knows about the baby. And she's trying to get ahold of your parents."

She pulled back, all the color drained from her face.

"I know, I know," I whispered. "So maybe we clear everyone out?" *And I keep you here until you agree that this wedding is a bad idea?*

She opened her mouth to say something—what it was, I'd never know—when Busta stopped rapping and Tes entered the room. The king. Everyone stopped what they were doing.

"Party peopullllllll!" he yelled, throwing his arms open. "Just a little break and then we'll get back to the party. Are we having fun yet?"

In response, a drunken cheer rose up from the living room, the grand staircase, the kitchen. Tes still had that class president swagger, overpowering all.

Also, he seemed remarkably sober and clear-eyed for someone who couldn't stand up straight not that long ago. Must have been some powerful water.

Or had Tes been putting it on? Acting drunker than he actually was to distract me and Mia and everyone? I loved my best friend, but I wouldn't put it past him.

The dirty Green Day tee was gone. In its place, Tes'd changed into a blue button-down shirt, perfectly crisp like it was fresh from the dry cleaner. He looked like his father, about to make an offer no one could refuse on a new Mazda.

"This winter," he intoned, his voice bouncing off the walls, "I got one hell of a surprise. My girlfriend, my beautiful Mia"—he gestured toward where we were sitting, and Mia, now under her boyfriend's spell, smiled and waved at everyone—"was carrying our child. And I was scared, but also fucking thrilled... Sorry, Mia, I know how you feel about cussing."

Everyone tittered, like we were adults at a wedding listening to the toast, except we weren't. We were just a bunch of kids getting trashed, our clothes mussed from fumbling in bedrooms that weren't even ours.

And I knew Tes, that glint in his eyes. He was steering us, manipulating the whole thing as confidently as he ran student council meetings. This would not end well.

"I wanted to have you all here tonight to celebrate our wedding at Springfield's fancy courthouse, because God knows our parents won't." Everyone laughed again, right on cue. "But now, I want to say something to Mia in front of y'all and God and everyone..." He made his way over to Mia, and she sat up straight, aware she was on display but also happy to do her lover's bidding.

Tes knelt in front of her, just as he'd done in the hallway after fighting with Xander—a supplicant. His face went from a magnanimous smile to a grin that was terrifying. Demented.

"Is it mine?" he asked.

A collective gasp, just like he ordered it.

Mia was still smiling, disbelief growing on her pretty face. "Wh-what?"

"You heard me," Tes said, calm as you please. "Is it mine?"

"Anyone home? I see cars in the driveway, but no one's talking—" Xander entered the living room, Cameron in tow. The two of them glanced around at the jocks and goths and drama kids, all of whom were completely silent. "Man," Xander said, grinning. "Who died?"

"Glad you came." Tes stood up and crossed the room to shake Xander's hand, like a politician. Cameron shot Xander a worried look. I scooted closer to Mia, tucked my arm through hers. I could feel her shaking.

I had a flashback to last spring's dance—we didn't get a prom until senior year, so it was a consolation prize of sorts. Xander wasn't there yet, but me and Mia and Tesla had twirled around to the *Golden Girls* theme. We sang and giggled tipsily thanks to the Champagne he'd sneaked in in a thermos. We'd gone as a trio and I didn't even feel like a tagalong. It had been all bubbles and laughter and slurred lyrics, just like the movies tell you high school is—perfect. For a moment, I'd imagined we were dancing at Tes and Mia's wedding, which wasn't hard because Mia was wearing her fluffy white dress from the quinceañera her extended family had thrown for her the year before. She said normally people didn't wear a quince dress to a dance, but I think she liked imagining it was her wedding dress too.

I wished we could go back.

"I'm sorry, man, for the shit we got into a while ago," Tes said.

Xander nodded slowly, like he wasn't sure what to believe or what he'd just walked into. I could have told him—*a trap*—but I was frozen in my spot on the couch, arm in Mia's, protector to the end.

"I wanted you here tonight so I could tell you, no hard feelings."

"Not a problem, man," Xander said with a nervous laugh, clearly aware of the house full of eyes on him. All the white people staring at the Black guy. Cameron didn't leave his side, giving us all the evil eye through her twin curtains of long dark hair. "But maybe let's shoot the shit without an audience?"

"Nah, I'm good," Tesla said, backing away. "I was just asking Mia about the father of our baby." He paused, looked down at his Chucks, and for a second, all his defenses were down before they snapped right back up again. "*Her* baby, I should say. Because I'm sure as *shit* not gonna be the chump who raises a kid that isn't mine, like my dad."

Wait, *what?*

And yet, oh God, it explained so much.

Tes looked exactly like his mother, but Max looked like their dad. *Max's* dad. Tes's mother had always come to his baseball games and Academic Bowl matches as we got older. His dad was a shadowy presence at best.

For the second time that night, my stomach dropped to my shoes. *Did you know this?* I asked Mia with my wide eyes. Equally wide-eyed, she shook her head.

"Not gonna repeat that pattern," Tes said to the company of frozen faces. No one moved. "So, I thought we'd get this straightened out here and now. Before I make the biggest mistake of my life." Those last words were directed at Mia, with a gaze I could only describe as murderous.

I thought of Tes, the gun in the study, the weird smile on his face.

I squeezed my eyes shut.

"What the *fuck*, Tes?"

My eyes popped open. Everyone gasped at Mia's angry tone, using not only a curse word, but the ultimate curse word. She shook off my arm, hoisted herself off the couch and waddled over to Tes, pointing her finger in his face. People cleared a path for her.

"Am I on trial here?"

He crossed his arms, grin replaced with narrowed eyes. "Only if you want to be."

"Cut the shit, Wrightwood," Mia snapped. Her serene face was now fiery.

Mia was generally the calm one. The peacemaker. The girl teachers never had to worry about. Piss her off, however? May God have mercy because she sure wouldn't.

Mia put her hand on her lower stomach, now less Virgin Mary and more angry fertility goddess. "What would *ever* make you think this baby wasn't yours?"

Everyone—all of St. Cecelia's and half the public school—watched, listened, and waited. I hadn't seen my classmates this quiet, this rapt, since the administration interrupted lunch period for the OJ verdict sophomore year.

"You have *no idea* what I go through every day," Mia announced through clenched teeth. Even her curls were standing on end. She was so freaking terrifying, the freshman admirers crowded around me as if I could ward off the bad vibes. One even reached for my hand.

"I am *huge*. I feel *sick*. There is something *growing inside me* and that's all I can think about. Nothing else is important and because we agreed it's a secret, because everyone would *freak the fuck out,* I can't talk to adults. I can't go to a doctor because I'm so scared someone will see me and tell my parents, or even worse, something will be *wrong* with the baby, and I can't do anything about it. I can't even tell my mom and dad because we had this *bright. Fucking. Idea* to elope tomorrow. And I *never* complained. Even when my clothes stopped fitting and I cried to Paulina just so you wouldn't have to hear, and you wouldn't dump me. I was that afraid of losing you."

Mia took a deep breath, and one hand was still on her stomach, but the other had her index finger pointed at Tes's chest like a dagger. "Not anymore. I'm not backing down. I'm just gonna ask you, in front of everyone, just what your problem is with the *mother of your child.*"

Silence. In the corner, someone started applauding but was quickly shushed.

And without missing a beat, Tes pulled a square of notebook paper out of his pocket, unfolded it, and brandished the note in Mia's face. "Look familiar?" he snarled.

Behind me, Xander muttered, "Oh fuck."

"W-where did you get that?" Mia stuttered.

Don't look at me, Tes. Don't look at me.

"Doesn't matter." Tes's voice rose. "Sure sounds like you and Xandy over there were together last fall. Around the time that, hmmmm…" He pretended to think, then gave her a death glare. "You got pregnant?"

"It wasn't like that." Suddenly Xander was at Mia's side, holding up his hands. Like a protection. A prayer.

"Xander," said Tes, his murderous gaze fixed on his former best friend. "I know Catholic school sex ed is shitty, but you do know how babies are made, right?"

"You have no idea," Xander said through clenched teeth. Cameron stood in the corner, face whiter than ever.

"Hey, Tes," I said. I couldn't sit on the couch, dumb and supposedly innocent, any longer. I was off the hook for the letter, but I knew something terrible was about to go down, and maybe I could make it less terrible. "Let's take a step back."

"Pal." Tes gave me a look that could only be described as patronizing. "Let the big kids handle this, okay?" He didn't even speak to Max that way. He gave an eight-year-old more respect than his best childhood friend.

I prepared all my best swear words, ready to let him have it. "Tesla, what the fu—"

"We kissed, okay?"

Several "oh my Gods" rang from the crowd. I wished they'd all freaking disappear. This drama, that wasn't even theirs, would be all over school come Monday. And Tes seemed to be enjoying every minute. Or he had been, until Mia dropped the kissing bomb. Now his face was pale. She'd admitted it.

All heads turned to Mia, in the center of the room, looking like the innocent target of an angry mob. I shivered.

"We kissed," she repeated, eyes fixed on Tes. Xander opened his mouth. "Let me finish, Xander." She looked around the room. "We would *talk*. About things that none of y'all would understand."

Well, *that* hurt.

"You could have talked to me," I said so softly I'm not sure anyone could hear me.

But Mia did, because she turned around, more tired than angry. "Paulina, I know you mean well, but has anyone in this town, in this *school*, ever asked if you speak English? Have they referred to your father as 'that Mexican lawyer' even though he's from El Salvador, or sent him hate mail from prison? Have they told you to go back to where you came from, even though you *and your mom* were born in the United States, and when you say that, their racist asses don't believe you, so you just ignore them but it never stops being so fucking painful?"

My revelation must have shown on my face because Mia said, "That's what I thought." She surveyed the room again before refocusing on Tes. The audience was hers, just like her star turn in *Jesus Christ Superstar*. "Xander *understood*. He knows what it's like to exist in a town that's almost all white. We feel it every single day, and there is *no* way to get it unless you're not white. Period."

"She's right," Xander muttered, glaring at Tes, at me, at all of us who had intentionally or inadvertently made him feel more different than he already did.

They exchanged a look, Xander and Mia. Not a long one, but one that projected love and understanding and a whole damn relationship right there in an eye-lock. Jane Austen would have been proud. I realized then, Mia also knew about Xander's son—probably before I did. I wondered if she'd told him about her pregnancy before she told me.

I'd been in the front row for her and Tes falling in love. We had a history. And yet I'd never seen Mia look at Tes like that.

"So yeah," Mia continued, redirecting that hypnotic gaze at the father of her baby. Looking down—like a queen would her least worthy subject—even though she was much shorter than him. "One night, it went further than talking. He kissed me, and I didn't stop him right away, and I'm sorry for that. We never had sex. We never even fooled around. Yes, he *liked* me liked me, but he never pushed it after I said no."

"I wrote her to get my feelings out," Xander said. "But that was it."

"That was it," Mia confirmed.

Everyone watched Tes. What would he do?

He crossed to a couch—which a group of sophomores quickly vacated—and slumped into it, his head in his hands.

He grabbed a decorative pillow, buried his face, and screamed.

Mia perched by him, not quite touching, and he mumbled something, then raised his head.

"Come again?" she asked gently, face the picture of loving concern.

"I said, I don't want to get married anymore."

The crowd started to murmur. Even more gossip fodder. I could practically *hear* the phone lines burning tomorrow.

Mia sighed. "I get it."

He gazed at her, eyes wet. "You could have told me."

"I know. I'm sorry." Mia's eyes were wet too. I was wondering if we should all clear the room, give them a moment when—

Crack.

At first, I wasn't sure what the sound was. It was vaguely firework-ish, but even the dumbest rednecks wouldn't bring them into this fancy house.

Then, one of the kids who skipped school at the beginning of every hunting season came running from the kitchen.

"Gunshot!" he yelled, eyes wild.

For a moment, Mia and I looked at each other, confused. Tes raised his head from his hands, dazed like he just woke up.

And then something real, something awful, occurred to me. In the next split second, every prayer I'd ever learned raced through my head.

"Max!" I heard someone scream. "Max!"

And it's only when we ran to the study that I realized the person screaming was me.

CHAPTER FIFTEEN

No one knew how it ended for Blair-Marie Elliott. According to her parents, though, they found her after a day and a half in a corner of the basement. Little. Helpless. No longer breathing. Her mom told the press through waterfalls of mascara running down her face, "It didn't feel real. And then it did."

Now I knew what she meant. Seeing Max's tiny, crumpled body didn't feel real. Until the moment it did, after Moose broke down the door. He was in front of the gun cabinet—the one I knew was there but didn't think to double-check when I shut him in. Eight years old, on the verge of his First Communion, a cracker melting on his tongue and sip of wine that would make him and his classmates giggle.

Mia jostled me and caught me by the waist. Her face went white. "Pal," she whispered. "Do something." Her big brown eyes met mine. "Pal! Paulina," she said louder, putting a delicate hand over my mouth.

I was still screaming.

Tes scooped up his brother. I could see the blood seeping down his button-down shirt. And that finally silenced me.

The house, still full, was now deathly quiet.

Why had Max aimed the gun at his own chest? Or had it just gone off? Had it been deliberate, the result of a bored little kid shut in a room while everyone partied and accused and cried around him? Would we ever know?

Mia dragged me by the arm, through the hallway as the population of St. Cecelia's made room for us, scooting up against the walls like trapped bugs and averting their eyes. As we ran alongside Tes, he mumbled to himself. As we got closer to the car, I made out the words, over and over like a dark mantra: *shouldhavebeenme shouldhavebeenme shouldhavebeenme.*

❖

"Go go go go go!"

As we made our way down the endless driveway, sneakers flopping on concrete, all I could see was Tes's back. He held a bleeding, silent little boy to him as we raced to the Bear, Mia in tow.

"Tes, you're drunk!" I recognized the voice behind me as Xander's. Cameron was behind him, her arm around a waddling Mia. "You can't drive."

"Don't tell me what to do!" Tes screamed, animalistic, like nothing I'd ever heard before.

Out of the corner of my eye, I saw Cameron whisper into Mia's ear. "Cameron will drive," Mia called. Keys flew through the air, which Cameron caught one-handed.

But once we reached the car, she hesitated.

I was the only one close enough to see her frantic eyes and hear her whisper, "I can't drive stick."

"Get in the back seat," I told her, my voice a good octave lower. "I can."

I didn't own a car, only used my mom's if it was snowing and absolutely not fathomable for me to walk or bike or ride with Tes. I got my license because it was the thing to do when you turn sixteen.

But when I was ten, months before he died, Dad took me outside of Havendale, to the country roads where every kid learned to drive, and taught me how. Once I succeeded, he said with a satisfied smile, "Now you can drive anything, babe." I never asked why he'd decided to teach a ten-year-old how to drive. Maybe he always knew he wouldn't make it to my teen years.

"GO!" Tes screamed from the passenger seat.

I stabbed the keys in in the ignition and shot out of the driveway. Tes clutched Max, burying his face in his brother's lifeless little neck.

"Fuck! Which way is the hospital? You're going the wrong way!" Tes cried.

I cranked the steering wheel and pulled back into the driveway. I could hear my friends in the back seat loudly slump to one side. Like dead bodies. *Don't think that, Pal.*

"Guys?" A tiny, plaintive cry from Mia broke through Tes's sobs as he buried his face in Max's neck again. "When we get there...I think I need to see a doctor too."

Tes's head snapped up. He grabbed my arm, his hand wet with Max's blood. I glanced at the rearview mirror but couldn't make out Mia's face in the dark.

"What's going on?" Xander said roughly.

I shot back out of the driveway at a death-defying speed, praying no cop would pull us over.

"It's..." Mia took a deep breath and let it out. "I don't think the baby's supposed to come this early."

"Goddammit!" Tes yelled as we skidded.

Black ice, from the late winter storm yesterday.

The road slip-slid underneath us. My adrenaline shot up and took me to a very dark place. A place where not only did I lock an innocent little kid in a room with a gun, but I took out everyone I loved in a car accident. Even now, things could get much, much worse. I focused hard on the darkened path ahead.

And then there was Ani, reflected in the headlights, right in the road outside Tes's house, waving her arms at us.

All I remembered after that one last glimpse of my ex-love, face illuminated in light, eyes bright blue and wide, mouth open, forming words I'd never hear, blond ponytail trailing like a fallen star, was:

Screams.

A large *thunk.*

My head smashing against glass.

The rest was silence.

Both joy and terror of good and bad
that makes and unfolds error
—*William Shakespeare*, The Winter's Tale

Part 2: Learn to Fly
Perdita
Chicago, 2014

I see the play so lies
That I must bear a part.
—*Perdita, William Shakespeare's* The Winter's Tale

Chapter One

February

"Happy birthday, baby! We got you improv classes!"

She shut off my Dixie Chicks to tell me *that*?

I turn over on my bed, where I've been lying on my stomach working on plans for my latest clock and staring at the bare tree outside my window, black twig etchings on gray sky. My moms' faces are eager. I'm not sure what reaction they're expecting.

All I can think to say is, "Um, my birthday's not for two months." Plus, I've been hinting since after Christmas that I want a new laptop or Lasik, not classes in something I'm 99.9 percent certain I'll hate.

Ma is undeterred, her smile growing wider. "Come on, Perdita! You can't be a real Chicagoan until you've taken improv, right?"

I raise an eyebrow at her, sitting up and pushing my curls out of my face for the millionth time that day. Where's my elastic? "Pretty sure I can. And have been. Since I was born."

Mum (she grew up in England, so she's always been Mum to me) gives Ma the here-comes-a-teenage-moment look. I've seen that look a thousand times since I started high school, and more than ever this year. Sometimes she even says it out loud.

Mum perches on the edge of my bed, smoothing her long floral skirt. Ma plops down with a bounce, her crazy purple plaid pajama pants sharply contrasting with my plain, navy comforter. Chaos and

Order: if we had a family band, that's what it'd be called. And come to think of it, Ma would be *all about* a family band, so I shouldn't ever say that out loud, or we'll be touring the country wearing matching outfits.

"Perdita," Mum says in her gentle voice with a hint of steel underneath. *Purrr-dih-tah:* I love when she says my name. Her eyes are almost ink-black to my light brown. "I know this might not be what you expected, but we want to do something as a family." She glances at Ma before continuing. "Since you started junior year, we feel like we never see you."

"It's the toughest year," I protest, as if it's going to make any difference. "You told me that when high school started." I glance over at my worktable, the various parts of my clock scattered atop graph papers full of sketches. I have to get this project about quartz versus pendulum just right. I've been building clocks for years, but if I can place at the statewide science fair, the possibilities are endless.

"Not the clock thing again," Ma groans, flopping back on my bed so her face is level with my hip. I glare down at her, and she holds up her hands in surrender. "Kidding!" Her expression is trying to be apologetic, but it's so goofy—typical Ma—I have to smile.

"That may be true." Mum pulls Ma up and keeps ahold of her hand. "But learning something new is a good way to get out of your own head." Ma rests her head on Mum's shoulder as Mum continues. "Weren't you just telling me that Samuel Morse was also a painter?"

"Samuel Morse was an *inventor*, not a scientist," I mumble, but Mum gives me the same raised eyebrows I've seen since I was three and refused to go to bed so I could watch "the show with the boys and girls." (*Friends* reruns on TBS.) I didn't win then and I'm not winning now.

Guess I'm taking improv classes with my moms.

If Ma had handed down this proclamation, I'd wheedle or plead and likely, she'd cave. People think that because Mum's this mild-mannered Shakespeare professor, she's the easier parent, and Ma, the ex-cop, must be a disciplinarian. In reality, the opposite is true. Ma could easily be talked into an extra Oreo before bed when

I was little and extends my curfew by fifteen minutes now. She's the one who initially adopted me and gave up her job in the field to be a desk jockey, pushing papers and working remotely, until she left altogether to go back to school for social work.

Mum is the one who named me though. She's the one with all the rules and order and tenure. When she talks, I automatically sit up straighter. Her students do it too.

I shake my head, pushing my glasses up my nose. "So when are we leaving for improv?"

"Be ready at six," Ma says, clapping her hands. She's the joker of our family, and now that I think about it, I'm actually surprised she hasn't signed us up for improv way earlier. "It's still cold as balls out, so we'll drive rather than dealing with the train."

Bouncing up from my bed, she realizes Mum and I are looking at her and rolls her eyes. "Yes, I'll wear big girl pants."

"Thank *gawd,*" Mum and I say at the same time, and burst out laughing.

"Wanna wind the clock before we leave, hon?" Ma asks Mum as they leave the room. About thirty seconds later, I hear the cranking that gets louder every year. I made my first clock when I was eleven, and it's old-school. We have to wind the thing once a day to make sure it keeps running. The three of us take turns. Like most kid-made things, it's pretty ugly—the face is crooked and the hands always look on the verge of falling off—but Ma and Mum refuse to throw it away. In our house, "I'll wind the clock" is equivalent to "I love you."

As I listen to the familiar tick, I text my best friend Lulu.

Guess what I got as an early birthday present?

She replies almost before I hit Send. That girl has faster thumbs than anyone. *New laptop? Lasik? That grandfather clock from that shop near Clark and Fullerton you are obsessed with because you're a weirdo?*

Oh right. I forgot about that beauty. Did I text Ma a photo even? *None of the above,* I type. *Improv classes. AS A FAMILY.*

Whatever, Lulu texts back. *Your moms are hilarious. I'd totally take improv with them.*

A year ago, I would have agreed with her. The odds have been stacked against me since I was born: most families aren't clamoring to adopt a little brown baby who was premature and as a result would forever have very bad vision (hence my thick specs). I don't know much about my birth, but I'm sure whatever lawyer or adoption agency practically threw me at Ma who, at the time, was a single Chinese-American police officer who'd just come out of the closet and wasn't speaking to her parents.

She was just finalizing all the paperwork, while simultaneously jiggling my little carrier and debating what to name me, when she met Mum, who was finishing up her MFA thesis from a booth at Clarke's just off the Belmont Red Line here in Chicago. Mum said hello, then picked me up like she was born to it and started humming an old song Rod Stewart made famous. (I listened to it a few years ago and it has weirdly misogynistic lyrics, but my moms still love it.) As the story goes, I quieted immediately, burrowing into her chest. We go to Clarke's every year on their anniversary, sit in the same booth even.

They quickly joined forces, and Mum the Shakespeare scholar suggested Ma name me "Perdita" which means "lost daughter" and ensured I'd never have to go by my first name *and* last initial at school. A few months later, I was one of the youngest participants in the Pride Parade, Mum proudly pushing me in a stroller festooned with rainbow flags that matched Ma's pants. We even made the *Trib*.

They're hilarious to you, I text Lulu, *because you don't live with them.* She and my other best friend Dot just love Ma's crazy pajamas and terrible puns, and Mum's decidedly nonacademic goal to try every single kind of Oreo that Nabisco can invent. The great thing about this is I can basically have Lulu and Dot over whenever I want. The bad thing is we often end up binging Netflix shows *en masse*, a family with two extra kids.

I used to love all of this: that my moms were so quirky and cool compared to other parents at U-High who work downtown and wear power suits and crunch numbers for fat paychecks. We jokingly call ourselves "The Diversity Bunch" because Mum's university, U-High, *and* the police department (back in the day) clamor to take our photos for their ads every year because I'm Latina, Mum is Black, and Ma's Asian. Queer women of color with a very obviously adopted child ticks a lot of boxes! (Ma and Mum love this because it means free family pictures. We have a whole wall.)

I know how lucky I am to have two parents who think I'm the greatest thing since sliced bread, have given me all the space I need to grow and just be, have taken me on vacations, and encouraged my admittedly strange fixation with clocks.

But lately...

I don't understand why Ma and Mum—who've been forthcoming about everything from how babies are made to why the prison system is corrupt, who learned Spanish and Mandarin *with* me so I'd feel connected to my heritage and family—always clam up when I ask about my adoption. I know my bio mom was really young and Ma met her while on the job, but that doesn't really narrow anything down. I've heard about crack babies, babies whose birth mothers were HIV-positive and transmitted to their infants...I mean, Ma was the cop who saw it all. I've always assumed I was in a less-than-ideal situation, but so were a lot of adopted kids. What's so terrible they can't tell me?

And another thing. Lately, I've been wanting to meet someone again. Romantically. I'm not a total newb. I had a girlfriend freshman year and a boyfriend as a sophomore—just hand-holding puppy love, nothing significant.

But junior year, I got serious: books, BFFs, and clocks only, no distractions. I want to be the world's foremost horologist, someone who studies time. It's not nearly as dirty as it sounds, but after one too many jokes at school, I now just say "time scientist." For a good six months, my interests felt *pure*. Anything else was a waste.

But I've seen Lulu and Dot texting whatever person they're obsessed with (and this can change week to week, with Dot especially). Lulu's cheeks turn pink in the most adorable way. Dot gets this secret smile as she types a reply or takes a selfie. As a wannabe scientist, I'm always intrigued by what I don't know. I've read plenty about the chemical rush, the endorphins, that seem unique to romantic love. It wasn't there with my exes.

Also last summer, I discovered how fantastic masturbation is and I started wondering what it would feel like if someone touched me that way. I'd like to experience that rush, not just in my parts, but in my heart.

For purely scientific reasons, of course.

Ma used to interrogate perps on the regular. She may be a softy at home, but I swear the woman can also read minds. I know, I just *know*, she senses me pulling away, wanting to date, and aching to know more about my origins. Hence the improv classes. It's her way of keeping me close *and* under her watchful eye.

Have I mentioned I hate improv?

I try to be quiet about it because it's basically Chicago's official art form and I don't want my citizenship revoked. And, of course, I've been to shows because you can't live here your whole life and *not* be able to direct people to the place in Old Town where Tina Fey got her start.

But how is playing silly games in front of an audience fun? I'm not a kid. I wasn't into games when I *was* one.

My phone buzzes and I look down. Lulu and Dot have sent me a pic. In it, they're both grinning and giving dorky thumbs-ups while flashing a sign with the words YES AND scribbled on notebook paper.

I have no idea what that means, I text. But I'm smiling.

"Let's go, P!" Ma's voice echoes through the hallway. My phone says it's six o'clock.

Time to improvise, whatever that means.

❖

Hi kid,

It's been seventeen years.

I started looking for you after I woke up hungover last Christmas. I had the mother of all headaches—definitely don't recommend—and not from something festive and Christmas-y like eggnog, just my old friend Jack Daniels. I really hope you haven't been hungover yet.

Anyway, I woke up that day wondering if you knew what happened, about the night all our carefully laid plans went to hell. Just like George and Lennie and the rabbits from Of Mice and Men, *which I bet you've read by now.*

I'm mostly sober, and I go to meetings, but I relapse once in a while. Holidays are the hardest, and when I slip, they're the worst.

I hope you're in a place where your holidays are nice, with presents and lights and people who make you feel wanted. At one point, I had all that too. Mostly.

If I were to find you, I don't know what kind of relationship we'd have. If I'd be welcome at all in your life.

I made so many mistakes.

I stopped writing to you for so long because I couldn't—losing my brother, then you so soon after—was too much. I blamed myself for both. I think about him every single minute of every day.

If not for therapy and meetings, I would never have accepted that his death wasn't something I could undo and was technically my fault.

But you...maybe that's something I can work on.

So I opened this notebook again, the same one I used before you were born. My handwriting is significantly worse now, sorry. Course, I don't know if you'll ever see it... And then I'll go back to meetings. I'll stop drinking, even though it gave me a little bit of warmth during these long, cold winters. I'll try hot chocolate instead—the good kind with milk, not water.

Maybe you'll read this someday.

On the other hand, I'm not sure I want you to.

How do I sign this anyway?

We'll settle for,

Someone You Still Don't Know

Chapter Two

Oof, there are so many white boys here.

Looking around this small class, I would guess my moms are the oldest by at least a decade. I am the youngest.

The rest are a sloppily dressed crew, guys and a few girls. Some of them reek of the cigarettes they were smoking outside a few minutes ago. We passed them coming in, me trying to pretend I wasn't with my parents and Ma trying and failing to hide her hurt *why won't you hold my hand anymore, Perdita* face.

Once we got inside, though, we bonded over the big picture of Tina Fey, whom all three of us love. I wouldn't mind learning to be as witty as she is, but I doubt surrounding myself with twentysomethings, who clearly have money (these classes aren't cheap) and are trying their best to hide it with their quirky Goodwill clothes, is the way to do it.

Besides, Tina's sense of humor probably can't be taught. I feel like I'm perpetually *not* in on whatever joke is happening in front of me. Mum calls it my overly logical mind. Ma just thinks I need to loosen up and study less. I call it awkward and I wish there were meds for it.

"Hey, improvisers! Let's get ready to rumbllllllllllllle!"

Oh God.

Ma says that same phrase sometimes when she's come home from a party and has had even a sip of alcohol. I think it's from an old nineties song. Really, I should *know* because our family soundtrack is basically all nineties all the time. And now it's coming from someone bursting into the room, who I assume is the teacher. Likely another white guy who's all too eager to tell me why women aren't funny.

I shift in my chair, crossing my legs in a power pose and ready to look over my glasses and down my nose at whomever I'm stuck with for the next eight weeks.

Oh. *Oh.*

Since when does Michael B. Jordan teach improv in Chicago?

"Hel*lo*," Mum murmurs.

Mum playfully pokes her arm with an overly loud "Shhhhhh!" because Ma is incapable of being quiet, *ever.*

"No need to shush!" the guy at the front of the class says, looking in our direction with the most gorgeous smile I've ever seen. I expect to hear a *ding* emanate from his gleaming, straight teeth. "In fact, in Improv One we'll do the opposite of shushing. I want you all to be comfortable with *not* being comfortable, taking risks, and doing very silly things with people you don't know. If you're a quiet person during the day, you'll be louder than a bomb here at night."

Oh no. I am a quiet person during the day *and* night, and I'm not good with people I don't know. This is going to be more painful than I initially thought. Between that statement and the fact that it's being uttered by the cutest guy I've ever seen, my face is now on fire.

"I'm Fenton," our teacher says with a grin, clapping his hands together like it's the first day of school. "You were supposed to have Hal Rosenblum, who's been here since the Bill Murray days, and will tell you more about *that* than you ever wanted to know. Lots of stories involving cocaine." Everyone laughs, even me. "Unfortunately, he was cast in the DC show and had to leave for rehearsals yesterday, so you're stuck with me."

"That's fine," I hear a girl murmur behind me. So I'm not the only one who's noticed our teacher could play a Marvel superhero. And I'm jealous? What the frig?

"Who here has taken improv?" Fenton asks. A handful of people raise their hands. One burly bearded dude raises two. "Fantastic. A mix of old guard and newbies, I like that. I'm old guard—started in the kids' program here when I was tiny—but new at teaching, so I'm a little bit of both."

Cool. Maybe this is an introductory day and he'll just stand up there and talk, and I can stare like a creeper while trying to act like I'm *not* staring like a creeper.

"But hey, you didn't pay *way* too much money for me to stand here and talk at you." He claps his hands again. "Everybody up! Let's make a big circle."

"Come on, P!" Ma grabs my hand, then Mum's, and rushes us to the circle like someone just offered her free clown pants.

Wait.

She either lied earlier or she forgot to change. She's still wearing the purple and pink plaid bottoms. "This is my daughter!" Ma exclaims to Fenton while pointing enthusiastically at me. So much for my plan to blend in.

"Well, hi, daughter!" Fenton says to me with a smile that says, *I get that you're embarrassed but your mom's also really sweet.* He's right on both counts. I simultaneously want to sink through this floor with its ugly gray carpet and grab his hand and never let go. I'm terrified of whatever we're about to do in this circle, humiliated my mom singled me out, turned on by the hottest guy I've ever seen, and we're only three minutes in.

If this is the whole "chemical rush" thing, Lulu and Dot can have it.

"So, the first game we're going to play is called Zip, Zap, Zop," Fenton explains once we're situated in a very sloppy circle. The bearded guy opens his mouth, and Fenton holds up a hand. "I'm sure some of you have played it before, but I'm going to explain the rules for everyone."

Fenton says something about nonsensical words and does this sort of hand-brush-clap at another person, but I'm distracted. His lips look really soft and my face is on fire all over again, so it's no wonder when I totally space and just keep staring. Suddenly, the room falls into an awkward silence.

"It's ZAP," Bearded Guy obnoxiously stage whispers.

Ugh.

Eventually, I understand the game, but I still can't get it together, and I'm the slowest one in the class by far. My reaction times are horrible. My moms are rock stars though. Even when Ma screws up, she laughs so loudly at herself that half the class joins in, and one girl with blue hair even compliments her pants. Mum is more reserved—I get that from her. She may be a Shakespeare scholar but she's not an actress, though she tries really hard to be fast and even gets a high five from obnoxious Bearded Guy.

We play some other games in the circle, and I'm hopeless at all of them. Why? Why is freezing necessary? I don't *want* people tapping me on the shoulder, dangit!

The worst is "What are you doing?" A person asks the question, and the object is to name one action while miming another. Easy.

I'm the last to go up, and my blood pressure is through the roof. When I try to play, I feel like a toddler who can't pat her head and rub her stomach at the same time.

"Say you're mowing the lawn!" Ma keeps loudly whispering suggestions from the sidelines.

I know she means well, but my face just gets even hotter. So nope. This is not easy when all eyes are on me, it turns out.

I really don't understand how anyone can find this fun. Though everyone around me, including my parents, is having a grand old time. I love winning—competitions and good grades—but I've always hated games. And no one even wins improv games, so what's the point? Finally, *mercifully*, class time is up, and Fenton dismisses us until next week. No doubt I'll be humiliated all over again.

Happy early birthday, Perdita.

We all start packing up to leave. Bearded Guy walks out with some girl whose glasses are way cooler than mine. Fenton waves and smiles in my direction.

"Hey!" he says. Surely his girlfriend's behind me, but when I look over my shoulder, there's no one else. Ma and Mum are already outside the room, probably entertaining their new fan club. I can hear Ma's loud chortle.

"Perdita, right?" Fenton asks, loping toward me with those mile-long legs. He's so tall and graceful, I feel like a Weeble in comparison.

"Yeah." It comes out aggressive, a bark as loud and nervous as I feel. I clamp my lips shut.

"Great name," he says. "*The Winter's Tale.* I love Shakespeare."

"Me too," I say. What? I *don't* love Shakespeare, but facing that smile, I'm powerless to disagree. I do love my full name though, Perdita Yu-Gilman. It's a freaking mouthful if you're not used to it.

Fenton perches on a chair. "Just wanted to say you did good tonight."

I laugh. I can't help it. He's got to be shitting me.

"I was the worst in the class!" I protest, temporarily forgetting all the blushy, odd feelings I've had since he walked into the room.

He laughs too. "You should have seen me when I started. I didn't know my zips from my zaps."

"You were also, what, eight?" I point out.

"Seven." He grins, and I can't help it—I grin back. It's just a dumb conversation, but now I feel like we have an inside joke. I mean, he didn't stop and chat with anyone else. My face isn't on fire anymore, but my whole body feels warm and my legs are a little shaky. How old is he?

"Anyway," he says, still grinning, "I'll see you next week?"

I wait a second, then realize it was a question. God, one cute boy and I'm a space cadet? "Oh! Yeah. Next week."

And upon hearing that bon mot, Fenton gives me one last knee-wobbling smile and saunters out of the room, taking my heart with him.

"Everything okay, P?" Ma asks when I find them waiting in the hall.

"Yeah." *I think I'm in love. Is this love or is this just infatuation? Probably infatuation. Come ON, Perdita. He's your* teacher *and he was just being nice so you won't ask for a refund.* I nod fiercely, like one of those Funko Pop toys with the bobbling head. "Yeah," I repeat.

"I think I know what this is," Mum intones, winking at Ma. "Never seen you look that way, Perdita."

"Look what way?" Ma asks. Mum pokes her arm, and I renew my desire to sink through the floor. "Ohhhhhh," Ma says, looking at me knowingly. "Someone's got a cruuuuush!" she singsongs.

"Oh my God, Ma!" I say, totally embarrassed but also kinda loving that I, square, bookish Perdita, thought a guy was cute.

Ma slings an arm around me. "Let's blow this pop stand, wife and daughter. We passed that Froyo place on the way here, and I need hot fudge *now*." Her smile is so big, I don't bother to tell her that no one calls it Froyo anymore. She takes Mum's hand and the two of them smile at each other.

And with that, I follow my funny, embarrassing moms, who are never going to let me live down my crush, out of the training center in search of dessert.

Chapter Three

I'm still thinking about Fenton on my way to U-High the next morning. This is the first year Ma and Mum are letting me take the train from our apartment in Lincoln Park by myself, and the Red Line is its usual rush-hour sardine can today. It's even more packed because we're all in our warmest winter gear. Snowpocalypse, the freak blizzard that actually shut down the city for a few days, happened a little over a month ago, but it's still freezing.

Squeezed in with the mass of humanity and sweating in my puffy coat that I can't take off because, well, I can't move my arms, I wonder what he's doing right now. If he's thinking about the girl with glasses and the Shakespearean name who couldn't get Zip, Zap, Zop right. I'm so lost in my own head I almost slam into the heavy wood doors and into the *other* mass of humanity that is U-High. Shaking off...whatever this is, I make my way through the hall.

"I have to tell you something," Dot says, catching up to me and Lulu in front of our lockers.

Dot's purple-painted lips are smiling, but her dark eyes are serious. Lulu and I look at each other and I raise my eyebrows. She shakes her head, a nonverbal *I don't know.*

"What's up?" Lulu and I say in unison, same tone even. We look at each other and giggle, and I start unwinding my scarf—layer one of approximately six hundred.

Dot looks down at the stack of books in her arms, pushing aside the pink streak in her black hair. "Soooo…I need you both to know that I'm nonbinary."

"Okay," Lulu says. "First of all, we love and support you."

She looks at me and I quickly chime in. "Yes, Dot! All of that. All the way."

"And second," Lulu says, tossing her blond bangs out of her eyes—she needs a trim. "Um, what exactly does nonbinary mean? I know I can Google it, and I *will*, but…" She trails off. I know how my bestie since kindergarten feels; we want to take this seriously, but Dot doesn't *owe* us an explanation.

"We want to know what it means to you, if you're willing to share," I finish. Lulu takes my hand and squeezes it gratefully.

Dot bites her lip. I wonder how her parents took this, or if she's told them at all. They're doctors and really big on *this* or *that, yes* or *no*, likely *male* or *female* too. They know Dot's a lesbian, but even that is very "don't ask, don't tell." It's my moms who give Dot girlfriend advice. "It can mean a lot of things, but for *me,* it means I don't identify as male or female. Sometimes I feel both, sometimes I feel neither, sometimes it's just all one big gray area. And that might change." Lulu and I both nod as other U-High students stream past us to homeroom. "But can you two start using they/them pronouns for me, instead of she/her?"

"Absolutely," I say. Lulu gives my hand another thank-you squeeze.

"Cool," Dot says. "I'm not gonna make a big announcement yet, and I'm still going to use the girls' bathroom, because, well, there isn't a gender-neutral restroom here yet, and I'm still kind of working this out myself, you know? But I'm glad you're both good."

"Hey, we love you," Lulu says. "Exactly how you are. Always."

"Love you both too," Dot says and pulls us in for a group hug.

"Guess I'm really the token hetero now," Lulu cracks, and Dot and I laugh.

I came out as bi in eighth grade, and my moms gave me the purple- pink- and blue-striped heart pin I always wear, transferring it from denim to down to wool as the seasons change. They've never said as much, but I think they were secretly relieved their daughter was also part of the queer club. My freshman ex Allie and I are still friendly acquaintances, smiling at each other across the room when we share classes. Spencer from sophomore year, however, called me a slut when I broke up with him. So Lulu and Dot "accidentally" broke an entire carton of eggs in front of his locker.

"No flag, no parade, no nothing," I tease her with a smirk. "Just you and the straight guys of the world."

"Damn privilege," Lulu says, and Dot bursts out laughing again.

The bell rings and that's our cue to disburse. I make a mental note to Google the crap out of *nonbinary* during free period and print out stuff for myself and to share with my moms if Dot comes out to them. Dot loves hanging out at my house because my moms just want us all to be happy, and Ma has strict Asian parents too. Even though Dot's Filipino, not Chinese like Ma, the two of them understand each other. Dot's parents expect them to be a doctor, even though Dot wants to study art and design and is incredibly talented.

I'm just telling Dot *Text me if you need anything* when I hear my name from a very authoritative voice.

I turn around. "Hi, Dr. Schneider. Gorgeous dress!"

I'm not kissing her ass: our dean dresses like a school-appropriate 1940s pinup, or maybe 1950s. Today she's wearing a red dress with a circle skirt and matching lipstick, and even though most of the higher-ups wear power suits, it all just…works. Ever since I met her at freshman year orientation, I've been completely intimidated by Dr. Schneider while also wishing she was my third mom. Or at least a very cool aunt.

"Thank you, Perdita," she says, red lips curling up. "I didn't know how to dress myself till I was thirty, so I appreciate any and all compliments. Walk with me?" It's not really a question considering she's the dean *and* advisor to the math and science clubs, but I nod anyway. We fall into step, Dr. Schneider's heels clicking against the floors of the emptying hallway.

"I'll write you a pass," she says, reading my thoughts. "Just wanted to catch you before today's science club meeting. How's the clock coming along?"

"Harder than I thought," I answer honestly. "Building isn't exactly my strength to begin with, and then I wanted to add that solar-powered component we talked about." She nods thoughtfully, chewing her lower lip. Her lipstick doesn't even smear; she's *that* put together. "But I think I'm figuring it out," I finish, hoping my words are true.

"I'm glad to hear that," she says, leading me into her office. "Can you close the door?"

I know I haven't done anything to get in trouble, but my stomach drops. Did she overhear me and Lulu talking to Dot? I hope we didn't out them with our words of support.

"So," she says, folding her hands on her pin-neat desk surface. On the shelf behind her is a silver-framed photo of her with her arms around a woman with short dark hair. The frame stays the same, but the person Dr. Schneider's hugging changes every six months. And sometimes it's a guy. "The Illinois Math and Science Symposium is awarding a scholarship to the summer physics program at Johns Hopkins based on state science fair projects."

Whoa. That program is, without a doubt, the Holy Grail for science nerds going into senior year. If you do well, you pretty much have your pick of schools. It's also outrageously expensive, which is why I hadn't even thought of applying. Mum and Ma do fine, but we're not exactly rolling in cash. My U-High tuition is waived because Mum's a professor, and Ma's former desk job means she's really good with paperwork. She filled out her own FAFSA forms for next year, so she's had practice with financial aid too.

"It's a new scholarship," Dr. Schneider says. This snaps me out of my reverie involving top-of-the-line lab equipment and my very own white lab coat with my name embroidered on it. Also custom goggles… "There's a catch, though. They want candidates to be well-rounded, so the scholarship application includes an essay about the implications of your project."

"Like a lab report?" That's easy enough.

"Not exactly. More of a personal perspective. Why this project is important to you based on your life experience, that sort of thing."

I can't help it. I groan, temporarily forgetting I'm in the presence of my role model and oh yeah, the *dean*.

"Sorry," I say, sitting up.

"It's okay, Perdita," she says, and a little smile plays on her red lips. "I know how you feel about personal essays. As does anyone who's had you for English."

"Grammar is great," I tell her, and I mean it. Grammar is rules, theory, stuff that makes sense. Subject here, verb there, and all the tenses are surprisingly soothing. I even like iambic pentameter's rhythm.

It's *feelings* that get me. If I were Juliet, I would have said good-bye to Romeo right around the time he proposed after knowing me for all of an hour. Ms. Wickman and I really got into it over that one. Why did they have to be so dramatic instead of just stopping and *thinking*? They had to know their actions would have consequences, that people would die.

Maybe this is why neither of my relationships worked out. Fenton pops into my mind, and I push the thought away. What would a charismatic movie star doppelganger want with a geeky high schooler whose big dream is to go to *physics camp*?

Or worse, what if I'm just not good at feelings? Am I a sociopath? Is there a test I can take online? Lulu would know. Not for the first time, I wonder about my biological parents, what their histories look like. What's in me that was also in them?

"The deadline's in a month," Dr. Schneider says. "I'm more than happy to write you a recommendation"—I nod furiously—"but requirements are requirements. I wanted to give you some lead time to get your thoughts together."

She scribbles a tardy pass for me and hands it over her desk. And I notice something I've never seen before: a series of silver scars, lengthwise from her wrist all the way up the soft skin of her forearm.

I know what those mean from the peer counseling training I did sophomore year. I signed up to beef up the college applications

I was already thinking about and, well, just because. Those scars in that place mean at some point, Dr. Schneider didn't want to live anymore. My heart aches just like it did during training. What did she go through? And now that I have this intimate info about the woman I've always admired most (next to my moms), I simultaneously want to ask a million questions and leave immediately, giving Dr. Schneider her privacy.

"Perdita?"

I tear my eyes away from the scars.

"Don't sell yourself short," Dr. Schneider says. "If you can build a clock, you can write an essay."

I nod and leave the office, my mind spinning. Since I got off the train this morning, my best friend has come out to me, I have a deadline for something way out of my comfort zone, and I found out my shero, who's strong, smart, *and* has amazing style, tried to hurt herself in the past.

I wonder what else the people around me are going through and if, like Dot, they'll soon feel comfortable opening up or if, like Dr. Schneider, they'll hide it in plain sight.

Chapter Four

I haven't even *been* through anything," I moan, flopping back on my bed as Natalie Maines's fiddle whines mournfully in the background.

"Uh, I think that's good," Lulu points out, passing me the plastic shell of rotisserie chicken. I dig in with my fork, making sure I get a bite with extra skin.

"Not when you have to write a personal statement, am I right?" Dot says, putting their rainbow-socked feet on my calves. I smile at them, happy someone gets it. "But I mean, you're going to have to for college apps anyway. Might as well start now."

"I'm just not a reflective person," I say, leaning back. Lulu's hands are in my hair. She loves playing with it, was jealous of my curls in elementary school, until I came to class one humid day looking like I lost a battle with an electrical socket. I can tell by the way she's dividing it into sections that she's going to make a loose French braid—my favorite. I sit back, grateful to have best friends that have listened to me whine about this stupid essay for almost a week now.

"This'll make Improv Hottie notice you tonight," Lulu says, expertly weaving strands together.

"Yeah, because male attention is the reason I do anything." I crane my neck as much as I can to give her a healthy dose of side-eye.

"It can be the reason you do *some* things," Lulu retorts without stopping her braiding, and I swear I can feel her eyes roll. "You're not, like, less smart if you want to look cute for your crush."

"He's not my crush!" I insist. Dot rolls their eyes too, humming the refrain of "Wide Open Spaces."

"Okay, fine. You're both right. I don't know what I was expecting from an improv teacher, but I really didn't expect the cutest guy I've ever seen."

"How old do you think he is?" Lulu asks.

I think of Fenton, his big smile and the way he encouraged everyone in the class, not just me. Those insane brown eyes, so deep I could drown in them. "I'm not sure. I'm hopeless at guessing that kind of thing. I don't think they'd let a high school kid teach an improv class with mostly adults. Maybe college?"

"Oooooo!" they chorus, and I flick chicken off my fork in Dot's direction, which leads to general chicken-flicking.

Deftly, Lulu holds on to the end of my braid. Ma appears and knocks on my open door. Today's pants are bright blue flannel with green frogs mid-ribbit, her usual Wednesday gear. She has a textbook tucked under her arm.

"What's new, ladies?"

I clear my throat, a hopeful signal that Ma will remember what Dot told her when we got here after school.

"People," Ma corrects herself.

Dot grins and I pat their knee.

"Besides chicken food fights." Ma smiles but raises an eyebrow in that parental way, letting us know we better knock it off.

Dot obediently starts picking up chicken and gathering it into a napkin, while Lulu shifts around, my braid still in hand, looking for a hair tie. I dangle my wrist in her face, and she pulls the elastic off and starts wrapping it around my curls.

"So, Constance," Lulu says casually. "Is this Fenton guy as hot as P says he is?"

"I never said he was hot!" I protest, grabbing the edge of my finished braid.

"Oh, he's hot," Ma confirms, winking at me. "I may be gay, but I'm not blind. I can speak for Jacqueline too. We were all pretty smitten." She checks her watch. "Speaking of Fenton, you've got half an hour before we have to leave for class, Perdita, and then y'all have to clear out. Cool?"

"Cool," Lulu and Dot chorus, and Ma wanders down the hallway, where her office and studying beckon. Over her shoulder she yells, "I'll wind the clock, baby!"

"You have the best moms ever," Dot tells me, putting the shell on the chicken.

I sigh. "I know. Believe me. But..." I trail off, wondering how to put this into words without sounding like an ungrateful brat. Dot's parents don't fully accept them, never have, and they're not even out as nonbinary yet. Lulu's are okay, but they're tax attorneys in the Loop and they work a *lot*. She's practically lived here since we were little. They have a whole townhouse not far from here, but it always feels cold and empty to me.

While I think, I get up and close the door. "Just...some things have been bothering me lately. I mean, Fenton's primo eye candy, but I still hate how Ma and Mum signed us up without talking to me first. When has comedy *ever* been my thing?"

Lulu suddenly finds her nails very interesting. After a pause, she says quietly, "I'd love if my parents wanted to take a class with me."

I knew I'd step in it somehow.

"I'm sorry." I sit back on the bed and put my arm around Lulu. She leans her head on my shoulder—the universal Lulu sign of "all is forgiven"—and I pat her long blond hair, tangling my legs with Dot's. I don't know what I'd do without my best friends.

"It's more than that," I continue haltingly. "You're right, Lulu, it's nice that my moms want to hang out with me and try something new. We usually talk through stuff like this first, though, and improv was sprung on me, like, an hour before our first class." I concentrate on the thin white stripes on Lulu's navy J. Crew boatneck—the girl loves her patterns.

"And lately, I don't know, I've really been wondering about my adoption." I remember the conversation in the office with Dr. Schneider and that personal essay. "The science geek in me—"

"Which is all of you," Dot interrupts, and I grin.

"Which is all of me, wants to know about genetics. If I'm vulnerable to any diseases or conditions. I know my mom was

Mexican-Salvadoran and my dad was white, but that doesn't really narrow much down in terms of what they and their families are like, you know? Not that it matters in the grand scheme of things, but I'm so, *so* curious about where I came from. My heritage."

I don't mention my perfect pitch. Even though I've never been interested in singing, the head of U-High's music department has been begging me to join choir ever since she heard me humming Green Day in the hallway sophomore year and pulled me into her classroom to test my range. That definitely didn't come from nurture: Ma is tone deaf, and Mum can carry a tune, but just barely. Was one of my bio parents a singer?

I tuck a stray curl behind my ear. "And more than anything, I want to know about my mother—the one who pushed me out. All I know is she was really young, and Ma found out about me through work, so I'm guessing bio mom had some issues. I'm not saying I want to meet her—maybe that's, um, not even possible—but I want to know *something*." I hear the catch in my voice and see Dot looking at me, sympathy in their silver-lined eyes.

Lulu kisses my shoulder before disentangling herself. "I have an idea," she says, blue eyes glowing. "And it might help with your essay too."

Now she's got my attention. "I'm all ears."

"What if," Lulu says, "you tied your questions into your essay somehow?" I can tell from the way she sits up straight that she's excited. "Like, clocks track time, and as you spend more time on this earth or something, you've become more curious about the time you came into the world. You're so good with logic, you can tie it together better than I'm doing. And present it *that* way to your moms. Parents will answer anything if you tell them it's for a school project. Especially yours."

She might be on to something. Mum and Ma put school above all else. Not that they're grade grubbers or obsessed with me getting into the Ivy Leagues—Ma didn't even start taking college classes until last year—but I have to maintain a certain GPA to keep my U-High tuition waiver. They've never had to push me because I'm such a nerd, but they'll do anything to help me excel. It's meant staying up all night to help me build a volcano in third grade and emailing all their relatives asking for photos for my fifth-grade family tree.

Hopefully, it'll expand to answering all the tough questions they've avoided.

"She's got her thinking face on," Dot observes. They twist their face into a caveman-like scrunch.

"Oh God, is that what I look like?" *Please never let me make that face in front of Fenton.*

Lulu's giggling like crazy, and I throw a pillow at her just as Ma knocks on the door. Our cue to get ready to leave.

"Ask them," Lulu whispers, sobering up, and Dot nods in agreement.

"I will," I promise.

After class.

Really.

❖

"Perdita!" Fenton says later that night, slinging his backpack over his shoulder and coming to meet me in the corner, where I've been oh-so-slowly putting on my coat, scarf, and gloves. I love the way he says my name, like it's his favorite dessert.

Blerg. I really do have it bad.

"What'd my most reluctant student think about tonight's class?" he asks, perching on a chair and crossing his mile-long legs. He must be at least six two, exactly a foot taller than me. It's more than height: Fenton has *presence.* He's probably a really good performer.

He waves a hand in front of my face. "Still with me?"

"Oh! Uh, yeah," I stammer. Pulling on my gloves, I try to think of a good answer. The "most reluctant student" comment means he's on to me. Has he been paying extra attention? Or am I just that obvious?

"Eastenders was fun," I answer, meaning it. Apparently, that's a really popular soap opera in England, and the game consisted of us making certain signs and gestures at each other—sort of like Zip,

Zap, Zop but with terrible British accents—and running around the circle taking each other's places. My favorite part was yelling, "Everybody outta me pub!" It signaled all of us to run around waving our arms while we formed a new circle. After a while, I stopped feeling self-conscious and started enjoying how silly we got to be. Plus, Mum channeled all of Monty Python in her half-British accent. It was pretty brilliant.

"Ha!" Fenton says. "I knew that one would get you." There's that smile again, and for a second, I forget my name.

"But the whole 'Yes, and' thing you were talking about? I don't get it." And that was frustrating to me. There's very little I don't get in a classroom setting.

Ostensibly, "Yes, and" means to just go along with whatever my partner in the scene is doing. We're both making it up as we go along, but we're not supposed to contradict each other. Things progress instead of stopping. When Fenton explained this, everybody nodded along except me. Isn't saying "no" a good thing once in a while? What if the other person says something totally out there that you *can't* play off of? Plus, Fenton said a lot of people use "Yes, and" as their life philosophy, and that's just screwed up.

I'd love to argue with him about it though.

"Hmm," Fenton says, looking thoughtful. "That might take some extra time."

Behind me, someone loudly clears their throat, and I don't even have to look at the doorway to know it's Mum. That's how she quiets down students, but rarely does she direct it at me.

I glance over, and she taps her slim silver wristwatch, cocking her head at the door. I think of the scars on Dr. Schneider's wrist.

"I think my moms want Froyo," I say to Fenton, reluctantly gathering up my stuff. Really? They can't let me have these few minutes on my own? And did I just say *Froyo*?

"Gotta answer the call," he says, and for a minute, we're looking into each other's eyes and it's better than my last three birthdays combined.

Another loud throat-clear from Mum, which makes me look over. Ma waves with a suspicious look at Fenton. That's new. Even the frogs on her pants look like they're not messing around.

I sigh, trying hard not to sound like a bratty kid. "Guess I'm being summoned. See you next week?"

He nods, now serious and intense. "Bye, Perdita."

I'm making the way to the doorway, which my moms have mercifully cleared, when I hear my name.

Fenton, standing behind me, smells like cinnamon and pine and holy shit I'm about to swoon.

"Here," he says, pressing something into my hand. His skin is on mine. Our hands look good together. I want to stay in this moment, our palms joined, forever.

Then he cocks his head toward the door. "Go find your moms before they kill me."

I don't look at the card until much later.

I have to come down to earth first.

❖

Hi kid,

Still don't have the courage to really go out there and find you.

By "out there," I mean the internet, not the ends of the earth like Indiana Jones in search of the Holy Grail. Do kids watch Indiana Jones movies anymore? I loved them when I was little: this archaeologist and adventurer who also got the girl (well, more than one girl). They made a new movie a few years ago, but it just wasn't the same. Not as offensive, though, so that's good.

Maybe you're more of a Star Wars *fan. Less stereotypes, more space. Or did you grow up on Disney?*

This all sounds very silly, now that I'm reading it over. But I wonder what movies I would have shown you if my plans with your mom had worked out. If watching my favorites through your eyes would have made them seem even cooler, or just sad and dated.

I really suck at writing letters.

I suppose I could set up an account and write you emails you'd never get. I have to send them all the time for work, and I can type and text like the wind, like everyone can these days. (Do you even remember a time without cell phones?)

But there's something more honest about pen and paper. I have to choose every word carefully. I can't erase every mistake with the tap of a key. And when I DO cross things out, I can really stab pen into paper, and that's so cathartic. Cathartic. A smart word for the kid of two smart parents, who is also most likely very smart. I hope you're in a house that encourages you. I was destined for greatness; that's what I thought when I was your age.

I was so far off.

Don't get me wrong. I have it pretty good. I sell cars—let's just say I had a connection that hooked me up after I barely passed college. Still have my degree, though, and a nice house I own, which is more than most, especially after everything crashed several years ago.

I was so sure I'd be Ivy League material, but that went to shit when I started drinking every day the summer before senior year. My parents ended up sending me to this Catholic boys' boarding school in St. Louis rather than back to where it all fell apart. Maybe they just couldn't stand to look at me—their other son—or maybe they felt guilty for abandoning us. They got divorced a few years later. My mom lives in California now, and I don't really see her.

My senior year was shit. I didn't fit in at the new school. I went from class president to total outcast—the internet was just becoming a thing, and even though Google didn't exist, people had heard about me, about what happened. I don't know if they blamed me, but they sure as shit didn't want to associate with someone so messed up. Deep in my heart, I couldn't really blame them.

My grades went to crap, papers and tests and pleasing teachers and all the factors that once mattered just faded into nothingness. Everyone else pulled it together, but I just fell far behind and stayed there.

I went to one of the state universities, my safety school. I crashed with buddies in dorms and apartments when even I knew I was too fucked up to drive, or (more often) when someone took my keys. Apparently, I'm a messy, sobbing drunk. When I get really bad, my buddy Scott told me, I freak out if I see an old Cadillac or hear a loud noise. I still can't stand fireworks.

After graduation, I came back to my hometown because I had nowhere else to go. Then I got this job, and I've been on and off the wagon ever since. Mostly on, since the DUI three years ago. Looking back, it's a wonder I didn't kill myself...which I think was kind of the point. When my dad retired, he turned the dealership over to me.

I still stay away from guns, but I don't want to get into that right now. Maybe someday.

It's the damnedest thing, kiddo. You think you're headed in this beautiful direction: the pot at the end of the rainbow is right there, like Lucky Charms. Sure, you have problems, or what you think are problems, and then after everything goes to hell, you look back and realize you never knew shit...

When you think you're always right, you couldn't be more wrong.

Now I'm talking in disaster movie clichés. I hope you're a better writer than I am.

I've been waking up lately, worrying you were put in a foster home where you're abused, or that you just got lost in the system somehow. I've read the statistics and they're horrific. In the past, when I allowed myself to think about you, I hoped you had a comfortable life where you had everything you could ever want and then some. As I get older, I realize I just want you to have people who love you, all the time. And hopefully, if I get the courage to do the research, to maybe, just maybe, track you down, I'll see you have it.

It's strange: reading over these last two letters, I realize I've said the word "hope" more than I have in the past seventeen years. And I have you to thank, wherever you are.

Love,
Someone You Don't Know

Chapter Five

March

"Omigod, he gave you his *number*?" Lulu squeals the next morning, words bubbling over one another.

She hands me back the card with just his full name, Fenton Alexander Johnson, email address, and phone number on it. Professional and adult. It's a very simple print, navy border and type on white card stock that's thick but soft. Made even softer now because I've turned it over and over so many times in my hands, even slept with it under my pillow last night. So embarrassing.

Still. He gave me his card. This feels like...something. I don't know what exactly, but I'm ready to find out. Even if that means I have to play Zip, Zap, Zop a million more times.

"You're the color of a farmer's market tomato right now," Lulu observes, flicking back her bangs.

"Would you trim those already?" I ask, desperate to change the subject, yet sort of wanting to talk about Fenton, the card, and those deep brown eyes forever. "By the way, Dot, I love your look!"

"Thanks," they say, sheepishly but proudly, looking down at their pressed gray trousers, slick navy vest and striped lavender shirt with the sleeves rolled up. "Thought I'd be dapper today."

"Super hot," Lulu offers.

Dot bites their lip. "I think my parents suspect something's up, just because I've amped up the style choices. Some days I'm really masc, and some days I'm femme. I think they want me to go back to my T-shirt-and-jeans phase from seventh grade."

"Hey, I'm still there," I volunteer. Between Dot's cool outfit and Lulu's chic forest green wraparound dress—Lulu's parents may be distant, but her mom has impeccable taste and lets Lulu raid her closet—I feel a little underdressed in my skinny jeans and plain gray Henley. I wonder what Fenton would think if I glammed it up a little. I silently curse myself for caring what a guy thinks of my wardrobe. Maybe Lulu could teach me to French braid my own hair so my curls don't stick out all the time?

"P!" Lulu says, snapping her fingers in front of my face. "Can you snap out of Fentonland for a sec?"

I shake myself. It's worse than I thought. "I wasn't *in* Fentonland, whatever that is." Lulu fake coughs *bullshit.* I ignore her and look at Dot. "What's up?"

Dot looks from side to side in the loud and crowded hallway, leans in, and lowers their voice. "I'm thinking of coming out to my mom and dad."

"Seriously?" I ask. "Do you think they're ready?"

They sigh. "Considering how they took the lesbian thing, I dunno, but I feel like I can't keep my whole identity from them much longer."

Valid point. The bell rings, and I give Dot a hug. Lulu immediately follows. "However they react," I say, "we're here for you."

Dot smiles. "Thanks. And by the way, have you texted Fenton yet, or are you just holding on to his card for posterity?"

Oh God. I hadn't even thought about next steps. "Should I text Fenton?"

Lulu rolls her eyes and Dot laughs. "Uh, how else is he supposed to get *your* number, dum-dum?" Lulu asks.

Oh. Right. And here I was waiting for a text to pop up on my phone.

Lulu shakes her head. "You little love novice. What *are* we going to do with you?"

I know I'm not all about feelings, but when she says *love,* my heart leaps.

❖

I'm on a walk with Fenton Alexander Johnson.
I'm on a walk with Fenton Alexander Johnson.
I'm. On. A. Walk. With. Fenton. Alexander. Johnson.

It's all I can do not to tell every single person passing by, and there aren't many. We're strolling along the lakefront, which most Chicagoans with brain cells don't dare to do until the first warm day of the year—which in this city can be anywhere from February to July—but today's unusual. It's in the forties, and when the winter's been this cold and Chicago earns its "Chiberia" nickname, we all go a little crazy when the temperature's above freezing. On the way to meet Fenton outside the comedy club, I counted three guys in shorts and flip-flops. Still, not even they brave the lake.

Like me, the weather's unpredictable this spring.

But Fenton could have suggested we stand and wait for the Red Line train at North and Clybourn, which, for some reason, always takes forever, and I still would have brushed my hair, put on some lip gloss Lulu left in my room, and told my moms I was going to Starbucks to study.

I can't believe I took the initiative and texted him right after school. I can't believe he replied right away: *Yes! Now you live in my phone!*

I can't believe that we had a whole rapid-fire text conversation that lasted half an hour, and quickly found out we had two weird things in common: a love for nineties music and a macabre interest in this screwed-up Blair-Marie Elliott unsolved murder that happened on the North Shore. I've always suspected the mom, who's dead now, even though people swear it was her brother who was only twelve at the time. Turns out Fenton agrees with me.

I *really* can't believe he asked if I was free and wanted to meet up, with none of the hard-to-get crap I've seen guys pull with my friends.

"Cold?" he asks, and before I can say yes, Fenton hands me his scarf. It's gold and burgundy, and it smells like him, like cold air and pine and some really subtle cologne. I wrap it around my neck and inhale. "I saw you pull your coat around you," he says. "Actually, can I help?"

Can he help? Shakily, I nod.

Fenton doesn't even touch me as he gently takes back the scarf and starts winding it slowly around my neck as I lift my hair up to help. Momentarily, I'm a heroine in one of the Jane Austen books Mum loves and that I've always rolled my eyes at. I thought going weak in the knees was surely something a romance author made up, but right now, I'm having trouble walking in a straight line.

"I like the colors on your pin," he says.

I smile. "They're the same as the bi pride flag, which is also the prettiest."

We walk in companionable silence for a bit, and despite my excitement, I'm not feeling as awkward as I expected. Still, I do need to know one thing, so I take a deep breath and try to pitch my voice lower so I won't sound even younger.

"Um, Fenton? Can I ask how old you are?"

"Oh, man." He looks down at his shoes, which are really nice considering his job. I don't think improv teachers are exactly rolling in money.

"I knew we'd have this conversation. Look, I know you're probably into the whole college thing..."

Wait, what?

I stop and turn to him. "Uh, I'm not in college."

The relief on his face is palpable. "Oh great, so you get it. My dad tells his friends I'm taking a 'gap year' and tries to sound all Euro about it, when really he's on my ass every second to start applying. But I want to prove to him I can do it, you know? Getting to sub a whole class myself was a total fluke, but I'm thinking this way, I can show him I'm starting to make a living and I can finally move out of his place..." He shakes his head, rubbing his hands together and blowing on them. "Anyway, sorry to make it all about me. What I meant to ask was, are you on a break from school too?"

He thinks I'm old enough to be taking a break from college.

Shit.

I could lie. But he sees my moms every week. I wouldn't be surprised if Ma has the whole class sing "Happy Birthday" to me in

April, or Mum brings Oreo cupcakes that spell the number 17. Or both.

"I always run my mouth and don't let anyone else get a word in," Fenton says in a reassuring tone. "Wanna keep walking?"

Trying to formulate the words in my brain, I nod, knowing distance will buy me some time.

"I'm sorry, Perdita. For dragging you out in the cold and then for talking too much like I always do when I'm really intimidated. You're just this put together girl I wanted to get to know—"

"Who's going to be seventeen in April," I interrupt. Now it's my turn to look down at my shoes, scuffed green Chucks peeking out of the hems of my frayed jeans. Fenton can't see it, but underneath my coat, I'm wearing a T-shirt that says ATHEISM RULES under a boring blue cardigan that used to be Mum's.

I wish I had a Look like Lulu's striped J. Crew tops and Essie-painted nails, or Dot's cool style—snappy suspenders and a bow tie one day, full-on wiggle dress and kitten heels the next. But no, I'm all jeans and polos and the occasional ironic tee, not unlike six-year-old me. I need a look that's all mine, with casual and fancy outfits and things I can just spontaneously pick out for dates because I'm pretty sure this is one? Maybe?

Maybe I need to grow up and stop thinking in makeover montages.

But first, I need to be honest with Fenton, who looks as baffled as I feel.

"You wanna sit?" I ask him, and he nods, serious for once without his handsome smile or his charming words. We park on one of the concrete steps, looking out at the choppy gray waves of Lake Michigan, the skyline of downtown and the Ferris wheel of Navy Pier in the distance. My scarf is warm around my neck.

We both start talking at once, and then laugh, diffusing the tension a little. "You first," I tell him. We're not touching, but it kind of feels like we are.

"Okay," he says, biting that luscious lower lip in a way that makes me want to...I don't know what exactly, something other than sit here in the cold feeling very awkward. "I guess you should know first, I'm eighteen. Just turned. Normally, the training center wouldn't let someone so young teach an adult improv class, but they got desperate. I graduated last year from Latin, was young for my class, and like I said, my dad really wants me to go to college. My mom doesn't care so much, but it's my dad who paid for school and all that, so he wants me to be serious. They had me really young, so I think he wants to make sure I'm on the right track and stuff. And like you"—Fenton looks my way and smiles, and it's different from his roguish grin, more serious, a little sad—"he's not sure how he feels about the whole improv thing."

I'm about to get lost in those eyes once again, but then Fenton says, "Now you."

"Um," I say, sucking in my lips. Eighteen doesn't sound much older to me. He hadn't even graduated high school a year ago. But I *know* that to Mum and Ma, it'll be a whole different story. "Yeah, I'm sixteen." Fenton sucks in a breath, and I hastily go on. "*Almost* seventeen. As in, my birthday's in April and not, like, six months from now." I muster a small smile. "I have to say, I love that you thought I was in college. I'm at U-High, by the way. One of my moms is a professor at the university."

"The one who *doesn't* wear the crazy pants?"

I think of Mum with her floral skirts—her favorites have pockets where she can keep tea bags and an Oreo or two—and her soft voice reading me Shakespeare when I was little and, truthfully, up until about a year or so ago. "Yup. Crazypants was a cop, but she quit last year. She's at Harold Washington now, wants to do social work after finishing her requirements. Help people in a better way."

"Do they know you're here?"

I know it wasn't Fenton's intention, but that question makes me feel every inch the sixteen-year-old. I feel guilty lying to Ma and Mum, for being so distant with them lately. Unlike Fenton's dad, they've never pushed me into doing anything big that I didn't really want to do. Improv classes don't really count. "They think I'm at Starbucks, studying. I have a really big project—I'm building a clock—and I want to enter this scholarship contest for a summer program at Johns Hopkins, so I have to write a personal essay to go with it."

"Damn." Fenton's face changes from slightly wary to an expression of thoughtful respect. "I guessed you were smart when you said U-High, and just, the way you *are* in general, but..." He shakes his head. "Wow."

I didn't know blood could actually race through my veins, but it does, pumping through me so my feet get all tingly in their Chucks and my cheeks warm. My fingers itch to hold Fenton's hand, like... Oh my God, he's taking my hand between both of his and trying to warm it up. *Please, don't stop!*

I now completely understand the goofy expression Dot makes when they text a new crush because, though I can't see my face, I'm pretty sure I'm making it *right now.* Hopefully, it's less scrunchy than my thinking face.

"Listen," Fenton says, his voice gentle and so soft I have to scoot closer, lean in. Our shoulders are touching, and I could die right here, right now, the happiest I've ever been.

"I like you."

Invisible person in the sky, strike me down because it really can't get much better than this.

"I hope this doesn't sound sleazy, but ever since I saw you try to play Zip, Zap, Zop, there's been...something about you," Fenton says, still rubbing my hand between his own.

Now I'm tingling all over and I have to concentrate on his words, but that means looking at his mouth and that means I'm a goner all over again.

Fenton says, "I thought you were beautiful"—Oh my God oh my God *oh my God.* I cannot scream right now without freaking him out—"but it was more than that. I like how you obviously love your moms. How you always try even though you're not sold on improv."

He gestures at my coat. "That pin you always wear, with those same colors. I know what kind of shit bi people get, 'pick a side' and all that, yet here you are, daring anyone to argue with you."

I grin. "Some people still don't think bisexuality is real, or they get the definition wrong—it doesn't mean only boys and girls—so I have to educate them."

"Yes! Like that!" He takes a deep breath. "I've never looked at a girl before and thought, *I have to know her.* It's why I kept stopping you after class, and then I gave you my card like a dork. Why I wanted to take you on a romantic walk and"—he shivers—"why I *completely* forgot about the lake effect and how it would be ten degrees colder where we are."

"Hey," I say, "nobody's perfect."

He laughs and...yup, there's that chemical rush, *whooshing* through me so intensely I shiver, and it's not from the cold.

"But..."

And with that one word, the air around us cools.

"I don't want to sneak around, you know?" Fenton gently returns my hand, voice now grave. "I'm guessing your moms might not want their sixteen-year-old with an older guy who's not even in college?"

He's got me there.

My heart sinks to my stomach. He has the power to arouse or devastate me with every syllable now, nothing in between. "N-no," I manage to stammer.

Fenton rolls his lips, contemplating. "Do you think," he says, slowly, "they'd be okay with it after your birthday?"

"Seventeen's the age of consent in Illinois," I blurt out.

"Whoa," he says, eyes wide. "Definitely *not* what I was implying, but, uh..."

"Oh God, no!" It's so ridiculous I start giggling, and after a minute, Fenton joins in. Pretty soon, we're both laughing for real, clutching our sides. He's got this amazing deep chuckle, and paired with my high-pitched giggle that sounds just like Mum's, echoing against the chilly lake air, it's like music.

"Sorry," I say, once we calm down. I raise my glasses to wipe a tear from my eye. "When your mom's an ex-cop, you know random laws like that."

I realize I never answered Fenton's original question, and something about his honesty makes me want to match it with my own.

"I can't really say whether they'll be okay with it or not." I take a deep breath, decide to go for broke with the whole honesty thing. *If he can't handle your truth bombs,* I remember Dot telling Lulu once about some guy, *he doesn't deserve you.* I think I even remember Ma looking up from her paperwork, nodding approvingly at the advice.

I push a stray curl behind my ears from where it's sneaked out of my beanie and look right at Fenton. "But I'd like to stick around and find out."

He smiles. "I'd like that too."

And then he stands up, offers me his hand again. I take it as I get to my feet. Our joined hands feel like a promise.

"So," he says, glancing at me slyly, "what do you suggest we do until April?"

I think for a moment. "Go to Starbucks. Then I'm only half-lying to my moms," I suggest. "Plus, I really want a hot chocolate."

Fenton nods, and we start walking to the nearest exit, which will take us to North Avenue near the comedy club and a giant Starbucks where, conveniently, I really do go to study. He's still holding my hand. "Hot chocolates it is. On me."

And then an idea pops into my head. A project to keep us both occupied and help me with my essay, especially if Mum and Ma still refuse answers when I ask—and I have a sneaking suspicion they will. Maybe he'll know where to start.

He can't think I'm too weird. This situation is already weird enough.

"Alsooooooo…" I drag the word out, and Fenton looks at me curiously before I take a deep breath and ask, "Wanna help me find my birth mom?"

Chapter Six

*T*his *is it*, I text Fenton. *The moment of truth.* Just like we'd strategized over hot chocolates.

After school today, I offered to help Mum fold laundry while Ma is at class downtown. The faster we get it done, the faster Mum can get back to grading midterms. Of course, I have an ulterior motive.

I see the little three dots pop up, and my heart leaps. I wonder if Fenton will always have this effect on me. I hope so.

Think she'll talk?

I type back as fast as my thumbs will go. *Who knows. Cross all your phalanges for me?*

Sounds dirty.

I giggle. *Fingers and toes. What did they teach you at Latin anyway?*

I was too busy watching stand-up specials on my phone. :)

Which reminds me... *Hey, we never talked about "Yes, and" the other day. Care to give an insider's perspective to an improv newbie who may or may not be coming around?*

I mean, screaming, "Everybody outta me pub!" *was* really fun.

For you, anything. Go talk to your mom and I'll think of something really good.

I debate sending some heart emoji but decide that's immature, not to mention *premature*. We can't officially date until my seventeenth birthday, we decided. He hasn't even kissed me yet. But that doesn't mean we haven't been texting every waking minute. The chemical rush I've been feeling is so strong, sometimes I see spots in front of my eyes and have to sit down. I even texted him a bunch of pictures of my clock in progress. He was really impressed.

I hear the buzz of the dryer. *Gotta go. Will report back.*

Good luck, P.

I square my shoulders and take a deep breath. Fenton's confidence and the memory of his smile bolster me.

I'll need it.

"You're quiet today, love," Mum observes as she crosses the arms of my favorite long-sleeved tee, perfect and meditative, the way she does everything. "Anything going on?"

You can do this, I remind myself. *They should have told you ages ago.* I cuddle a warm and fluffy towel for strength before concentrating on matching corner to corner, the way Mum taught me when I was very little and loved making piles: one for each of us three, plus kitchen and bathrooms. Sometimes we listen to Counting Crows or Foo Fighters, but today the living room is quiet.

"I have this essay for school." Best to lead with that, start easy and academically. Use school, like Lulu advised and Fenton agreed. "Really, it's for a scholarship competition, for this summer science program at Johns Hopkins." I look over, and she's crunching into an Oreo. "Mum! You're going to get crumbs all over everything!"

"I'm sorry!" she says, spraying even more crumbs. Eating is one thing Mum *doesn't* do with the utmost grace. My diplomat grandparents are always horrified when they visit from overseas, and I think that's part of the reason she does it, a small rebellion against a very itinerant and restrictive childhood.

"They're candy corn flavored, love. Limited edition." She digs in her pocket and offers me a slightly flattened cookie. I shake my head. "Anyway, a scholarship! That's wonderful. I know you don't love essays, though you're going to have to write them for college soon."

"That's what Dot said too," I reply, picking up the towel's matching washcloth. "And I want this essay to be really good, you know? Personal." I take another deep breath, intent on touching hem to hem, a perfect square. "I was thinking about my clock, and how I've always loved time, not just as a scientific construct but as a concept. Like, that's how we measure *everything,* from the day we're born to when we die, you know?" She nods, dark eyes completely focused on me.

That's it, Perdita. Reel her in. I feel a pang at how manipulative I'm being, which is quickly replaced by resolve. I could be so close to getting answers.

I deposit the folded washcloth into the right pile and grab another. "And I was thinking," I say, matching corner to corner as Mum sips her tea, "about *my* time. When I was born. And how I don't know much about that time. And how that's what I'd like to write about."

Crunch.

Mum bites into the flattened Oreo, her back turned to me.

When she does speak, her voice is even and measured. "We've told you, love. When you're eighteen, you can take one of those ancestry tests or get in touch with the attorney who took care of the adoption. That's the law." She faces me but isn't meeting my eyes.

"But it's not *against* the law to answer my questions, at least enough so I can write my essay." Mum's not lying—they *have* told me all this since I was old enough to know I didn't look like either of my moms. It's not like adoption as a concept is a big deal. I just want details.

Eighteen is over a year away. It's not even about the essay anymore. It's about *me.*

The floodgates open, and I can't stop talking. "Mum, I know this is hard for you and Ma, and I'm guessing something went wrong when I was born and that's how Ma found out about me. Maybe she was even there for…whatever happened?"

Mum says nothing, keeps folding a washcloth, smoothing out the corners with unnecessary force.

But she's not totally shutting me out, so I press on. "I know how Ma wasn't looking for a kid at all, how she'd just come out and started a new job, and then suddenly she was becoming a foster parent and going through home visits and all the licensing and paperwork. I know the story of how you two met, and how Ma *definitely* wasn't looking for a girlfriend, let alone a partner, and how our family was this whole big wonderful surprise—"

"And you can't write an essay about all that? Seems like the story's got everything you need. Lots of drama." Her voice could cut glass.

I've never heard that tone directed at me.

The corners of her mouth turn down. "I'm so sorry, my love. I didn't mean to snap at you like that."

"It's okay." Maybe I can use her remorse to my advantage. "But can you blame me for asking, Mum? I'm so, *so* happy things worked out the way they did, for all of us, but I thought this would be a good excuse for me to learn more. For my scholarship essay," I add lamely.

Mum glances at one of Ma's Chicago Police Department shirts in her lap. It's a million years old. The cotton fabric is worn thin, the logo faded. Ma still wears it all the time, and will until Mum "accidentally" rips it and it becomes a dust rag. "Perdita," she says, and her voice has weight. Almost as if she's about to tell me someone died.

I lean forward, hoping for anything, even just a cookie crumb.

I want to know who I am.

"You *know* who you are," she says, clenching her jaw, and I realize I've spoken aloud. Mum gestures to the wall of Diversity Family Photos, all of us with dark hair of various shades and big happy grins. There's the two of them hugging a toddler, then a grade schooler, then fourteen-year-old me (my first year at U-High; they still use it on their website).

There are wrinkles by her eyes I'm only now just seeing. Oreo crumbs collect at the corner of her mouth. "I don't know why you want to bring this up when we've given you everything, so much more than you would have had with…"

I realize I'm perched on our couch, literally on the edge of my seat. "With who, Mum?" I ask, hearing the plaintive whine in my voice and hating it but forging ahead. "With who?"

She knows. She's seen my birth certificate. What isn't she telling me, and *why*?

Mum puts the various piles in the laundry basket, ready to disperse them to their respective rooms. The exact way she's done it since *she* was little and folding laundry made her feel at home, wherever that was any given year. "Put your clothes away, will you, love?" she asks. Her voice has returned to normal, but she's avoiding my gaze. The spell she was under just moments ago is broken.

"That's it?" I ask. "You're still not going to tell me?"

"There's nothing you need to know," she says, and now her eyes lock on mine, eyebrows raised practically to her hairline. I know that look. It's the one she's given me so many times growing up when I tried to get something out of her—a candy bar, a later bedtime, an extra episode of "the show with the boys and girls"—to no avail. The look that says, *case closed.*

I can't believe this.

I understand why they haven't always been forthcoming with me. Adoption is a long process and Ma never hesitates to take me through the logistics, but she clams up when I ask about the people on the other end. I'm not sure you *can* explain "addict" or "criminal" or whatever to a little kid. But I'm not little anymore, and the more I ask, and the more they say no, the wilder the possibilities in my head get.

What if my adoption wasn't legal? I've heard of black-market babies—it's not as much of a thing anymore, but maybe I slipped under the radar. Ma says she wasn't looking for a child, but what if she was lying and she...bought me? Or even, oh God...

"Was I kidnapped?"

Mum's head snaps up. My words hang in the air.

"Why would you ask that?" Her words are careful, her tone measured.

"You didn't say no." My eyes narrow, and now I'm staring at a smaller, more pinched version of Mum. One without as much power over me. One without secrets.

And she rolls her eyes. My serious, thoughtful mother, to whom I just asked a life-altering question, discounts me as if I just asked for something completely ludicrous like a fake ID or a sleepover with Fenton. "Then I'll say it now: *no*, you were not kidnapped. Your ma was a *cop*, for God's sake."

"Yeah, and cops do bad things, sometimes because they think they're above the law, sometimes because they know how to get away with it. She left because she couldn't put up with that anymore." Mum's eyes widen, and I know I'm pushing it. I shouldn't have brought up kidnapping because now her defenses are up. I've accused her and Ma of being criminals.

Mum reaches for my red polo shirt, her hands closing around it as if she's afraid it will run away. "I'm not doing this without your ma, and frankly, Perdita, that was a really difficult time for her, which is why she doesn't like talking about it."

"Not even to me, her daughter?" I ask. I know this is now futile, but God help me I can't stop. "Not even so I can write about it, but just so I *know*?"

"I'm sorry," she says, and she sounds anything but. *Case closed.*

It's then I realize I don't hear the tick-tock, as familiar to me as breathing. No one's wound the clock today. Mum's just sitting there, folding laundry with more determination than ever, smoothing every pleat like she's mad at it. She doesn't seem to notice the absence of sound, of time, of the consistency that's comforted me since I was eleven and built the clock, so proud even though now it looks really janky. Her indifference winds up and punches me in the gut.

I grab my pile of clothes and glare at her, heading to my room while calling over my shoulder, "You have Oreo on your face."

❖

"*This* is your dad's office?" I ask in awe as Fenton unlocks the door and leads me in.

"Ridiculous, right?" He sighs, and I try not to gawk at the minimalist paradise: the windows with a breathtaking view of downtown, the sleek furniture and well-placed abstract art on the walls. Welcome to the Gold Coast. "Only the fanciest for Alexander Johnson, new money."

"What does he do?"

"Hedge fund." I give Fenton a questioning look, and he shakes his head. "Don't worry, I don't understand either. Doesn't keep

Dad from trying to explain it every second. He wants me to work for him, make this a father-and-son joint. Provided I go to college, of course." He takes my hand. "But that's not why I brought you here. My dad's assistant can find *anything*. He's a Google master. Olympic gold medal level." Fenton raises his voice. "Smith, you around?"

"Fenton, my man!" A short, dark-haired man practically materializes in front of us. Everything about him screams *fancy*, from his perfectly messy coif to his neatly maintained goatee, to the shirt and pants that look casual but probably cost more than my tuition. "Long time no see," he says, and Fenton lets go of my hand to give Smith one of those half-hugs guys do.

"Dad's known Smith since high school," Fenton explains once they break apart.

Smith snorts. "Ugh, that school. That *town*. He saw me through all the shit—I'm talking literal *shit in my locker*—and then some." He turns to me. "Once I transitioned ten years ago, this kid's dad made sure I had the right insurance, helped me navigate all the paperwork, even hooked me up with the best doctors."

"That's awesome," I say, and I mean it. I'm also realizing there's a whole new side to Fenton. The rich kids at my school dress like he does—old, worn jeans and T-shirts—and Fenton has that same air of confidence, like he knows he's going to be okay no matter what. I bet his dad's condo is even fancier. No wonder he hasn't moved out yet.

"Oh shit, I'm being so rude right now," Fenton says, taking my hand again. "Smith, this is my…" He hesitates, and I don't miss the little smirk on Smith's face. "This is Perdita."

"Great name," Smith says, shaking my other hand. "I did *Winter's Tale* in college. Camillo."

"The king's friend who tried to right wrongs," I say without even thinking.

"Yeah! I loved that role." His smile widens, and I feel instantly at ease. "You know your stuff."

"It's my mum's favorite," I tell him, feeling a pang in my heart when I imagine her stony face refusing to tell me the truth yesterday, followed by genuine hurt when I gave her the silent treatment this morning. I haven't seen Mum since—I took a cab to the address Fenton gave me right after school. Improv tonight is going to be awkward.

"Speaking of which," Fenton says, "Perdita wants to find her birth mom, and her parents don't really want to talk about it, so we were wondering if you—"

"Do I hear my wayward son?" a voice booms out from the hallway. Once Fenton's dad comes into view, I can see where he got his height and his self-assured walk. From his casually knotted tie to the sound of his shoes hitting the polished floors, this man exudes confidence. Like Idris Elba playing James Bond.

Even his smile looks like Fenton's, taking over his whole face and crinkling up his eyes.

Until those eyes land on me and his smile freezes.

Fenton doesn't notice. "Hey, Dad, this is—"

"*Mia.*" A whisper, as if he's seen a ghost.

Smith's head swivels toward me and his eyes go wide. His left hand, festooned with a thick silver ring on the wedding finger, goes to his mouth. "Holy shit," he mumbles.

Fenton's dad straightens up, the horrified expression disappearing as quickly as it came. The fog lifts from his eyes, replaced by pure hardness. "You need to leave." He points at me, big and intimidating. I inch toward Fenton, who takes my hand. "Both of you. We'll talk about this later, Fenton. Smith?" He cocks his head toward the hallway. "My office. Now."

Those shoes clack along the floors, just as self-assured as they were a minute ago. Only now, I see Fenton's dad's shoulders are hunched. And the hand he hasn't shoved in his pocket is shaking.

Smith turns toward us. "I'm so sorry."

"What the hell just happened?" Fenton interrupts. "And who's M—"

"Not now," Smith says, lowering his voice to a whisper, his face frantic. He looks at me. "I can't help you, Perdita. I'm really sorry, but…" He trails off, clearly at a loss, looking back toward the hallway. "I have to go."

"Wait!" I say as he turns away to join Fenton's dad in his office. My head is spinning. My almost-boyfriend's dad, who's never before laid eyes on me, called me *Mia*. Why would he do that? What's going on here?

And why do I get the feeling this is a clue to my past?

"Please," I say, stepping up to Smith, whose back is to me. "He's your employer. Your friend. I get that you want to protect him." I take a deep breath, still so confused, but my intentions are growing clearer in my mind, sharp as glass, crisp as the snow that just fell outside this morning despite the fact it's late March. "But can you look up something for me? Anything? Just give us five minutes?" My voice breaks. "I'm so tired of not knowing who I am."

That last part wasn't planned. But once the words escape my mouth, I feel down to my bones how true they are. Personal essay be damned, I want to know where I came from *now*, not in a year.

Smith turns around. Something in his handsome face changes. I'm not sure if it's the desperation leaking out of my pores or what, but he takes a deep breath, glances over his shoulder, and lowers his voice so much that I have to lean in. Fenton moves closer, threading his fingers through mine.

And Smith says one phrase, almost inaudible:

"Havendale, 1997."

❖

Mia,

I saw you today.

Remember that old Mamas and the Papas song we used to wail before choir? You loved Cass Elliot's harmonies more than anything. I think I fell for you over and over again, to be honest.

Anyway. Smith, who you knew as Cameron, just left my office after making triple sure I wasn't going to jump out my third-story window. I assured him I was fine. I may or may not be lying. And without even thinking about it, I pulled up a blank Word doc and started banging away on the keys of this very sleek laptop. We would not have believed in 1997 that something like this could exist, that we'd all just carry around our computers, our lives on our backs like digital turtles. Right now, this platinum shell, the clicking as my fingers meet keyboard, are all that's keeping me sane.

I guess you had a daughter. And somehow, she met my son.

She's really short like your mom was. Is? Has that same crazy curly hair as you, the hair I got to touch the one time we kissed. I never forgot how soft it was and how that surprised me. I watched her clench her jaw like...he did when he was stressed out. She is both you two and something brand new. When Fenton was born, watching him grow, I felt that same way.

It took a long time for me to stop thinking of you every day. After the accident, I never saw you again. I have no idea where you are, or if you're still alive.

I don't know what to tell my son, if I tell him anything at all. How do I bring this up? "By the way, Fenton, I have no proof except the fact that I almost threw up when I saw her, but your new girlfriend is the daughter of the girl I always wished was my girlfriend, except she was with someone else and went into labor when we were all in the car with a little boy who'd gotten too close to a gun, and I couldn't talk about any of it outside my therapist's office for ten years." That should go over well. Our relationship is challenging enough as it is. He makes me realize what a little shit I was at times.

And at the same time, I'm happy. Really happy.

That may sound strange. But she—your girl—gives me hope that you're out there. Or even if you're not, a little piece of you is. That you never really left.

Xander

CHAPTER SEVEN

"This is your room?"

As Fenton hesitates in the doorway, I see the space I've inhabited my whole life with new eyes: a clump of past Pride Parade signs ("If God Hates Queers, Why Are We So Cute?" is my personal favorite), the piles of clean clothes Mum and I folded before the argument started, my desk that's looking more and more scattered as my clock project (*sans* essay) intensifies, my unmade bed with crumpled blue sheets and the flowered comforter I threw off last night when I got hot. Oh God. Is he looking at my bed?

"Um, sorry for the mess!" I squeak, pushing past Fenton and frantically throwing the comforter over the whole thing. *Oh crap.* My laptop's under there, and that's the whole reason we're here. I throw back the covers and retrieve it, then remake the bed.

I look back and he's smiling impishly.

"Sorry." I look down at my *Star Wars*-socked feet—we have a no-shoes apartment—feeling shyer and more self-conscious than ever.

"Hey," he says softly. "I heard a messy room is a sign of genius."

I roll my eyes. "You did not."

"Guess you'll never know," Fenton says, and everything in me both relaxes and amps up. I'm feeling the chemical rush big-time. "You wanna invite me in?"

"Oh!" I say. "Yeah." *And* he has good consent ethics. Be still my fluttering heart.

Fenton makes his way to my desk, which has become more of a worktable since I started high school. I tend to do my homework on my bed. I wish I could stop thinking the word *bed*, so I sit on it, figuring out of sight, out of mind.

Fenton's still studying the various pieces and papers that make up my clock. "Tell me about this." His voice is soft, inviting, beckoning me off my bed—*aaaagh!*—and toward him like a moth to a flame.

I edge up to my pride and joy, breathing in his sharp boy smell mixing with the permanent strawberry-vanilla of the scented candles I keep in my room. "Well," I say, pushing my glasses up my nose and looking down at the batteries, microchips, and doll-sized gears. I'm afraid I'll combust. "What do you want to know?"

He turns to me, voice soft like mine. "Why time?"

I look into his deep brown eyes, and a flood of warmth rushes through me. Maybe it's why my story comes out so quickly, a jumble of words that make up a story only Dot, Lulu, and my moms know.

"When I was eleven"—I run my hands through my hair and pull it into a ponytail just to have something to do—"we went to London on my spring break to visit my grandparents. We go every couple of years or so. And it was rainy, like it always is there, so we ended up at the National Maritime Museum because it was the closest building to duck into and the café next door was closed." Gingerly, I brush aside a set of gears and rest my butt on the side of the desk, gesturing so that Fenton knows he can sit in the chair. He sinks down, those incredible eyes focused on me. I pull the elastic out of my hair and let it fall to my shoulders, just to see if Fenton notices. My curls fall around my face. He's looking.

I remind myself to breathe. "So yeah, we're in this random museum and I hear someone talking about horology, and I remember laughing because, you know, I'm eleven and anything that sounds remotely dirty is *hilarious*..." Mum had glared at me, not amused at the spectacle I was making, but I could tell Ma was trying not to laugh too.

"But something about that word intrigued me because I'd never heard it before, you know? So we follow the voice into this room off the hallway, and the lady speaking at the front—she was like a Disney movie version of a British person, really tall and thin with a tweed suit and big glasses—she smiles and kind of beckons us in." Fenton nods, still all ears. Boys never focus on me like this. "So anyway, turns out this was the annual meeting of the Antiquarian Horological Society."

Fenton laughs. "That's a mouthful."

I smile, remembering. "Yeah, and it's basically a fancy way of saying a group of people who are obsessed with old clocks. Or," I clear my throat and try to imitate Eleanor that first day, "the art, science, social history, and technology of timekeepers." Fenton laughs again, and this time I join him.

"And, I don't know," I say, making another ponytail and this time securing it with the hair tie I had around my wrist. "I'd never thought about clocks as this sort of living thing, little pieces working perfectly together to give us all a construct that we think we're in charge of, but we're really not. I just really...connected with that."

"Because it's like you," Fenton said, touching my hand. It's the gentlest, lightest brush of skin on skin, but it sets every one of my nerve endings on fire in the best possible way. "You're...um." Here's this smooth, confident older guy struggling with what to say to me. "Short, but you have this big brain that does it all."

And maybe I'm just the nerd to end all nerds, but "big brain" is the most romantic descriptor I've ever heard.

"And..." I say. Now I'm fumbling, trying to stop myself from jumping on the chair and putting my mouth on his mouth. "I built that clock in the living room when we got back." Fenton's eyes widen, like he's impressed. "And now—this is gonna sound really dorky—I'm the youngest-ever member of the Antiquarian Horological Society."

He grins. "That's one for the résumé."

"Eleanor is very proud," I say, grinning back. "So I'm doing a whole comparison of quartz versus pendulum, and I'm building the quartz clock to go with it." I don't mention the personal essay because I'm in this sweet, squishy little bubble with Fenton listening to me nerd out and I don't want to pop it.

Fenton stands up. For a second, I worry I've geeked out *too much*. Antiquarian Horological Society, really? But instead, he moves closer.

I scoot off the desk, drawn to him.

"You're amazing," Fenton breathes.

Time stops.

His lips are barely touching mine, light as a feather...

"What are you doing here?" It's Ma. And she's using her cop voice.

Shit.

Fenton and I break apart, knocking something to the floor behind me. *Please don't let it be the battery that took me forever to find online.*

Mum's wearing jeans, so she must have come from class. I didn't hear the front door open. She folds her arms over her polo shirt, looking at Fenton, then at me, face stony. "I'm waiting," she barks.

I'm not sure who she's addressing, but Fenton says, "I apologize, Ms. Yu. I, uh—"

"We weren't doing anything," I offer, hearing the panicked whine in my voice. "I was just showing him my clock."

Ma's face is impassive. She doesn't believe me. And maybe, considering we were pretty much about to kiss, she shouldn't.

"I have another errand to run before we go to improv," she says, giving me a *this is not over* look. She glares at Fenton. "I'll walk you out, hm?"

It's not a request. With an apologetic glance over his shoulder, Fenton is gone.

I realize we never Googled "Havendale, 1997."

And now, I don't have the heart.

Chapter Eight

Improv isn't going well. And it's all my fault.

Mum looks wounded. Ma keeps glaring at me, and they pointedly sat as far from me as possible. I'm really in for it once class is over, and yet, I'm not sorry. Fenton and I weren't doing anything wrong, and if Mum is hurt, it's her fault for not telling me anything.

I respond by glaring back at Ma.

As if that weren't bad enough, Fenton sent me a text during class break.

Just heard from my dad. He's really freaking out about us possibly dating but won't tell me why. WTF? He's never done that.

I widen my eyes at him from across the room, but now my moms are staring daggers at *him* too, so we don't dare approach one another. *Is it because I'm younger than you?*

It can't be. I didn't tell him your age, and I don't think Smith found out either. He's good but not that good. It's weird 'cause Smith seems almost afraid of you too.

Why would they be afraid of me?

He called me Mia. I don't need Google to know that means something.

I bet my moms could tell me, but of course they won't. Right now, they're huddled in a corner, glancing at me, then at Fenton, and whispering. We've never had any rules about boys in my room, but we will now. I'm tempted to just go for broke and ask *them* who Mia is, in front of everyone, so they can't evade me. Instead I text Fenton.

Can you talk to Smith again?

I tried. He won't budge. :(I guess I can't blame him? He's really loyal to my dad. A brief pause, then another text comes through: *My dad's all talk though. And I'm eighteen. He can't tell me who not to see. Still, he never freaks out like this.*

What exactly is everyone hiding?

Fenton shuts off his phone then claps his hands. "Okay, kids! Back to work we go." But he sneaks a glance at me, and his eyes are as worried as mine.

What are we going to do?

❖

The car ride home is dead quiet. Of course we're stuck in a traffic jam, which just ups the angry vibes pinging all over, bouncing off of the cold, frosty windows.

"I think we should drop out of the class," Mum says. Her voice cuts through the air like glass piercing my heart.

I can't help it—I snort. My moms glance at each other before projecting twin glares at the back seat. Even in the dark, I can tell it's more than just the typical "Perdita's having a teenage moment" look.

"Why?" I ask. The one syllable comes out snotty and defiant, like a teenager on one of those old sitcoms Ma loves, even though there are no families like ours on them.

"She asks *why*," Ma mutters, turning back and riding the brake as the taillights in front of us glow red.

"You're the one who wanted to do improv," I snap, crossing my arms and staring out the window.

"I didn't know our teacher would hit on my daughter," Ma says, voice louder. I can see the crease of her brow in the rearview mirror, though she won't look directly at me.

Really? "He's not *hitting* on me," I say. "We haven't done anything." Ma looks over her shoulder, and I see her eyes glinting. "Fine, we almost kissed, but that was the first time anything like that has happened. We're just friends." *For now.* "And FYI, he's not even nineteen and I'm days away from turning seventeen. He graduated from Latin *last year.* It's not like he's forty. I know what I'm doing."

Something occurs to me. "Is it because he's a guy?" My voice is getting high and hysterical, and I hate it, but I don't think even the deepest of breaths could calm me down right now. "If he were, I don't know, Felice, you'd be rolling out the red carpet."

"Perdita." Mum looks back, illuminated by a slash of streetlight. "That's not what Ma is saying, and you know it."

What she's not saying: *Keep the peace. Don't make things worse.*

Maybe she's right.

But then Ma snorts again, inching the car forward. The fact that she's not even listening to me, that Mum's just sitting there—asking me with her big eyes to calm down instead of addressing the real issue—just sets me off.

"It's not even about Fenton, is it?" I ask. My voice is sharp, and I sound, disturbingly, like Mum in the rare moments I piss her off. I don't even know what I'm doing wrong, except asking questions I should already know the answers to.

"You want to punish me because I'm wondering about my adoption," I continue, focusing on Ma's face in the rearview mirror. "Which I've been wondering about since way before Fenton. Which is *normal.* Especially considering you've never told me shit except that I'm Mexican-Salvadoran, and really, I don't even know if *that's* true. I've never seen my birth certificate, or my adoption papers. I know absolutely nothing about my mother—"

"*We're* your mothers," Mum breaks in. The hurt in her voice is so raw, I can feel it in my bones.

"And don't you forget it," Ma mutters through gritted teeth, inching the car forward again. "Shit," she says when we see the red light up ahead.

"I don't understand why you're doing this, love," Mum says. She smooths her skirt with hands that even I can see from the back seat are trembling. "Acting out, sneaking an older boy into your room, asking questions about a time your ma doesn't like to remember—"

"Oh my God, this is *not about you!*"

I don't recognize my own voice coming out in a strangled cry, like my throat had to twist the words, garble them, before releasing them into the overheated air of our family sedan. "You think I woke up one day and said, 'Oh gee, I think I'll hurt my parents' feelings by asking about my heritage.' I could do a whole lot of things if I wanted to hurt your feelings. I could drink every weekend like half my class. I could blow off homework and lose my tuition break. I could screw around and get pregnant like my *real* mom probably did—"

"*ENOUGH!*"

As she screams that one word, Ma brakes so hard I lurch forward.

Mum's hand is between my head and the seat. She's reached back to protect me.

"*Connie,*" she whispers, her eyes huge and shining in the late winter dark.

"Jesus Christ, you almost hit that c—" But when I crane my neck to look at Ma, my boisterous cop mother wearing flannel pants with rainbow fish on them under her puffy parka, I see that she's resting her head on the wheel.

Sobbing.

Until this very moment, I've never seen her shed a tear. Not in fifth grade when Mum had pneumonia and I suddenly remembered I had an art project due the next morning. Not at a marriage equality rally when one of her best friends spoke about getting tear-gassed at city hall.

Not even at their tiny wedding in Massachusetts before it was legal here. It was just the three of us in some random suburb at the home of Mum's friend who was a justice of the peace. They didn't want to wait anymore. I twirled around with a flower crown on my head—the height of glamour for a six-year-old—and Ma looked at me and Mum, her eyes shining as she said, "I do." Afterward, we bought a cake at a supermarket and ate it sitting on the back of our car in the parking lot, still all dressed up, overdosing on super-sugary frosting and singing along to Rod Stewart. The flowers are dry now, but the crown still hangs on my mirror.

"Perdita," Mum says, and squeezes Ma's shoulder, then rubs her back, making circles, like she used to do for me when I was little. Without looking me in the eye, she continues, "*This* is what thinking about that time does to your ma. *This* is why we don't talk about it."

Ma sobs louder and she sounds like a kid almost, but deeper, more guttural. Like she lost something really important and she'll never get it back.

I blurt out, "I'm sorry."

And I *am*. I really am. But even though I feel like shit about making Ma cry, I must keep searching. Now more than ever because something is very clearly up.

Still. I'll hear the echo of her sobs as I toss and turn in bed tonight.

"Put it in park, Connie," Mum whispers. "We're stuck anyway; we can switch. I'll drive us home."

Ma nods, still crying. Her sniffling cuts through the annoyed honking horns around us.

I look to the winter sky, an endless black void.

We don't say a word through the rest of the drive. Thankfully, traffic picks up.

When the elevator opens on our floor—Ma staggering like she's drunk, dried tears all over her face; Mum practically holding her up; and me trailing behind, feeling ever the lost daughter—we see something completely unexpected.

A figure sleeps in our doorway, head propped up against the frame at an angle that can't be comfortable. An overstuffed duffel bag sits next to them. They're wearing sweatpants and an old T-shirt, disheveled like they got dressed too quickly.

"Dot?" I say softly, the first word I've uttered since the car.

At the sound of my voice, Dot startles awake. They look at all three of us with haunted eyes.

"My parents threw me out."

CHAPTER NINE

Needless to say, it was a long night.

My family doesn't unpack the car incident, which is highly unusual for us. Both Ma and Mum make it a point of talking things out when we disagree—especially when said disagreements result in yelling or tears. But there wasn't time, what with getting the whole story from Dot—which is pretty much exactly what you'd expect—then making up the guest bed, all of us knowing how bad this is and not trying to make light of it by saying we were having a sleepover. I mean, their parents blocked Dot's number. So, yeah.

My moms talked late into the night. I could hear them through the wall. Ma was going on about contacting her friend at the Department of Children and Family Services first thing in the morning. Mum made a list of what we'd need for the guest room. At one point, Mum said, "Dot can live with us, right?"

She'd barely finished the question when Ma replied, "Obviously."

As I dozed off, tears ran down my cheeks.

A rustling sound woke me at about 4:00 a.m. Dot was in my doorway. "Can I keep you company? Just for tonight?" They looked down, fiddling with the afghan we'd grabbed from the couch with the periodic table knitted in. "I feel about five years old…"

By then I was already scooting toward the wall, shoving my blankets back and patting the empty space. "Come here." Holding hands, we fell back asleep.

Last night and this morning, the three of us, Mum and Ma and me, were a quiet but united front. We were not going to deconstruct the worst fight we'd ever had, and we probably never would.

I don't blame Dot for this. How could I? Much as my moms hate me right now, there's no way they'd *ever* throw me out of the only home I've ever known. They'd never block my number and leave me to fend for myself. That's the cruelest possible shit, and I can't even imagine what Dot is going through.

We filled Lulu in last night via text. And when we get to school, she's waiting at Dot's locker with a big box of Do-Rite Donuts and, "All the hugs you can handle, if you're up for being touched." Dot was.

Dot wants to go to Dr. Schneider, to fill her in on the situation and potentially stave off any bullying, and Lulu volunteers to go with her. They head down the hallway, Lulu's arm around Dot's shoulder, the red-and-white donut box in her manicured hand. I watch them, my heart full of love for my best friends in the world.

Ma is going to try to get ahold of Dot's parents today—not to talk sense into them because we're way beyond that—but to let them know Dot is okay and is with us, where Dot will likely be for the foreseeable future. Now I'm not sure I want to go to science camp, even if I win the scholarship. As tense as I still feel around Ma and Mum, I don't want to leave my friend when they need me most.

I'm still going to keep looking though. The words *Mia* and *Havendale* are now tattooed on my cerebral cortex, waiting to be linked to other clues. I know they're out there.

During my free period a couple of hours later, I see Dr. Schneider's door open.

"Knock-knock," I say, rapping on the frame.

She looks up with a smile. "Come on in."

First things first. "Did Dot talk to you?" I ask, closing the door and taking a seat. There's a new framed poster above her desk: a map of the stars. I have the same one in my room. A glazed donut sits primly on a white napkin, waiting to be devoured—I'm guessing it's from Dot and Lulu's meeting earlier—next to a small statue of a woman draped in loose, flowy clothing.

"They did," Dr. Schneider says, closing her laptop and folding her hands. "Very glad Dot has friends like you and Lulu. They'll need you both."

"I've got Dot's back," I reply. A lot of kids are out at U-High, and it's not a big deal. We're in Chicago, after all, and part of a major university with people from all over. The school has a float in the Pride Parade every June. Still, Dot's the first nonbinary person I've known, and that's probably true for a lot of people here.

"Good. The administration and I will be talking to your moms and DCFS. Just to make sure Dot stays safe and has everything they need." Dr. Schneider swallows hard. "I shouldn't say this in front of you, Perdita, but I wish I'd felt comfortable relying on others when I was young and first realized I was queer. I ended up transferring to U-High—I'm not sure if you knew it, but I'm an alum—and the environment wasn't perfect, but it was so much more accepting than where I came from. There are still problems all over, of course, but…" She exhales. "Situations like Dot's…are so much better than they used to be."

For a minute, she doesn't look like the put-together adult I admire. She's not just the leader, advocating for her students and pushing for every single grant the math and science clubs have ever gotten, but someone like me, unsure of the world and her place in it. I wonder what she went through.

Is that where the scars on her arm came from?

"My ma didn't talk to her parents for a while," I offer. "They didn't disown her or anything, but they just didn't understand. Probably around the time you were having trouble too. But they came around after I was adopted." Gran and Gramps wanted to get to know me, and they've never said as much, but I know they missed Ma too. They adore Mum. We spend every Christmas with them downstate and take them out to shows when they visit. There's a framed photo in our apartment of Gran holding baby me aloft, both of us all smiles as if we'd finally found each other.

I'm still mad at Ma, but that doesn't mean I don't respect her. She knew her parents wouldn't be okay with her loving women, at least initially. I feel a weird urge to give Dr. Schneider a hug, but she's the dean, so I stay in my seat.

She closes her eyes, and when she opens them again, she's the Dr. Schneider I've known since seventh grade, efficient and well-dressed. "Anyway. How's the essay?"

"Actually, I came in here to talk to you about that," I say, leaning back in the chair, my heart sinking. I don't want to disappoint her, but I'm really not sure what to do here. "The direction I wanted to go...isn't happening."

"Oh? Why's that?"

And I don't know what it is—maybe it's lack of sleep, or the fact that my moms and I are on the outs, or these new feelings for Fenton that are *far* deeper than a chemical rush—but sitting here in an office with a person in authority, one I also trust, during free period when I really should be finishing *Hamlet*, in this surprisingly comfortable leather chair, between bites of the donut she eventually pushes toward me, I tell Dr. Schneider everything. All of it: from improv class to my walk with Fenton to Fenton's dad's reaction toward me to last night's blowout that almost resulted in a car accident. At first, Dr. Schneider asks questions, but then she goes completely quiet with the laser-sharp focus that everyone knows is classic Dr. Schneider.

I've been concentrating on the donut, then the napkin (which I've been systematically shredding), then the little statue, as I tell the story. It's not until I finally get to the end that I look up and see Dr. Schneider's face.

I swear to God, if I were the tinfoil hat type, I'd think all the adults in my life were conspiring against me.

Dr. Schneider looks like Fenton's dad: same expression, blood drained out of her face. She's twisting her hands and cracking her knuckles, which I've never seen her do, *ever.*

For a minute, we stare at each other—or more precisely, she stares at *me* like *I'm* the science project. Like I'm a specimen under her microscope and she's scrutinizing me, not in a disrespectful way, but like a discovery that she genuinely wants to make, for the greater good.

"Perdita," she asks slowly, "when were you born?"

Okay… "Nineteen ninety-seven," I answer.

"What day?" she asks, almost before I'm finished answering.

"April fifth. Um, Dr. Schneider? Are you okay?" I have to ask because now she looks borderline catatonic and I'm wondering if I should call 911.

"Perdita, you'll have to excuse me," she says, sounding strange. Her tone is quiet and unsure, as if she's fighting her way out of a dream. "I need to make a call." She must see my face, because she musters a smile that's meant to be reassuring, probably, but just comes off as pained. "Come by tomorrow and we can talk more about the essay." Another tight, odd smile, and I understand I'm being dismissed.

On my way out, she tells her admin, Rose, to hold all her calls.

"Sure thing, Paulina," Rose's words fade as I make a beeline for my locker.

We're not supposed to text during the day, but I have to talk to someone, and Dot and Lulu are in class. Besides, Dot's dealing with enough.

So I just had the weirdest convo with my dean.

I'm praying Fenton's by his phone and I'm not disappointed. He texts like the wind too.

Tell me.

I give an abbreviated version and he replies, *If I were a conspiracy theorist, I'd say some shit's going down and that shit involves you.*

That's what I thought! Despite all the weirdness going on, I love how we're on the same wavelength, and that he's so firmly in my corner. *This is like a Lifetime movie with a paranoid housewife.* Oh God. *Not that I watch those,* I hastily type.

That's a shame cuz I totally do. Gotta know if my computer is trying to kill me or if the husband I ordered online is really a jewel thief.

I giggle and the sound echoes through the empty hallway. *Not that I want you dead, but free sparkles* would *be cool.* The bell rings. *I gotta go,* I type.

Starbucks later? Near the comedy club? You deserve a hot chocolate.

Deal, I type, feeling the smile on my face.

He has my heart.

Chapter Ten

April

"You ready?" Fenton whispers.

My fingers hover over my phone. Around us, tourists are buying tickets, and a few stray comedians are doing funny vocal warm-ups: tongue-twisters about weather and whether and even a mini-game of Zip, Zap, Zop. The energy is palpable. Fenton was running late, so instead of Starbucks, we're at the comedy club attached to the training center, just feet away from the improv classroom and half an hour before Fenton's gig.

My moms think I'm at the library.

I scooch just a little closer to Fenton so our thighs press together, and the resulting *zing* goes up through my sneakers. I don't know what I'm going to find, but I'm glad I'm going to find it with him.

"Ready," I say, and we grin at each other before I open Google and type in the words.

Mia, Havendale, 1997.

And my phone dies.

"Goddammit!" I yell and several patrons, as well as a group of flannel-clad improvisers, look at me. I clap a hand over my mouth, my face on fire.

"Relax," Fenton says quietly. He touches my shoulder and hands me his phone, search results already shining through the screen.

Our eyes go wide as we read the article. It's shitty quality, more an image of an article—this was 1997 after all. But my eyes go blurry with tears anyway.

Car accident in the earliest hours of a Saturday morning.

A little boy, shot with his father's gun, bleeding out in the front seat.

One girl killed.

And after barely making it to the hospital: a baby.

There aren't any names because they were all minors. But I know, I just *know*, the baby was me.

Is me.

❖

My kid,

I told my therapist about these letters, how I've started them up again because you're about to turn the same age I was when everything happened. He was supportive. Encouraged me to write down the whole story if I could. Even if you'd never read it. So here goes.

We were at St. Cecelia's, a Catholic school in a small town, Havendale, Illinois, where I still live.

Catholic school is weird. It's basically its own little kingdom, with rules and regulations and uniforms and God. I didn't know what a specific experience I was having until I was out in the world and meeting kids who didn't have monthly Mass and could wear whatever they wanted every day. How wild to learn there are people who didn't see priests and nuns as these sort of strange magical beings who knew all and could do no wrong.

Until they did.

One of our priests was suddenly not there anymore... They caught him with a little boy, which we didn't know until way later. It took years before people knew this was a constant problem.

It was also the nineties, a strange and violent time. People act like things were simpler then, but I don't think simpler times have ever existed.

I'm getting off track. Basically, your mom and I were boyfriend and girlfriend. We were juniors. She was really scared, of course, and kept the pregnancy a secret. Because she was a very faithful Catholic, she never even considered an abortion. Meaning, kid, you were wanted all along.

Once I found out she was pregnant, I wanted to marry her. I only felt close to my little brother, Max, and I figured Max could be part of my new family because our parents were just...absent all the time. Looking back, this was all so dumb of me.

What's even dumber is how paranoid I got about another guy in our group. I suspected he might be your father. Deep down, I knew it wasn't true, but I was really afraid and mad that my dad hadn't done a good job. I took it all out on someone else. It's not an excuse, just an explanation. It's especially not an excuse for what happened to my little brother. One night, when I was paranoid, I loaded my dad's gun.

And I forgot to lock his safe.

My little brother found it while I was interrogating my girlfriend about our baby. About you.

I will never, ever forgive myself.

On the way to the hospital, your mom went into early labor. We ended up hitting another girl—a girl who loved your auntie Paulina ran in front of our car. Nobody else knows this, but I persuaded her to come. She'd been awful to your auntie, and I stepped in, screwed up another life.

The shock of early labor, the impact of the accident, and some complications that may have been preventable had your mom gone to a doctor, put Mia in a brief, but still scary, coma.

You and Mia were airlifted to a bigger hospital in St. Louis pretty quick. Soon after that, Mia's mom's restaurant was shuttered, and they disappeared. I never saw Mia again. I never saw you, period. They gave me papers, and I signed them.

I have to stop now.

I'm sorry.

Love,

Someone You Could Know

Chapter Eleven

Fenton stayed with me until his show started. People laughed and drank around me. And I finally understand the whole hype around improv.

Maybe it's because I just found out I survived a car accident before I was even out of the womb, or that I was born in Havendale, a place I've never heard of until recently, or that nothing is as I thought even two months ago… Whatever it is, I'm really happy to be here, watching. And I'd feel that way even if Fenton weren't onstage.

His team, Not Tom Hanks, has been together almost eight months and it shows. They're not like our class, fumbling around while sussing out everyone else's personalities. Fenton and his seven teammates pick up each other's cues and words with ease, moving around the stage almost like they're dancing. And there *is* something fantastic about knowing how in-the-moment improv is: what we're watching won't—*can't*—be replicated. As soon as a joke is made, it disappears for good, leaving only the memory of laughter in its wake.

During the last moments of the show, Fenton plays a stoner dude with a girl with blond hair that's crazy curly like mine and a guy with a ton of freckles playing the girl's dad. The running joke is that they keep forgetting they're in the driveway, and even though it's just the three of them and two folding chairs onstage, the whole theater can't stop laughing, including me. Fenton caps it off with, "Wait, are we still in the driveway?"

Lights down, and the crowd goes wild. During curtain call, Fenton looks right at me and smiles. He once told me ninety percent of improv is bad. I just saw the other ten percent, and I see why everyone endures the rest.

It was a kind of magic.

I take an Uber back late, still on a high from the show. My moms didn't wait up. The clock isn't wound, and reality slams right into me.

For the first time in years, I wind the clock myself. I hope Mum and Ma get the message.

❖

As soon as Dot and I arrive at school, I get called to the office before we can even meet up with Lulu. I *know*, somehow, this has something to do with my bio parents.

A package for me, overnighted via FedEx, sits on Dr. Schneider's desk, and she excuses herself. I guess I'm supposed to open the bent box, white and orange and purple. Inside, there's an old-looking, red spiral-bound notebook with a folded letter taped on the front.

Kid.
Not "kid."
I know who you are now.
Dear Perdita,
You're my kid.
Today I am sitting at my desk, pushing paperwork for a used Chevy Lumina for an older couple, and my phone rings. It's my best friend from high school.
She and I stayed in touch, nothing huge, just occasional Facebook messages, and sometimes when I'm up there for a conference, we have dinner. The fact that she's calling me in the middle of the day means something is wrong. When I saw her name on the display I flashed back to that awful night. PTSD kicked into full gear, and for a second, I wished I still drank.

Clutching my latest sobriety chip, I answer, hoping like hell she's just calling to shoot the shit.

But with her voice low and urgent like I hadn't heard in decades, she tells me to go to the U-High website—specifically the science department page—to look at the photo of a student working in the chemistry lab. A student she'd known for years.

Now she's shocked she never saw it before, but she figures she's been at the school so long, worked with so many teens day in and day out, and focused on their brains, their hearts, more than what they looked like. Pal's always been cerebral like that.

She tells me to do it right now—doesn't give me time to ask questions. And says that if I want to know more, I'll have to figure it out myself. She can't risk her job or, more importantly, her ethics. But maybe, she says, this could be the first step in making things right. For all of us.

The second I saw those curls poofing around your lab goggles and that grin that reminds me so much of my little brother, I knew.

You are my daughter.

I'm getting ahead of myself. I know we'd have to take a DNA test, and supposedly they're very easy these days, you can buy them at Walgreens even. But, Perdita, there's no way you aren't mine. And Mia's. She's your mom.

Was.

Maybe you know all this, and maybe your mothers (I did some more digging) have told you everything. Maybe you've already ripped up this letter or burned it. And maybe it's selfish of me, but writing this letter has helped me more than years of AA and therapy combined. If I don't ever hear back from you, believe me, I understand. You owe me nothing, Perdita. Nothing.

I guess there's a chance you don't know any of this. So...

Your dean knew you when you were just a speck of cells. She was your mother's best friend, and mine. I'm not surprised she's in charge of a whole school because when we were your age, exactly your age in fact, she was in charge of all of us. And she paid the price.

We didn't speak for a very long time.

It wasn't like now, with Google and social media, where you can find almost anyone. It was harder to keep track. Easier not to be found if you didn't want to be. Still, even now, I've never found a trace of Mia. She wasn't in good shape the last time I saw her. I fear the worst, but I'll never know.

I'm not sure what to do from here. I'd like to know you. I understand if that's not something you want, right now or ever. You look so happy in that picture. Smart. The best of your mom and me.

So here's what I'm doing: my name and all my info are at the bottom of this letter. I'm enclosing a notebook full of all the other letters I wrote to you too, and the newspaper article about the accident. (No one's names are included because we were all minors, but trust me, this is us. This is you.)

You are under no obligation to get in touch. You can burn it all and go live your life. You might have done so already.

But if you're still reading, and you'd like to get to know your loser of a dad, you know where to find me.

Love,

Someone You Could Know: Tesla Wrightwood

Chapter Twelve

Tesla Wrightwood.
    That's my dad's name.
I have a dad.

These thoughts are so basic. They are just a handful of syllables, popping around in my brain like that plastic corn popper toy I had as a kid. A handful of syllables that change absolutely everything.

The FedEx package screams OVERNIGHT. I find the newspaper article, laminated, preserved in plastic. I try to wipe smudges from his freshly-typed letter. I imagine the printer ink is still wet. But they've soaked through the paper, blurring a *T* or an *l*. Tears?

My dad was named after a physicist.

If this weren't so messed up, it would almost be poetic.

Mia.

How do I make sense of all this, my life turning upside down in just a few weeks?

What are the dos and don'ts? Tesla says there wasn't a Google when he was my age, but Google probably can't help me with this either.

Somewhere in the fog of that day, I decide not to go home after school. I'm unsure of my actual plan but text my moms some bullshit excuse about a science club meeting and dinner at the cafe near U-High. Dot's spending the night with Lulu, whose parents are gone for the weekend again. Sounds like she and Tesla have/had that in common. I have the opposite issue—moms who are constantly in my face, who tell me anything and everything except the one thing I want to know.

Sitting in Old Town, the same Starbucks where Fenton brought me for hot chocolates, the one I've secretly been thinking of as "our" place, I stare out the window and watch people go by: wannabe comedians, tourists filing into the mainstage show. Twentysomethings linger in front of a bar across the street, looking way cooler than I ever will. I've grown up here, but I've never taken Chicago people-watching for granted. Ma taught me to appreciate it when I was really young.

Ma.

Mum.

Tesla.

Fenton's dad.

Smith.

Dr. Schneider. (Thinking of her as Paulina—a person with a first name, a person who was once young and in Catholic school and knew about me—is still odd.)

They all know things I don't.

I can't go home.

I end up joining Lulu and Dot. We watch Netflix romcoms. We split a rotisserie chicken. We talk about anything and everything— except parents. I don't tell them about the notebook full of letters I have yet to read.

Early in the morning, my eyes open and I sit up, looking at Dot snoozing peacefully next to me on the air mattress. Lulu's in the bed above us, her adorable tiny snores the only sound. I smile, quietly scrambling to my feet. Just-risen sunlight streams in through the windows as I pad in my socked feet through the empty hallway, phone in hand. I slept better than I have in weeks.

Once I've reached the kitchen and started a pot of coffee, I text Fenton. *Two questions: are you free today and do you have a car?*

Time to get answers.

Chapter Thirteen

In the end, it's Bearded Guy who saves us.

Fenton's car is in the shop, and he's been crashing on Bearded Guy's couch while things between him and his dad cool off. I brush aside the guilt I feel about coming between father and son. I need to get to Havendale today. I need to find my father.

Fenton, to his credit, doesn't ask me why I don't just call or email my dad. I'm grateful because I don't know those answers myself. The old Perdita would have taken the logical route after discussing it with Dot, Lulu, *and* my moms. Then again, the old Perdita didn't know anything about her birth parents.

Things change.

Bearded Guy hands over the keys to his battered old Pontiac. "But take care of it," he says to Fenton, eyes serious under all that yeti-like facial hair that's way more scraggly than it is in class. "Mopsa's my baby."

"You bet, Otto," Fenton says.

Otto looks at me, framed in the doorway of the tiny apartment. Behind him, there are overflowing baskets of laundry and a cat meowing. "By the way, I'm sorry I talked down to you that one time in class." He smiles. "I had you pegged all wrong, nerd girl. You're doing good."

Still slightly patronizing, but I'll take it. He *is* lending us his car after all. I smile back. "Thanks, Otto. We'll bring back Mopsa in one piece, promise."

"Cool." He fist-bumps me, gives Fenton that weird handshake-half-hug combo, and we're headed to the parking garage.

As we pull onto Clark Street, Fenton plugs my dad's address in the GPS. "Our first road trip," he says, grinning at me. I realize I'm smiling ear to ear and I hold out my hand. He takes it, keeping his other hand on the wheel and his eyes on the road. His palm is rough and warm against mine.

We're on Lake Shore Drive when I realize something. "Hey," I say, and Fenton looks over, turns down the Dixie Chicks' first album.

"Something wrong?"

"No," I say slowly. It's the date on Otto's car radio. As we idle in late Saturday morning traffic, Lake Michigan shining true blue on our left, I lace my fingers through his. "I just remembered it's my birthday."

"Well then," Fenton says, his voice low. Slowly but surely, he lifts my hand to his mouth, brushes his lips against my knuckles. I get shivers all over in the best possible way. "Happy birthday, Perdita."

Birthdays usually started with Ma's chocolate chip pancakes, silly cards, and at least one embarrassing attempt at singing "Happy Birthday" in two-part harmony.

Today I'm turning seventeen with a boy my moms don't approve of, my phone turned off, in a car that's not mine, hurtling toward a person I've never met in a town that, until a few days ago, I didn't know existed.

And the boy just kissed my hand. So despite all the uncertainty around me, I'm feeling fine.

For a while, we just drive and listen to music. The highway melts around us, sunshine on gray pavement. Before turning off my phone, I texted Lulu, Dot, and my moms in a group message: *Gone to find my father. It's okay. I'm okay. I'll be back soon.* I wish I could have told my best friends more, but I don't want them feeling pressured to keep secrets or lie to my moms. I know this isn't exactly the right way to go about it all, but honestly? Ma and Mum should have been truthful with me a long time ago. In a way, it's their fault I'm doing this.

"Hey, P?" Fenton says once we're finally out of the city. "Can I ask you something?"

"Anything, chauffeur," I say sweetly, trying to ignore the growing pit of dread in my stomach. It's part guilt for leaving my parents and friends high and dry, and part fear that he's about to say something I won't like.

Fenton keeps his eyes on the road but turns down the Dixie Chicks, whose perfect three-part harmony about abusive husbands and revenge fades away. "I've been thinking," he says. *Crap.*

"At first, I understood why you wanted to do this," he says slowly, as if he's trying to process the words as he utters them. He's careful with each and every syllable. Methodical in a way that Fenton the improviser often isn't and Perdita the scientist always is. "I mean, I read the letter, and it's some heavy shit. I still don't know how my dad's involved, but I agree with you—he and Smith know too much *not* to be. And"—he glances at me once more before he absolutely has to look back at the road—"I care about you. I want this to work out, however you see that happening."

I like all this so far.

"But," he says, and I *knew* there was a but. "This is…a lot. You're basically a runaway. I mean, I know you texted your moms, but I'm sure they're freaking out. I know my dad would be. Did you tell them anything?"

"How could I?" I don't mean for it to come out so snappish, but my defenses were already up. "They wouldn't tell me jack when I asked nicely. Ma almost crashed our car rather than give up any intel." Now I'm really gaining steam. "I *have* to do this, Fenton. I have to find my father. I have to know who I really am."

"Perdita," he says, and his voice has a gravity I've never heard before. "I'm not in your situation, so I can't completely know what you're going through, but…" He hesitates.

I sigh. "Go ahead."

Fenton looks over at me again and bites his lip. We're really moving along, passing an exit for the town of Dwight. In two and a half hours, with good traffic, we'll be in Havendale, and then…what exactly? I was so sure about how this would all go down when we got into Otto's car, but now...

"You *know* who you are already," Fenton says, eyes fixed on the road, not daring to look at me. I can tell he's afraid of how I'll react, that I just might completely flip out. For the first time, I feel the year-plus age gap between us, every damn day of it. "You have two moms who, yeah, are kind of overbearing"—I snort at the understatement of the millennium—"but they love you," he finishes. "I could tell when your ma introduced you to me that first day, all loud and proud. And even then, you...you just seemed so sure of yourself."

He's got to be kidding. "That first day? I sucked!"

"But you knew it. And you came back. And you were all, this isn't my thing but I'm gonna give it a try and keep an open mind. Maybe you don't see this, P, but you're so freaking *confident.* You love time and science and hot chocolate, and you hate writing about yourself. Most people our age don't know shit about themselves, but you've got it all figured out."

"Obviously not *all* of it," I say, trying to keep the snappishness out of my voice. I know he means well, but if I wanted a lecture, I'd have stayed at home. "As you pointed out, I'm running away as we speak."

Fenton looks at me sideways. "Am I talking down to you?"

"A little."

"Sorry." He pauses. "But your relationship with your mothers is something special, and I'd hate to see you end that over a fight." We pass into another lane. "My dad and I aren't close. I think since I stopped being tiny and cute, he hasn't been sure what to do with me."

I realize now that I don't know much about Fenton's family. "Did your parents break up when you were little?"

"They were never really *together.*" He takes a deep breath. "My grandma sent Dad away for a while after my mom had me. She said she didn't want him to ruin his future."

"Oh wow." It's all I can think to say. I can't imagine my parents sending me away, no matter what I did.

"Yeah." Fenton keeps his eyes on the road, but his voice catches a bit. "I was just a baby, so I don't remember him being gone, but he doesn't talk much about that year. He was still in high school—they had me really young—and I guess a lot happened. That's when he met Smith, who *also* won't talk about that year."

Havendale. I think of the newspaper article, the letters from Tesla I haven't yet read. Did Fenton's dad and Smith know him?

Were they in the accident too?

"Anyway," Fenton says, flicking on the turn signal before passing into the other lane, "he moved back to spend more time with me. At least, that's always been the story. He came around a lot when I was really little, I remember that much, but when I was around four or five, something shifted. He wouldn't get down on the floor to play with me anymore. Instead, he'd sit on the couch and judge." Fenton's small smile fades. "He was getting really driven, all about his career and being the provider, and I was just this goofy kid who didn't get good grades."

"Is your dad why you went to Latin?" I ask. That school's not only rigorous, but really expensive.

Fenton laughs. "Yeah, he insisted. I'm a legacy because he ended up going there his senior year. I lived with my mom until high school, then right after I got into Latin, she remarries and gets pregnant again in one fell swoop. So I'm fourteen, in a brand-new school with way richer kids than I'm used to, living with a parent I hardly know. Improv freaking saved me."

Wow.

"So I guess we're learning all kinds of shit about each other today," Fenton says in response to my silence. "All I'm saying is, I support you in this. Obviously. It's why I got Otto to lend me his car, even though, let's face it, your moms are probably going to cut off my head. Slowly." Despite the seriousness of it all, I giggle. Call it gallows humor. "I just want you to remember that you already have it all. This thing with your dad is gravy. No matter what, you know yourself better than you think. I see it. And I hope sometime soon, you will too."

I don't know if I totally agree with him.

But maybe, just maybe, Fenton has a point.

"Why do you like improv?" I ask. He never answered that. Our texts always get consumed with flirting or puzzling out the mystery of my adoption. And after hearing about his family history, just as complex as my own but in different ways, and seeing him kill it onstage last night, I need to know what else makes him tick.

He thinks for a second. "I like the sense of play, of feeling like a kid all over again in the best way. Improv's always been an escape for me, from whatever I was dealing with, until it became a way of life. Amy Poehler's called improv her religion, and I feel that way too." I can sense from the way the air shifts that he's not done, but I wait.

A couple of minutes later, my patience is rewarded. "I like that there's structure and spontaneity, all at once. I never thought about the structure part, really, until I started teaching and broke it all down." He looks at me, almost shyly. "Until I met you." He grins, eyes back on the road. "You're *all about* that structure. You take comfort in it."

I'm throwing structure to the wind today. Fenton, who's usually spontaneous, is keeping me grounded.

"Yes, and?" I playfully tap him on the knee, shocking myself with this boldness, and he grins full and wide while keeping his eyes on the road.

"'Yes, and' starts with the affirmation, the yes. You can't add on to something that's not already there, you know? And you can't just make shit up without a good solid base to start from."

Despite all the drama, I know one thing:

We really are good for each other.

"I think so too," Fenton says, reaching for my hand, and I realize I've spoken my thoughts out loud.

"Your dad paid for everything, huh?"

He doesn't let go of my hand, but I can feel his fingers tense. "He did. Why?"

"Sooo…" I look at Fenton, whose jaw is set as he stares at the empty road ahead. "Your dad paid for improv. Since you were a kid."

"Until I started work-study my last year of high school, yeah." He glances at me, handsome face a little befuddled. "What's your point, P?"

I focus on the green-and-white road signs. His hand is still warm in mine. "I know I only met him once, but your dad seems like a pretty smart guy. Like, if he's paying for classes all these years, he knows it makes you happy. So obviously he wants you to *be* happy. He just might not be great at showing it."

Fenton's quiet, listening.

"It's possible," I continue, my thoughts catching up with my words, "he wants you to work with him so you'll have a steady gig, and so he'll have you around more, both of which would make *him* happy." I squeeze Fenton's hand, look away from the window and over at him. "But, you know, there are other ways you guys can spend time together, if you want to."

He's still silent. I wonder if I've gone too far, and I try not to panic.

"Goddamn, Perdita," he says, but his tone isn't mad. In fact, it's full of...wonder. "I never thought of it that way."

Giddiness floods through me, but I try to keep it cool. "So, maybe you two should talk."

He nods slowly, a grin overtaking his face. "Maybe we should." Now Fenton squeezes my hand back.

Motioning at the radio, he says, "Feel like A Tribe Called Quest?"

"Perfect," I reply and cue them up on my phone.

❖

As we drive, edging closer and closer to our destination in the most comfortable of silences, I sit with Q-Tip's smooth voice and my own jumbled thoughts.

I may not have wanted to hear what Fenton had to say, but that doesn't mean he's wrong. In both our cases, our relationships with our parents aren't perfect. Ma and Mum and Fenton's dad were all thrown into unexpected situations—suddenly in charge of little lives when they weren't much older than Fenton and me. Fenton's dad was still in high school, even. I'm not a parent, but I know this much: there's no set rulebook.

Maybe all three of them were just doing their best.

And look at us: a girl with the best friends in the world at an amazing school, and a guy who wants to spend his life making people laugh. We've always been loved. Always.

I still don't understand what happened when I was born. I want to know the truth, and I still want to meet my father…I think. I'm fully aware I may be grounded for life for running away this morning, with a guy no less.

But more than anything, I want to hear Ma's voice.

We are all we have.

I reach for Fenton's hand, turn my phone on and ignore the flash of texts and missed call notifications. He glances over at me as I'm dialing. Squeezes my hand. Mouths *I've got you.*

I know he does.

The phone doesn't even ring before she picks up.

"Ma?" I ask. My voice sounds smaller than normal, as if I'm little again, wanting reassurance and comfort after a nightmare, asking her to chase the monsters away.

"Baby," she says.

Never have I heard two syllables so packed with worry, anger, and pure love all at once. Were I not already sitting, that one word would bring me to my knees. I bite down hard on my lip; I almost draw blood.

But what I don't expect, as I brace myself for the worst kind of punishment, is the question that comes next.

I put the phone on speaker.

"Sorry?" I ask, still not sure if I heard her right.

"You're going to meet your father, aren't you?"

I can't quite read the tone in her voice, but it's not anger.

"That was the plan," I answer honestly. And then a rush of words come tumbling out, one over the other, like warm clothes in a dryer. "I'm so sorry I worried you, Ma. I know I shouldn't have taken off like that, and please don't blame anyone but me. Fenton's a good guy and he was only trying to help. When we left, I was so sure that meeting my dad would solve everything, but now I'm not sure of anything at all. And I know I've pissed you off so much in the past couple of months and I'm really, really sorry about that, but we're like an hour and a half outside of Havendale and I just…I want my moms." I swallow hard. "My *real* moms."

It's just then I hear it. In the background, my homemade clock ticks and tocks.

Even in the height of their worry, fear, and anger, they wound it.

I love you.

I'm getting snot all over my phone. For the second time this crazy morning, Fenton kisses my knuckles, and now I'm swooning *and* sobbing and basically a hot mess. Guess I do have feelings after all.

"Then we're coming, P." Ma's even-voiced, even-keeled, reassuring, and decisive all at once—exactly what I need.

And now my face is a full-on faucet. Because she can't see me, Ma continues.

"First, keep your damn phone on."

I laugh a little. Fenton does too.

"Your mum and I are getting in our car right now, along with Dot and Lulu because you have the best friends in the world and they're not letting us leave them behind." I hear Dot and Lulu chattering cheerfully in the background. And, oh my God, why did I ever think I needed anyone except the people who already care about me?

Mum says something that makes Ma laugh.

"What did she say?" I ask.

"Hit Send," Ma replies. Before I can ask, she clarifies. "I've had an email to you in my drafts folder forever. I've added to it over the years. I just…wanted a place to write down my memories of when you came into the world, in a place where you couldn't find it." She paused. "And, you know, just in case something happened to me. Your mum knows. She thinks you need to read it now, and she's right."

After we hang up, I turn my phone back on. Ignoring the flurry of texts, I pull up my inbox. And there it is.

I look at Fenton. "Keep driving. I'll read it aloud to you."

He nods, eyes steady on the road. "What all's in there?"

I scroll down and down and down before scrolling back up, and inhale. "Everything."

❖

Hi P,

This is weird, writing an email to my own daughter. Right now, you're five and you're fast asleep after we let you watch a Friends *marathon on cable.*

Your mum thinks I need to let this all out. If it's up to me, you'll never know about the place we left behind. Never utter the word Havendale in our happy lesbian home.

Just in case, she says. And you know what, she's right. If anything, it'll keep me from waking up at three a.m.

It started the night before you were born. Officer Nakamura, who you know because he ended up transferring to Chicago too, and I were hanging around the station like we usually did. Not much happened in the very conservative cow town of Havendale, but I was happy enough to be there. Even if people sometimes lumped us together as "the Asians"—even though I'm Chinese-American and he's Japanese-American—well, it was better than hearing my parents tell me how wrong I was for loving other women.

Anyway, that night a couple came in with a little boy. He was so small, still missing his baby teeth. I could see the gaps even from where I was standing behind the desks. They all looked like they hadn't slept in a week. Officer Nakamura led them into a room, and they didn't emerge for a long time. Finally, the family left, looking even more tired.

I asked Officer Nakamura what happened. Before he answered me, he collapsed in the nearest chair in the nearly empty station, pinching the bridge of his nose and looking exhausted.

It was a priest, he said. At St. Cecelia's.

Then I had to sit down too.

Officer Nakamura went quiet, but I couldn't stop asking questions. Who? Should we go to the church now? Did he live nearby? How could we help?

In the midst of my nervous flurry, I thought of my own parents and their tiny house in Bloomington-Normal, the college town where I'd grown up. I'd lived there until I came out and it wasn't okay with them, and I moved out and enrolled in the police academy because I didn't know what else to do. Now, I'd never wanted to call them more—just to hear their voices.

Eventually, Officer Nakamura held up a hand, effectively shushing me.

I asked him to repeat himself. And he did. There were tears in his eyes when he told me this had happened before. He'd been around longer than I had, heard it from other cops. Even went to church at St. Cecelia's before he heard about it the first time. Usually, the family went to the parish with concerns or allegations. Then the priest would be gone, moved somewhere else.

I couldn't believe it.

Officer Nakamura looked at me and said, "Believe."

I couldn't sleep when I got home, which didn't bode well for me the next night, or morning really. The car accident. That's when your birth mother, Mia Rodriguez, went into early labor.

Hours later, I saw your face for the first time.

You were three months premature, weighing only four pounds, but strong as an ox and a silent little fighter. Soon they'd airlift you to St. Louis and I just...followed.

Normally, only family gets into intensive care units, but I flashed my badge and said I needed to further question the girl's parents. I definitely didn't.

I felt drawn to them, your mom and grandparents. Back in Havendale, a little boy, about the same age as the one I'd seen in the police station, had had an accident with a gun at a party. He didn't make it. I cried for him the whole ride to Missouri. Officer Nakamura drove me, face full of empathy. He and his wife had lost a baby two years before. Like me, he didn't quite understand why I'd insisted I needed to see the Rodriguez family again. But he got it. I never forgot that.

Soon, my unofficial questioning became just talking. For a few days, I bonded with Mia (once she got out of the coma, which was thankfully brief) and Lin and Carmen, bringing them food and watching TV while they slept. They even put me on the approved visitors list. I was the only one. They didn't want their family in Texas to see them like this, they explained. They were updating everyone over the phone. They were also moving back there as soon as Mia was well.

When her parents left the room, Mia confided in me.

My heart broke for this kid. This golden girl, who'd been too scared to tell, and how a car accident changed all of that. I was twenty-one; she was seventeen. I think she felt I understood her, more so than her parents.

Somewhere in there, Mia asked me to adopt you.

I wasn't sure at first. I told her I was a twenty-one-year-old lesbian cop way out of my depth. I was an only child, not speaking to my own parents. How could I possibly be a parent?

Then Mia said something I never forgot.

"Because you're kind," she said. Her brown eyes focused on me and only me. "Her mother should be kind."

There was convincing to be done, and likely a lot of arguing. Mia's parents were older, but they would've raised you as their own, among extended family. But your mom was headstrong. She wore them down. She worried about raising a baby when she still felt like a baby herself, while also picking up the pieces of an accident that had traumatized so many, including your father, who'd lost his beloved little brother. She didn't want the type of family secret where eventually you'd find out your "sister" was actually your mother, and your "parents" were your grandparents. She wanted everyone to have a fresh start: her parents, her friends, her former boyfriend, but most of all, you.

Mia's parents treasured her. I think they felt guilty that they hadn't noticed the pregnancy at all. She'd been through hell and back. Mia knew all along they would say yes to whatever she wanted.

Of course, adopting a baby isn't the easiest thing, especially as a single, Chinese-American lesbian. There were laws. There was even more paperwork. Everyone had to sign their rights away or take on new rights. I still wasn't speaking to my parents, but I knew they'd say I was crazy. And they would've been right.

I both didn't understand what I was doing and understood it perfectly.

I didn't name you for a long time, just called you Baby. It was on your birth certificate until we changed it later. I figured we'd get to it. Hell, you could name yourself if you got old enough and I was still undecided.

Per Mia's wishes, she and I never spoke again. After they left, I rented a shithole apartment in the worst part of St. Louis, visited you daily, staying until they kicked me out. I watched as you grew stronger, bigger, just as I knew you would. You were strong just like your birth mama.

I called Officer Nakamura, who hooked me up in so many ways. He pulled some strings to get me a desk job at the department in Chicago. He helped me rent a place nearby.

Every sleepless night, I thought about the boy at the police department. The one whose parents had trusted their faith, as was probably ingrained in them from a young age. And look where it had led all three of them. I told myself, over and over, like nighttime prayers, that I would protect you at any cost. I wouldn't talk about that time in my life, in our lives. I would always believe you and keep an eagle-eye out for anyone who wanted to hurt you.

And above all, we wouldn't be going to church. Any church.

I turned out openly gay. And a mother. Both of which I didn't expect. Both were my identity. Even in those hardest first weeks, when I was technically your foster parent and not yet your ma, I wouldn't have had it any other way.

I worried when you cried. I fretted when you slept through the night because what if the quiet meant you were no longer living? Our apartment was the size of a closet. I talked to so many social workers, had so many home visits, I lost count. Hillary Clinton wrote a book about raising kids and said it took a village. I was *your village for the first few months, and I took that very seriously.*

At the same time, it felt...natural. Not easy, *of course, but I really thought I'd feel less capable than I turned out to be. Somehow I, who'd never changed a diaper in my life, knew exactly how to feed, bathe, and clothe. When I didn't, I called Mrs. Nakamura, who didn't have a child but had a lot of nieces and nephews. More often than not, though, if I thought I was on the right track...I was.*

You and I were meant to be together.

That's not to say you didn't cry. Because you did. A lot. You were vocal from day one if the nurses in the Havendale and St. Louis hospitals were to be believed. Making your needs known. *Even though I was intensely proud of you for speaking up for yourself when you couldn't yet say words, I'm not going to lie to you. The crying was tough.*

My desk job was mostly paperwork. Your fostering, on track to an adoption, was mostly paperwork. When I think back to those hazy first days, I think of tears you couldn't yet cry, and drying ink. A profession I never fully believed in, but for so long felt was my only, steady option.

And that's where Mum comes in.

You'll know this story; it's all of our favorites. You're fourteen now, a freshman at U-High, but once in a while, you still ask to hear it at bedtime. You could be thirty and I would always, always say yes.

One night, at our favorite diner in Lakeview, you—who were still Baby at this point—would not stop squalling. I tried everything: a bottle, pacifier, feeling the diaper. Trying to ignore the increasingly frustrated looks of the patrons, I jiggled you up and down, murmuring what I hoped were comforting words, but just knowing *that you would pick up on my sleeplessness, my stress, my ongoing dread that the adoption would never happen, that the Rodriguez family would change their minds and I would never see your face again.*

Suddenly, another face appeared.

A woman with gorgeous dreadlocks and bib overalls, and the sweetest smile directed right at you.

"Little lost one," the angel crooned, "what are we going to do with you?"

She held out her arms. "May I?"

I'm not as smart as you are, P. Since then, I've asked myself why I willingly handed my baby to a complete stranger. Or listened, enthralled, when the woman started murmuring to my now equally enthralled infant.

As it turned out, she was singing. A song I vaguely remembered listening to in the back seat of the car when I was little. A song about wishing you knew the things you knew now when you were younger. I found myself humming along as your crying subsided, then stopped.

"Do you mind?" the woman whispered, gesturing to the seat across from me. I was still transfixed by this almost-Biblical tableau of mother and child—we've been to the Louvre and even the Renaissance artists didn't get it right. I nodded like the dumbass I am, and the woman sank down with the grace of a dancer.

Looking down at you, the woman smiled and whispered, "I always thought that song was called 'I Wish.' Turns out it's 'Ooh La La,' like the hook. Funny, right?"

"'I Wish' is Stevie Wonder," I found myself saying, louder than I'd intended. What can I say? I have good taste and I had a crush.

"I'm Jacqueline, by the way," the beautiful woman said.

"Constance. Connie." Thank the Flying Spaghetti Monster I didn't propose right then because I sure thought about it. In the space of two minutes, your mom cast a spell on both of us. Soon, she'd bring back the goofy optimism in me I thought was lost forever.

"And who's this?" Jacqueline kissed your little head.

It might have been the sleep deprivation and the paperwork combined with this woman sitting opposite me, but the vibes I was getting were that Jacqueline and I were alike in vital ways. Or it could have been the way Jacqueline was looking at me and the way you were curled on her chest, your soft sighs clueing me in.

Whatever the reason, I heard myself saying, "Why don't you name her?"

To her credit, your mum didn't laugh. She took it seriously. Her eyes rolled toward the ceiling as she contemplated what was likely not the question she'd anticipated when she offered to comfort a random baby in a diner.

Then she smiled, and it was like the first sunshine of spring. Small, but powerful. Life-changing.

"Perdita," your mum said. "Lost daughter. Who eventually is found." Now she looked at me with dark, laughing eyes. "I'm getting my PhD in Shakespeare."

"Perdita," I repeated. It was beautiful. The first syllable sounded like a cat's happy sound, the last two like an entrancing Italian aria I'd heard on a classical station. A name I'd never known that suddenly seemed like the only possible choice.

Against Jacqueline's bosom, you—Perdita—stirred, then relaxed again.

Behind us all, the diner's wall clock gave a loud, decisive TICK.

I will always protect you.

Ma

Chapter Fourteen

As we get closer to Havendale, there's nothing but wide-open spaces in front of me. It's not that I thought they didn't exist. I just wasn't expecting the sense of wonder.

Field after field stretches before us, neat rows of rich black dirt. Above that is the largest, bluest sky I've ever seen. The colors are so vibrant they almost jump. When I was younger, I had a book where kids looked up and said what shapes the clouds look like—a hippo, a bird, whatever. I remember laughing, because there's no way you can see this much sky in Chicago unless you go to the beach and it's an especially clear day. I've even been to Michigan a couple of times, and a beach in California right on the Pacific Ocean. But it was nothing like this endless expanse of sky.

"Listen to this," I tell Fenton, pulling up intel on my phone. "At this time of year, seeds are going into the ground for early planting. The fields are tilled." I glance out at the dirt rows, lines so neat and precise. "Everything's waiting to grow."

Somewhere in the midst of falling for Fenton and finding my father, spring arrived.

"By the way," Fenton says, while we both take in the magnificent Midwestern surroundings. He reaches into his backpack and pulls out a slightly squished pack of Hostess cupcakes. "Happy birthday, Perdita."

Our fingers brush. I know what he's really asking me. "So we're doing this?" I say.

We hit a four-way stop sign thirty miles outside Havendale. I have to look away from the cupcakes to meet Fenton's gaze, those deep dark eyes. The best face in the world.

"If you're still in," he says, "I'm still in."

Without any delay, I touch my lips to his. His hand goes to my cheek, then my hair, and I swear I levitate off the seat. I always thought I'd take off my glasses, shake out my hair like a librarian in an old movie, before someone kissed me. Turns out, I don't need to. I'm just fine where I am.

Our first kiss, and we're surrounded by dirt and sky with a pack of gas station cupcakes on my lap.

It's perfect.

❖

As we get closer to Havendale, I Google the town, which I've done before, but this time I find the link to their local paper.

"Hey, Fenton," I say, and he glances over at an underpass. "Listen to this." I read from the announcement. "Today, in the garden of St. Cecelia's Catholic Church, they'll be dedicating three new statues. One to Mia Rodriguez."

We planned to just show up at Tesla's house and kind of go from there. It's maybe not the world's best-laid plan, to ambush him like that, but I'm tired of waiting around. I know that a statue dedication means Mia may no longer be alive, but at least this way, I'll have an answer. And I can pay tribute to the woman who gave birth to me.

"What do you think?" Fenton asks me as I scrub cupcake crumbs off my face with a dusty napkin I found in the glove compartment. "Want to go to the ceremony?" He doesn't even finish the sentence before I'm nodding so hard I'm afraid my glasses will pop off. I text my moms the new plan, plus the address of the church.

And then I see the sign:

ENTERING HAVENDALE

POP. 19,172

A NICE PLACE TO CALL HOME

"Ready?" Fenton asks as we stop at a red light on the main drag. Traffic's practically nonexistent and we'll be right on time.

This is meant to be. All of it.

In response, I kiss him again, and it's even better than the first time. We break apart to see the light is green.

"Okay," I say, more to myself than to Fenton. "Let's go meet Mia."

❖

Because of a particularly long red light, and some extra kissing, we end up being a little late and have to scramble for parking. Finally, we find a spot and get out of the car, making a beeline for a group of people milling around a well-manicured patch of land in front of a couple of squat brown brick buildings. St. Cecelia's Academy, reads the swinging sign. The school's much smaller than my own but carries a dignified air, as if it knows exactly who it is.

I see him right away: tall white guy, khakis, hands tucked in his pockets. Nothing about him really stands out, but I *know* him. His sheepish smile and strong jawline, the way he stands, weight on the back foot, just like me.

This is my father.

I nudge Fenton and cock my head. "Tesla Wrightwood," I whisper. "Do you want to go up to him?"

I shake my head. "Let's just listen to the ceremony first."

We're at the back of the crowd when a tall Asian man with a bushy mustache, glasses, and a friendly smile addresses everyone. He stands next to three columns covered with cloth.

"Good afternoon. For those who don't know me, I'm Father Dorcas," he says. "Seventeen years ago, a devastating accident occurred in the St. Cecelia's community. Several of our students were in a tragic car accident. Second grader Max Wrightwood died at the hospital, and Ann Marie Donoghue, a promising varsity volleyball player, was killed instantly. St. Cecelia's had never known such pain, and every year since, we have gathered together to remember the victims in a moment of silence."

As we stand quietly, Father Dorcas looks out over the crowd, and for a second, I swear he spots me, but then his eyes pass over. "Mia Rodriguez, also a junior and a gifted vocalist, was in the car and went into premature labor. At the time, Mia was frightened of telling her parents or anyone in her life, aside from a few friends who were sworn to secrecy. Because of this situation, St. Cecelia's established a full sex-ed program, teaching our students about not only procreation, but also about consent, protection, and other matters." He smiles again. "*Very* controversial for a Catholic school, but we stayed strong, and now our students are even better prepared for the future."

I see another figure approach: a tall redhead in a bright blue dress with a full circle skirt. Making her way through the crowd, she then finds Tesla and touches his shoulder. He gives her a tight hug, and she takes his hand and squeezes it.

Oh my God.

"That's my dean," I whisper to Fenton. "Mia's best friend, and Tesla's." We grin at each other, and I take Fenton's hand just like Dr. Schneider took my father's.

"These statues have been a long time in the making," Father Dorcas continues. "The Wrightwood and Donoghue families have given generously over the years, and this year, they wanted to add something beautiful to our beloved memorial garden. St. Cecelia's Church takes great pride in its garden, and we knew that what you are about to see would be a welcome addition as well as a remembrance of April 5, 1997."

"Oh shit," Fenton says, his voice low and urgent. I look where he is and see two other figures approaching.

It's his father, along with Smith. His father, who called me Mia. Smith, who told us *Havendale, 1997.*

The pieces of the puzzle are coming together.

"Hello, son," Alexander Johnson says, giving Fenton an awkward side-hug. Smith smiles at us both. "We'll have to talk later," Alexander whispers to Fenton, "but I've given your comedy career some thought. I think we can work things out." Fenton grins, wide, and my heart warms a lot toward his tall, proud dad.

Alexander's eyes light up when he notices Dr. Schneider standing with Tesla. She glances over her shoulder and waves. Suddenly, I see them both as teenagers—and something more.

"And now," Father Dorcas announces, "I have a special surprise." He's full-on beaming, and I wonder what he has in store. "Three months ago, just as we were finalizing these plans, I got a phone call from our sister parish in Guatemala. One of their nuns, who had just transferred there after years of relief work in Africa, wanted to speak with us urgently. I was not at St. Cecelia's at the time of the car accident, but knowing its history, I had to sit down when she got on the line. We are incredibly grateful to God that she has done His work overseas, and that after surviving the accident against all odds, she is with us today." He steps back. "Please welcome Sister Mary Lucía, or as she is known to some of you in our congregation, Mia Rodriguez."

Shrieks.

Tears.

Gasps.

Fenton squeezes my hand as a beautiful woman with wild hair just like mine steps out into the early evening light, shielding her eyes. She pulls the fabric off the statues, revealing three bronze figures so exquisitely crafted they almost look real: a tall girl with a ponytail and a volleyball poised in one hand, her other hand ready to strike; a little boy, face upturned to the spring sky; and another girl with crazy curls, her mouth open as if in song. All three, frozen in space and time, ready for their lives to begin.

I look at the woman with the curls in her plain navy blue dress, then back at the third statue.

It's her.

It's me.

My moms are holding hands and finally here. I rush into their arms, and tears rain down our faces. We can't take our eyes off of Mia. This day that started out frightening and uncertain ends up sacred.

Any words Mia was about to say are cut off as Dr. Schneider, pulling Tesla by the hand, rushes up to her. Alexander and Smith follow suit, and a tight circle forms around her. There's squealing and laughing, then all go silent as they hold onto one another. It almost seems like they're praying.

And then, I swear, the crowd parts as I make my way up to the statue and this circle of friends. I can sense my moms and Fenton behind me. The air is filled with the aromas of mowed grass and fresh flowers, the murmuring of the congregation, and the gentle evening light. All of this feels holy as the group releases their clinch on Mia. In the distance, church bells clang clear and true, sounding out the hours, one by one.

Mia's eyes widen as I approach. Her brown eyes meet mine, and the connection is immediate, intense, and every inch of perfect.

Somewhere, a clock is ticking.

EPILOGUE

April 10, 1997

My lost daughter,

Someday I hope you understand what I'm about to do.

People will think it's my parents or your dad pressuring me to give you up. Babies shouldn't have babies and all that.

What no one knows is that we, me and your dad, talked on the phone last night. I'm getting better, but they're keeping me "for observation." He's not allowed to visit, by his folks or mine. But we needed to figure things out on our own. We needed to talk about you, our daughter.

I'd shooed out my parents, with their constant sacrificing and their love that was beginning to smother. They didn't know that, through our friends and a whole intricate process I won't bore you with, your daddy and I had arranged for him to call me.

We talked for five hours, from black night to sunrise outside my hospital window.

We still love each other, that's certain. We are in deep mourning for poor Max.

We fought. We cried. We went back and forth all night. At one point, we were sure we could keep it together, you and our friends around us. But even as we were making these breathless plans, we knew the dream—the house, Max, you—was over.

You are alive, a little small but overall healthy. That's all we could ask and more than we deserved. We knew better than to push our luck. Well, his luck and my faith.

I have to trust God will take care of you, now more than ever. But as I learned from reading Where the Red Fern Grows *in freshman English, I must meet God halfway. I have to let someone else take care of you.*

I found her. At our lowest, God sent her to me.

The second I met Constance, the cop who was at the scene of the accident that could have killed us all, I knew. I knew with the same certainty I had on my first date with your father that I'd found your ma.

I'm still not sure what it was: her capability in handling everyone from inquisitive officers to pushy nurses who made sure we knew they didn't approve of unwed mothers, particularly "the Mexicans," to friends who meant well but were getting in the way. She had everything from a death glare at casual racism to a commanding air around old white officers who'd been around way longer. Constance was young, but she was in charge, and everyone knew it. No one would ever mess with you on her watch.

At some point in the chaos, I reached for her hand, and she held it. The second our palms touched, she never let go until I was ready. And I imagined how she'd do the same for you.

Every day, I pray that I'm right.

Today, I will leave the hospital in St. Louis and go back to Texas with my parents. I'll see the sunrise up close. You will stay here until you're a little bigger, then go with Constance. She offered me an open adoption: letters, phone calls, pictures of you—as much contact as I want. I wanted to say yes, but I need you to have more than a teenage mother who trusted both too much and not enough.

I don't blame myself for your uncle's death, or the car accident that followed. But I've messed up so much: not going to the doctor when you were growing inside me, not setting boundaries with your dad when he was having struggles of his own, not understanding my dearest friend when she was, in her own stoic way, crying for help. I can make things right by giving you a new reality without these awful memories, with a mom who is capable, loving. She can do right by you in all the ways I can't.

I used to write off bad things as God's will. When Paulina lost her faith, mine grew stronger by the day. My faith hasn't disappeared, but it's changed. In the past few days, coming out of the dark, holding you in my arms, kissing your forehead one last time, I've learned much of God's will is intermingled with our own. We fail, over and over and over, but we try. Try to light up the dark night, stars in our own personal universe. We always try. We always keep on.

My parents would have gladly taken you, raised you as their own. I had to fight them and the whole system to give you to Constance. Eventually, they all listened. Lin and Carmen Rodriguez would do anything for me, their only daughter, and I know Constance, who is strong and true and kind, will do the same for you.

You're my daughter. You always will be. But as much as this will haunt me every day of my life—I may be a teen mom, but I'm not stupid—I have to let you go. I have to give you, and Constance, the chance to light up the night together.

I know this to be true as well: I have to learn to light up the night on my own. I'm not sure what this will look like. But I need to try, and that's why I have to let you go. For both of us to have the fresh start we deserve. I am putting all my faith in the idea that we will find each other again, someday, when the time is right.

Your dad and I signed the papers. I just held you in my arms for the last time. I touched your soft cheek, said a Hail Mary, and wished you the best possible life. I can't relive this moment too vividly, or I'll break down and change my mind, and that won't do either of us any good. Both you and I have to be strong. My family will be here soon to get me. I can't bring myself to say good-bye, so I'm sitting on my bed looking out my window at the stars.

And in this letter you'll never see, I write my wishes for you. I kept them in my English notebook from what feels like a lifetime ago, and tonight, I send them out into this wide, dark universe.

That you find friends as wonderful as mine.

That you believe, in God or Buddha or family. Just believe.

That you find something you love as much as I love music.

Speaking of love, that you fall into it headfirst.
That someday, somewhere, you will want to find me.
That someday, somewhere, you will succeed.
That, like the lost stars we all are, you will light up the world.
Forever,
Your first mama,
Mia

About the Author

Lauren Emily Whalen is the author of two books for young adults: the novel *Satellite* (2017) and the nonfiction book *Dealing with Drama* (2021). Her queer YA short story "I Saw Her Again" appears in the holiday ghost anthology *Link by Link* (2020). Lauren is a freelance writer, professional performer, and very amateur aerialist who graduated from Catholic school and is an unabashed devotee of the Bard. She lives in Chicago with her cat, Versace, and an apartment full of books.

Books Available from Bold Strokes Books

A Different Man by Andrew L. Huerta. This diverse collection of stories chronicling the challenges of gay life at various ages shines a light on the progress made and the progress still to come. (978-1-63555-977-4)

All That Remains by Sheri Lewis Wohl. Johnnie and Shantel might have to risk their lives—and their love—to stop a werewolf intent on killing. (978-1-63555-949-1)

Beginner's Bet by Fiona Riley. Phenom luxury Realtor Ellison Gamble has everything, except a family to share it with, so when a mix-up brings youthful Katie Crawford into her life, she bets the house on love. (978-1-63555-733-6)

Dangerous Without You by Lexus Grey. Throughout their senior year in high school, Aspen, Remington, Denna, and Raleigh face challenges in life and romance that they never expect. (978-1-63555-947-7)

Desiring More by Raven Sky. In this collection of steamy stories, a rich variety of lovers find themselves desiring more, more from a lover, more from themselves, and more from life. (978-1-63679-037-4)

Jordan's Kiss by Nanisi Barrett D'Arnuck. After losing everything in a fire, Jordan Phelps joins a small lounge band and meets pianist Morgan Sparks, who lights another blaze, this time in Jordan's heart. (978-1-63555-980-4)

Late City Summer by Jeanette Bears. Forced together for her wedding, Emily Stanton and Kate Alessi navigate their lingering passion for one another against the backdrop of New York City and World War II, and a summer romance they left behind. (978-1-63555-968-2)

Love and Lotus Blossoms by Anne Shade. On her path to self-acceptance and true passion, Janesse will risk everything—and possibly everyone—she loves. (978-1-63555-985-9)

Love in the Limelight by Ashley Moore. Marion Hargreaves, the finest actress of her generation, and Jessica Carmichael, the world's biggest pop star, rediscover each other twenty years after an ill-fated affair. (978-1-63679-051-0)

Suspecting Her by Mary P. Burns. Complications ensue when Erin O'Connor falls for top real estate saleswoman Catherine Williams while investigating racism in the real estate industry; the fallout could end their chance at happiness. (978-1-63555-960-6)

Two Winters by Lauren Emily Whalen. A modern YA retelling of Shakespeare's *The Winter's Tale* about birth, death, Catholic school, improv comedy, and the healing nature of time. (978-1-63679-019-0)

Busy Ain't the Half of It by Frederick Smith and Chaz Lamar Cruz. Elijah and Justin seek happily-ever-afters in LA, but are they too busy to notice happiness when it's there? (978-1-63555-944-6)

Calumet by Ali Vali. Jaxon Lavigne and Iris Long had a forbidden small-town romance that didn't last, and the consequences of that love will be uncovered fifteen years later at their high school reunion. (978-1-63555-900-2)

Her Countess to Cherish by Jane Walsh. London Society's material girl realizes there is more to life than diamonds when she falls in love with a non-binary bluestocking. (978-1-63555-902-6)

Hot Days, Heated Nights by Renee Roman. When Cole and Lee meet, instant attraction quickly flares into uncontrollable passion, but their connection might be short lived as Lee's identity is tied to her life in the city. (978-1-63555-888-3)

Never Be the Same by MA Binfield. Casey meets Olivia and sparks fly in this opposites attract romance that proves love can be found in the unlikeliest places. (978-1-63555-938-5)

Quiet Village by Eden Darry. Something not quite human is stalking Collie and her niece, and she'll be forced to work with undercover reporter Emily Lassiter if they want to get out of Hyam alive. (978-1-63555-898-2)

Shaken or Stirred by Georgia Beers. Bar owner Julia Martini and home health aide Savannah McNally attempt to weather the storms brought on by a mysterious blogger trashing the bar, family feuds they knew nothing about, and way too much advice from way too many relatives. (978-1-63555-928-6)

The Fiend in the Fog by Jess Faraday. Can four people on different trajectories work together to save the vulnerable residents of East London from the terrifying fiend in the fog before it's too late? (978-1-63555-514-1)

The Marriage Masquerade by Toni Logan. A no strings attached marriage scheme to inherit a Maui B&B uncovers unexpected attractions and a dark family secret. (978-1-63555-914-9)

Flight SQA016 by Amanda Radley. Fastidious airline passenger Olivia Lewis is used to things being a certain way. When her routine is changed by a new, attractive member of the staff, sparks fly. (978-1-63679-045-9)

Home Is Where the Heart Is by Jenny Frame. Can Archie make the countryside her home and give Ash the fairytale romance she desires? Or will the countryside and small village life all be too much for her? (978-1-63555-922-4)

Moving Forward by PJ Trebelhorn. The last person Shelby Ryan expects to be attracted to is Iris Calhoun, the sister of the man who killed her wife four years and three thousand miles ago. (978-1-63555-953-8)

Poison Pen by Jean Copeland. Debut author Kendra Blake is finally living her best life until a nasty book review and exposed secrets threaten her promising new romance with aspiring journalist Alison Chatterley. (978-1-63555-849-4)

Seasons for Change by KC Richardson. Love, laughter, and trust develop for Shawn and Morgan throughout the changing seasons of Lake Tahoe. (978-1-63555-882-1)

Summer Lovin' by Julie Cannon. Three different women, three exotic locations, one unforgettable summer. What do you think will happen? (978-1-63555-920-0)

Unbridled by D. Jackson Leigh. A visit to a local stable turns into more than riding lessons between a novel writer and an equestrian with a taste for power play. (978-1-63555-847-0)

VIP by Jackie D. In a town where relationships are forged and shattered by perception, sometimes even love can't change who you really are. (978-1-63555-908-8)

Yearning by Gun Brooke. The sleepy town of Dennamore has an irresistible pull on those who've moved away. The mystery Darian Benson and Samantha Pike uncover will change them forever, but the love they find along the way just might be the key to saving themselves. (978-1-63555-757-2)

A Turn of Fate by Ronica Black. Will Nev and Kinsley finally face their painful past and relent to their powerful, forbidden attraction? Or will facing their past be too much to fight through? (978-1-63555-930-9)

Desires After Dark by MJ Williamz. When her human lover falls deathly ill, Alex, a vampire, must decide which is worse, letting her go or condemning her to everlasting life. (978-1-63555-940-8)

Her Consigliere by Carsen Taite. FBI agent Royal Scott swore an oath to uphold the law, and criminal defense attorney Siobhan Collins pledged her loyalty to the only family she's ever known, but will their love be stronger than the bonds they've vowed to others, or will their competing allegiances tear them apart? (978-1-63555-924-8)

In Our Words: Queer Stories from Black, Indigenous, and People of Color Writers. Stories selected by Anne Shade and edited by Victoria Villaseñor. Comprising both the renowned and emerging voices of Black, Indigenous, and People of Color authors, this thoughtfully curated collection of short stories explores the intersection of racial and queer identity. (978-1-63555-936-1)

Measure of Devotion by CF Frizzell. Disguised as her late twin brother, Catherine Samson enters the Civil War to defend the Constitution as a Union soldier, never expecting her life to be altered by a Gettysburg farmer's daughter. (978-1-63555-951-4)

Not Guilty by Brit Ryder. Claire Weaver and Emery Pearson's day jobs clash, even as their desire for each other burns, and a discreet sex-only arrangement is the only option. (978-1-63555-896-8)

Opposites Attract: Butch/Femme Romances by Meghan O'Brien, Aurora Rey, Angie Williams. Sometimes opposites really do attract. Fall in love with these butch/femme romance novellas. (978-1-63555-784-8)

Swift Vengeance by Jean Copeland, Jackie D, Erin Zak. A journalist becomes the subject of her own investigation when sudden strange, violent visions summon her to a summer retreat and into the arms of a killer's possible next victim. (978-1-63555-880-7)

Under Her Influence by Amanda Radley. On their path to #truelove, will Beth and Jemma discover that reality is even better than illusion? (978-1-63555-963-7)

Wasteland by Kristin Keppler & Allisa Bahney. Danielle Clark is fighting against the National Armed Forces and finds peace as a scavenger, until the NAF general's daughter, Katelyn Turner, shows up on her doorstep and brings the fight right back to her. (978-1-63555-935-4)

When in Doubt by VK Powell. Police officer Jeri Wylder thinks she committed a crime in the line of duty but can't remember, until details emerge pointing to a cover-up by those close to her. (978-1-63555-955-2)

A Woman to Treasure by Ali Vali. An ancient scroll isn't the only treasure Levi Montbard finds as she starts her hunt for the truth—all she has to do is prove to Yasmine Hassani that there's more to her than an adventurous soul. (978-1-63555-890-6)

Before. After. Always. by Morgan Lee Miller. Still reeling from her tragic past, Eliza Walsh has sworn off taking risks, until Blake Navarro turns her world right-side up, making her question if falling in love again is worth it. (978-1-63555-845-6)

Bet the Farm by Fiona Riley. Lauren Calloway's luxury real estate sale of the century comes to a screeching halt when dairy farm heiress, and one-night stand, Thea Boudreaux calls her bluff. (978-1-63555-731-2)

Cowgirl by Nance Sparks. The last thing Aren expects is to fall for Carol. Sharing her home is one thing, but sharing her heart means sharing the demons in her past and risking everything to keep Carol safe. (978-1-63555-877-7)

Give In to Me by Elle Spencer. Gabriela Talbot never expected to sleep with her favorite author—certainly not after the scathing review she'd given Whitney Ainsworth's latest book. (978-1-63555-910-1)

Hidden Dreams by Shelley Thrasher. A lethal virus and its resulting vision send Texan Barbara Allan and her lovely guide, Dara, on a journey up Cambodia's Mekong River in search of Barbara's mother's mystifying past. (978-1-63555-856-2)

In the Spotlight by Lesley Davis. For actresses Cole Calder and Eris Whyte, their chance at love runs out fast when a fan's adoration turns to obsession. (978-1-63555-926-2)

Origins by Jen Jensen. Jamis Bachman is pulled into a dangerous mystery that becomes personal when she learns the truth of her origins as a ghost hunter. (978-1-63555-837-1)

Pursuit: A Victorian Entertainment by Felice Picano. An intelligent, handsome, ruthlessly ambitious young man who rose from the slums to become the right-hand man of the Lord Exchequer of England will stop at nothing as he pursues his Lord's vanished wife across Continental Europe. (978-1-63555-870-8)

Unrivaled by Radclyffe. Zoey Cohen will never accept second place in matters of the heart, even when her rival is a career, and Declan Black has nothing left to give of herself or her heart. (978-1-63679-013-8)